Sweet Beginnings

A Moonrise Bay Story

Beth Curley

To the women who have felt trapped by love and their light dimmed- may you find the strength to leave, the courage to heal and the heart to love yourself first. You were meant for more than to shrink yourself for someone else's comfort.

Contents

Prologue

Gracie

"Shit". I muttered, fumbling with my keys and the pizza box in my hand. It had been a long day at the bakery, and all I wanted was to come home, open a bottle of wine, eat pizza, and lounge in my oversized tub with my fiancé. Sure, I'd been looking forward to seeing my mom tonight, but when she called to cancel our plans, I was a little relieved. It had been a crazy week at work, especially since we were technically heading towards the off-season now. I was running the bakery with a skeleton crew, but with kids returning to school and summer ending, August on the North Carolina coast was turning into a busy month. With plans canceled, I picked up dinner from my and Michael's favorite pizza joint and planned on surprising him with a romantic night starting in that giant tub.

Walking through the front door of the townhouse I share with Michael; I wondered why the house was dark. It was after 7, and Michael should be home by now.

Heading towards the kitchen, I was going to check my phone for missed calls once I put all the shit in my arms down. Turning the corner, I dropped everything in my hands.

The pizza I had longed for all day, making a resounding splat on the floor. I couldn't believe the scene unfolding in front of my eyes. There was Michael, pants down around his ankles, dick buried deep into one of my best friends, Madison, who was bent over the kitchen island in all her resplendent glory.

The custom-built turquoise blue island with the beautiful white quartz countertop that took months to pick out when Michael and I remodeled the townhouse two years ago. All eyes were on me now. Was that panic on Michael's face? Was that a fucking smirk on my so-called best friend's mouth? That bitch!!!

"By all means, don't stop on my account." I angrily bite out. "I wouldn't want Michael to suffer from blue balls for fuck's sake." I was frozen in place. I wanted to pick up something, anything, and throw it at the two of them, but my body couldn't move. I watched in anger as Michael released himself from Madison and struggled to walk towards me while pulling his pants up simultaneously. I would think this situation was hilarious if it weren't happening to me.

"Baby, shit, Gracie. I'm sorry.   I, I..." Michael stammered, struggling to find the words, but he couldn't say anything that would make what was happening any better. Madison, still smirking, pulled her bunched-up skirt down and stood, arms folded over her DD-sized chest. I was always jealous of Madison's ample figure when we were kids. She had always been the pretty one between us. She was all legs and boobs with hair, the perfect blend of strawberry blonde to match her sea-green eyes.

I wasn't ugly, but I was less popular than Madison in high school. I always felt like I was living in her shadow. At 5'4, I was at least four inches shorter than her. Straight caramel brown hair and eyes that could only be described as brown. Plain ole brown. That's why I was shocked when Michael, the star quarterback, asked me out instead of Madison. We have been together since our senior year, and I thought we were happy. Michael had just proposed this past Valentine's Day, for fuck's sake.

"Madison, if I were you, I'd wipe that smug look off your face, or I'll do it for you." I hissed while balling my hands into fists at my sides. I could feel the rage simmering down in the depths of my soul. I was one second from knocking that bitch straight on her ass. I turned my seething rage on Michael and bit out the words I never thought I would say to him in a million years.

"Get the hell out of my house Michael; take your whore and get out of my house." Michael and Madison had the good sense to grab what things were in their immediate vicinity and leave. As I heard the click of the closing door, my body slowly slumped to the kitchen floor, and I began to sob. How the hell had I gotten to this place? Betrayed by the two people I thought I was closest to. How long had the two of them been screwing each other? I could barely stand looking at the beautiful kitchen I had created. It had always been my sanctuary. Even as a young child, I loved being in the kitchen. Now all I could see was Madison and Michael doing God knows what to each other in my safe space. I begrudgingly grabbed my bottle of pinot noir and dragged myself upstairs to the master bath.

This room, with its muted gray and white tones. Large soaking tub and standalone shower that was big enough for an entire family. The his and her sinks staring at me almost mockingly. Michael and I had built a life here, or at least I thought we had. Now what?

First things first, I was still taking a damn bubble bath. I needed to wash the ick away and drown my sorrows in this bottle of wine. With my air pods in and Taylor Swift's Folklore album on full blast, I stripped off my clothes, filled the tub with lavender bubble bath, unscrewed the cap of the wine bottle, and lowered myself into the glorious water. I'd figure out life tomorrow. Tonight, I was drinking wine, listening to my generation's greatest breakup songwriter, and wallowing in my utter disaster of a life.

Halfway through "My Tears Ricochet," the ping of my iPhone sounded through my air pods. Glancing down at the phone, I saw a message from Piper, my other best friend.

Piper: "*What the hell Gracie? I just walked into the Pirate's Chest, and who do I see at the bar? Madison and Michael eating each other's faces off. I've got half a mind to walk up and pull that bitch's weave out.*"

Me: "*Ugh, I can't believe they left here and went straight to a bar. It's a long story, Pipes. I'm currently wallowing with a bottle of wine, bubble bath, and Taylor Swift.*"

Piper: "*Girl, get out of the tub. I'm bringing more wine and Chinese food, and we can wallow together. I'll be there in 30.*
Me: "*All right, I'll leave the front door open for you. Love you Pipes.*"

Piper: *Love you more, Gracie*

I climbed out of the tub, wrapped myself in a towel, and headed into the bedroom. For a moment, I just stood there, staring at the bed that, just a week ago, I had been wrapped in Michael's arms naked. How could I have been such a fool? What was I going to do now? How would I face everyone in town tomorrow, now that Michael and Madison were seen making out at the bar, for fucks sake? Moonrise Bay is a small town of about 1000 residents in the off-season. Everyone knows everyone's business.

Ugh, angrily, I pulled the sheets and comforter from the bed. For a moment, I thought about burning them. Then I thought maybe I'd pull all of Michael's clothes from the closet and add them to the flaming pile. I wouldn't do that, of course. That wasn't my style. No, I wouldn't be burning anything, but I wouldn't allow Michael back in this townhouse to pack his things. He may have lived here for the past couple of years, but this was my house. I owned it outright and wouldn't allow Michael to darken my door again.

Dressed in my favorite pj's, a tank top, and pumpkin-covered pajama pants, I headed downstairs to wait for Piper. She burst through the front doors, anger radiating on her face, arms full of wine and Chinese food containers, looking ready to murder someone.

One thing I could always count on Piper for was her undying loyalty. Even though Madison, Piper, and I had been friends since grade school, I had been the glue that kept the friendship together. Madison had been the more popular of us girls, but Piper and I had always been closer. Looking back, I couldn't figure out why we had remained friends with Madison. She had undoubtedly begun to look down on us as we had gotten older. After graduation, each of us girls had gone our own way, but after college, we had come home to Moonrise Bay. Maybe that's how we became friends with Madison again. Piper and I kept in touch after high school, but we had only heard from Madison sporadically in those years.

"Girl, what the fuck?" Piper groaned as she unloaded her haul on the living room coffee table, and I finished debriefing her on the scene I walked into earlier tonight. Like me, Piper was petite, but she had a spunky attitude that made her seem larger than life. She wore her golden locks in a sharp bob, and with her cat-eye glasses, she totally rocked the funky librarian look.

"I just can't believe those assholes decided

to take their sham of a relationship public on the same night you found them screwing in your kitchen. I knew Madison was a complete bitch, but Michael. Jeez, I didn't see that coming."

"You and me both, sister," I added, grabbing the container of pork dumplings and a pair of chopsticks. "It took everything in my body not to punch Madison in her smirking face, but I didn't feel like getting arrested tonight."

"What's next, babe? I know what happened is still fresh, but you need to start thinking about what happens next. Revenge? Murder? Total ruination? Lighting all his shit on fire on the front lawn? I'm down to help with whatever plan you come up with." Piper stabbed a piece of Mongolian beef with her fork and laughed deviously. That's why I love her. No matter what, I knew Piper always had my back.

"Honestly, Pipes, I can't even focus on anything beyond gorging myself on pork dumplings and pinot noir. I want to pass out on this sofa so I don't have to think about Michael and our bed. I thought we were building a life together. I thought we were the success story of high school sweethearts, you know. I know we had our problems over the years. I thought we were past this kind of bullshit, and he'd grown up. I never thought he would do something like fuck my best friend in our house." I angrily wiped the tears that had begun to fall down my face as Piper wrapped me in her arms.

"I mean, we were just making our wedding plans last night, and now I know it was all just a joke to the two of them. He made me a fool to the whole damn town. How do I walk into the bakery tomorrow? What do I tell my mom? What the hell do I do now?"

"You walk through that bakery with your head held high, Gracie Henderson. You have nothing to be ashamed of. That's on Michael and Madison. They're the ones who should be hiding out. Not you, babe. As for what you do now, you pack up all his shit and leave it on the porch, or better yet, dump it all on Madison's front stoop. He's her problem now." Piper clinked my wineglass and drank the rest of hers, still holding my hand. "Now, what's this bullshit about sleeping on the sofa? Hell no, girl. I'm putting clean sheets on the bed, and I brought my pj's. We're finishing this food in bed with our wine and the "Reputation" tour movie. We need some inspiration from the best."

Piper grabbed the food and the wine and led the way. I knew she would stay up with me all night if that's what I needed. I knew that the morning wouldn't be so scary after all with Piper by my side.

****

Nathan

I was woken up by the sound of someone pounding on my front door. Glancing at my phone, I wondered who would be stupid enough to knock on my door at two in the goddamned morning. Grabbing my sweatpants from my bedroom chair, I trudged down the stairs and angrily opened the door. Michael pushed past me, smelling like a brewery and cheap perfume running his hands through his hair.

"Oh man, I screwed up Nathan and didn't know where else to go."

"How about home to your fiancé?" It's not that I didn't want to help Michael, well, maybe just a little bit. During our entire friendship, I had cleaned up Michael's messes. I'm tired of his bullshit. We're fucking adults, for Christ's sake, and I guess it's time he starts acting like one.

"That's the problem, Nate. I can't go home to Gracie. She's the one who kicked me out after she found me in the kitchen with Madison." Michael flung himself down on the couch in my living room and threw his face in his hands.

"What do you mean Gracie found you and

Madison in the kitchen? Please tell me you're not sleeping with Madison, Mike. What the hell are you thinking? She's supposed to be Gracie's best friend, and you're supposed to marry Gracie next spring. For fuck's sake, what's wrong with you?" I could barely control my anger. Michael, who had always had everything handed to him, breezed through high school because he was a star athlete. College seemed to be a snap, and when he graduated, his dad had a job waiting for him in the family real estate firm. Not to mention, he had the perfect girl. Gracie Henderson was sweet, funny, talented, and beautiful. Maybe not hit you in the face gorgeous like Madison, but if I admitted it, I'd always thought she was far more beautiful than Madison was. Whiskey brown eyes and long caramel brown hair. She had the perfect girl-next-door vibe about her. I couldn't believe Mike was stupid enough to throw her away for someone like Madison Burke. At least he had the good sense to look upset about his situation.

"I don't know what happened, man. I proposed to Gracie, but then I felt trapped. I'm only 28 years old, for crying out loud, and I've only been with a couple of girls. I've been with Gracie since high school, and then there were a few in college that I never told Gracie about. I don't think I'm ready to say forever to someone. Madison and I were working late in the office one night. We had a couple of drinks, and one thing led to another. She's everything Gracie isn't Nate. She's exciting and adventurous. We have a lot of shit in common too. Gracie is happy to spend the rest of her life in this small town. Madison is like me and dreams of something bigger than Moonrise Bay. I guess I didn't realize that Gracie wasn't what I wanted anymore until Madison, and I guess I was too chicken shit to tell her. I never wanted Gracie to find out this way, man." Michael blew out a long breath, waiting for me to say something, anything. I didn't know what to tell him. I wanted to punch him in the face for hurting Gracie, but if I'm honest, I had never thought Michael and Gracie would work out. Honestly, Gracie was too good for frat-boy Mike.

"You're an idiot, Mike. Moonrise Bay is a small town; you were bound to get caught sooner or later. I can tell you one thing: you're not moving in with me, and I'm not cleaning this mess up for you like I did with the girls in college. You're on your own this time, jackass. You can sleep here tonight, but after that, you can figure your own shit out. The couch is yours; I've got to be at a job site by 7 am, and I'm going back up to bed. Lock the doors before you go to sleep, and do not let Madison Burke in my house." With that, I headed back up the stairs to my bedroom and closed the door and Mike's problems behind me.

In the back of my mind, a small part of

me was happy. Gracie was single after ten years. I knew I couldn't rush things. I knew her life had just blown up, but somewhere, a part of me knew this was a sign that Gracie would be mine.

Two Months Later

Save Our Date

Michael and Madison

are getting married

February 15, 2025

Moonrise Bay, North Carolina

Chapter 1

Gracie

I woke with a pit in the bottom of my stomach. After getting that damned "Save The Date" card in the mail, Piper and I had pulled an all-nighter. We cried, drank copious bottles of wine, and sang Taylor Swift songs at the top of our lungs. Finally crashing around 3 am, we fell into bed, and I didn't even remember falling asleep. Now, with a pounding headache, I knew I needed to peel myself off the sheets, shower, and attempt to get ready for work. Thank God Louisa and Miquel were opening the bakery. At least I had been able to sleep in a bit. After showering and doing the rest of my morning routine, I threw on my Beach Buns Bakery t-shirt and a pair of black yoga pants, grabbed my bag and the keys to my Scout, and headed out the door. Jeez, wincing against the bright sun hitting my face, I muttered to myself, "Why the hell couldn't it at least be as gloomy outside as I feel? Not fair, not fair at all."

Driving down Coastal Drive towards the small downtown area of Moonrise Bay, it hit me how much I love my little town. Moonrise Bay is the quintessential beach town, with little Cape Cod-style houses littering our waterfront. We weren't an oceanfront town, but we do sit on the Intracoastal with a little bay that is the signature point of the town.

The bakery is in a shopping area in the heart of downtown Moonrise Bay. Main Street is truly the heart of our community, littered with colorful buildings and storefronts. On one side, you had The Moonrise Diner, The Pirate's Chest Bar and Grille, and everyone's favorite, Shiver Me Timbers Ice Cream Shop. On my side of the street sits my little bakery with its white picket fencing and pink gingham awning. The Secret Garden Nursery, The Little Nook bookstore, and The Red Wagon hardware store surround me. We're a quaint town but a tight-knit community. We all look out for each other.

As soon as I pulled up to the bakery, I knew this would be a day I would not want to leave my office. I was exhausted, hungover, and not in the mood to face the nosy gossips of Moonrise Bay. That is the downside to living in a small town. Everyone knows your business, and everyone has an opinion.

Stepping out of my truck, I glanced towards a truck parked in front of the bakery.

Sitting on the tailgate of his pickup truck, looking sexy as hell, was none other than Nathan Sundry. Nathan had been one of Michael's closest friends since high school. Before Michael and I started dating, I'd had a crush on Nathan. Over the years, he and I had gotten pretty close. Since he and Michael were best friends, Nathan was always around. You didn't see one without the other. We had all become one big group. Michael and Nathan, me, Piper and Madison. That is until we all went away to college. Nathan had stayed in Moonrise Bay and worked for his uncle in construction. They were now partners in that same business. Nathan and his crew of guys were some of my best customers. I swear those guys were in here every morning and every afternoon before we closed. I could see Nathan had already been to the bakery this morning, as evidenced by the cinnamon cruffin and the large coffee he was enjoying.

"If you're here about the "Save the Date," don't worry, Nathan; Piper got me good and drunk last night. I don't want to talk about them anymore. I know he's your friend, but your friend is a fuck-up, and I'm not in the mood to hear any excuses about why those two thought it would be okay to send me, of all people, a "save the date" other than wanting to rub my poor, lonely nose in the fact that they're now getting married."

I saw Nathan wince at the sharpness of my tone.   Nathan and I had always had a closeness he didn't share with anyone else, and I could tell it hurt him that I thought he was there on Michael's behalf.

"Come on, Gracie, you know me better than that. I can't resist these cruffins. I had a little break from the job site and thought I'd pop over for a pastry and coffee and check in on my favorite baker. That shithead friend of mine screwed up this time, but I'm not here to help him. I'm here for you."

Wow, I stood there stupefied for a moment. I knew Nathan didn't approve of the way Michael lived his life. I wasn't stupid. I knew Michael had cheated in college, and I knew Nathan had covered for him.   Maybe I was foolish since I had always ignored the obvious. Standing in front of this Nathan, I wasn't sure what to think. Bros usually stick together, but here he was, angry with Michael and checking on me. Nathan, with his quiet, brooding intensity. I had such a crush on him before I started dating Michael. Nathan never paid any romantic attention to me in high school, but I definitely paid attention to him. Nathan, with his sandy blonde hair and eyes the color of the ocean after a storm, filled my dreams when I was in school.

"Well, that's a surprise since you always covered for him when he was in college." I stared Nathan down, but he didn't look away. With one hand in the front pocket of his jeans and dragging the other through his hair, Nathan blew out a deep breath.

"You knew about that, unh? I'm sorry, Gracie. I've always felt guilty about helping Mike, but he's my friend…"

"I know Nathan. I don't blame you. It hurt, and I'm not going to lie; it makes me wonder how sincere you are now. I've never asked you this, but did you know? Did you know he was screwing around with Madison? Did you know he was planning on marrying her?" I bit the bottom of my lip, hoping he didn't know.

"Not this time. Mike was playing this one pretty close to the chest, I guess. He came by my place after you caught them together, and I told him in no uncertain terms that I wasn't cleaning up his mess this time. He's on his own. I am here just for you."

"Thanks, Nathan. Believe it or not, that means a lot to me. I still feel like he's ruined my kitchen for me. Remember how long it took me to design that space? Now, all I see when I walk in there is the two of them doing…well, you know what they were doing."

Nathan hopped off the tailgate and stood directly in front of me. He slowly placed a strand of hair that had come loose from my ponytail and tucked it behind my ear. We stood like that in the parking lot for what felt like an eternity. Neither one of us spoke. He gently rubbed his hands up and down my arms and then pulled me in for a hug. He smelled like heaven. Like a rainstorm in the summertime. I could get lost here. Wait, wait. What am I thinking? This is Nathan. This is Michael's friend. I can't cross that line. I can't even think about crossing that line. I pulled away from the embrace and stepped back, blowing out a deep breath.

"I've gotta get inside and face the music, I suppose. Thanks for stopping by and checking on me, Nathan. It feels good to know that you've got my back." I smiled weakly and headed towards the door of the bakery. I could feel his eyes on me as I walked away, but I didn't dare look back. What the hell is going on? One thing's for sure; I absolutely am not getting involved with another man right now, even if it's the painfully gorgeous Nathan Sundry.

****

I tried to keep to the back of the bakery most of the day. I couldn't stand the well-meaning stares of the morning regulars. Of course, everyone in town heard that Michael and Madison were getting married. They'd probably sent a 'save the date' to whole town. I knew it was only a matter of time.

Towards the late morning slowdown, I retreated to the safety of the kitchen. I had some new recipes I wanted to test for the holiday season and decided now was as good a time as any. I knew Louisa and Miquel could handle the lunch crowd. I couldn't run this bakery without the two of them. They had been with me since the beginning. Louisa was a single mom in her late thirties. Her deep brown skin and jet-black hair only accentuated her striking beauty. The fact that she was still single was mind-boggling to me. Miquel was all sass and attitude. He had also gone to high school with me, and when we met, it was an instant friendship. I amd also close friends with his boyfriend, Alan, who runs the nursery next door. Alan had come to Moonrise Bay on vacation a few years ago and fell in love with both the town and Miquel. He bought the nursery, and the rest is history.

I couldn't just sit in my office any longer. I needed to do something with all this pent-up anger. I was so frustrated that I was back to letting Michael and Madison make me angry. Working my way from behind my desk, I walked into the kitchen, bringing my idea book with me. Today was a good day to make bread. I always loved getting my hands on a big mound of dough. I grabbed the ingredients for Parker House rolls with a twist. This time of year,

I made my own pumpkin puree. With the amount of pumpkin desserts requested from my customers, I found it easier to make my own. Grabbing it from the walk-in fridge, I added it to the recipe and poured the dough onto the work counter. Working the dough on the lightly floured surface was therapeutic. My hands in the soft dough, as I gently folded it over itself repeatedly. It quieted my mind. I poured all my emotions into kneading the dough and felt a calm wash over me.

I put the batch in the proving drawer and turned on the radio to distract myself. Sitting down at my tiny desk, working on next week's menu, I heard the words all bay residents hated hearing. Tropical Storm Watch in effect until Friday evening.

It was Tuesday now, giving me only a few days to prepare the store for the impending weather. The bakery closes at 3 pm, so I decided to finish the bread recipe and menus at home. I gathered my notes, ingredients, and equipment, ensuring everything was packed securely.

Before leaving the bakery, I called Louisa and Miquel to the kitchen. I cared deeply for my employees and thought of them as more friends than people who worked for me. I told them both about the storm warning and that I wanted them to go home and make sure that they had everything they needed to protect their homes and families. I asked if they would come early tomorrow morning to create a plan to protect the bakery from the impending storm. Louisa and Miquel nodded in agreement and headed home to make their preparations. They both seemed to appreciate the concern.

As I closed the bakery, I couldn't help but feel a sense of responsibility, not only for my business but also for my employees and community. Like most storms forecasted for this part of the coastline, I hoped that it would shift and be no more than a few days' worth of heavy rain.

I reached in my bag for the car keys and heard my phone ding with a text message.

Piper: Storms a brewing. Seems like Michael and Madison tempted fate too many times, and

Now Mother Nature is paying back, hahaha.

Me: You're not wrong about that girl!!!! Tropical storm party at my place tonight? I'll make my special pasta.

Piper: You had me at Tropical Storm party.

I pulled up to the front of my townhouse and stared in disbelief. Michael was sitting on the front stairs waiting for me. I couldn't decide if I wanted to back up and keep driving or drive full steam ahead and run the bastard over. Seeing as I have a carload of groceries and work, I decided neither option was good. I decided to rip the band-aid off and get this confrontation over with. I knew it was coming one way or another. I may as well get it done. Michael approached the car when he saw me struggling with my bags.

"Truce Gracie? At least so I can help with all this stuff."

I just shrugged and grabbed my arm load, heading to the front door and leaving the door open for Michael to follow behind.

I love my townhouse. Walking down the entryway, it opens to a large bank of windows overlooking the bay. Tucked into the windows is a little sitting nook full of plush cushions in tones of sea greens and sky blues. A soft blanket slung over the back to make for a cozy reading area. I think this is one of my favorite spots in the house. To the left is the beautiful kitchen full of white cabinetry and that hand-crafted turquoise blue island. I don't think I'll ever look at the kitchen the same way again. To the right is the living room/family room. Soft grey tones on the walls and my Pottery Barn plush white sectional make the room inviting. I notice the number of framed pictures of me and Michael, bite my lip and realize I still haven't taken those pictures down. I couldn't even begin to tell you why they were still there. That would be remedied tonight, for sure. I place my bags on the island and turn to Michael.

"If you're here to get your things from the storage shed, go ahead and do it. I don't want you back in my house, Michael. Otherwise, I have nothing to say to you. I think everything was pretty much said when I got the damn mail yesterday."

"I don't know what to say, Gracie. I know I'm sorry won't even cover how much I've hurt you, but I really am sorry. I never meant for any of this to happen, let alone you finding out the way you did. I just…"

Seething with anger, I almost spit the words in Michael's face as I say, "What the fuck Michael. You didn't mean for me to find out this way?? You're sorry?? You're sorry, all right. A sorry sack of shit is what you are. We were just making our wedding plans a few months ago, for fuck's sake, and now you're marrying her!!! Was that all a lie? Did you ever plan on marrying me, or was the plan to humiliate me?"

Michael grimaces at the anger of my tone.

"I don't know what you want me to tell you, Gracie. I thought I wanted marriage with you. I did, but I think I just thought that's what we were supposed to do. We've been together for so long that everyone expected us to get married, so I asked. When things started between me and

Madison, I realized that you and I had become more like roommates than lovers. You and I wanted different things out of life. I want more than small-town living, Gracie. I didn't know how to tell you."

"So, you fuck my friend instead? You're a gutless piece of shit, Michael," I spit out. "I'll take some of the blame, though, because I'm the stupid, naïve girl who stayed with you all these years even though I knew about the other girls in college. Here's the thing, Michael: I undervalued myself. I always felt so special that you picked me over all the other girls in high school. The big football star choosing the science nerd over the cheerleaders and popular girls. I think that's why I stayed all these years and kept a blind eye to the cheating. But you know what, Michael? I'm so much better than that. I'm so much better than you; you don't deserve me. So, no more of your bullshit. Grab whatever shit you left in storage and get the hell out. If that's too much for you, I'll call Nathan to pack up your crap and bring it to you."

Turning from Michael, I walk towards the patio doors and say, "I let you take ten years of my life; I won't let you take anything else from me." With that, I walk outside and wait for Michael to leave.

****

Piper entered the townhouse with a whirlwind of energy and brought a haul of supplies worthy of any good tropical storm party. Her arms were loaded with booze, snacks, and other treats.

"Please tell me that wasn't Michael I saw leaving," Piper exclaimed, her words a mix of curiosity and annoyance. "What the hell did that loser want?"

I couldn't help but chuckle at Piper as I helped unload the supplies. "Ugh, eff my life. He thought he could come here with some bullshit apology and explanation, but honestly, I don't want to hear anything he has to say. I let him take what he needed and told him I'd have Nathan come for the rest of his things."

Piper rolled her eyes, clearly unimpressed by what Michael had to say. "I hope he heeds your warning and stays away," Holding up her small fists, Piper continues, "Otherwise, he'll be on the receiving end of one Piper Jackson. Now, let's crack open that bourbon and get this party started. We're here to have a good time before this storm rolls through."

The two of us settle in, bound and determined to put the Michael situation on hold for the night, and enjoy each other's company and the supplies Piper brought. With the first of many drinks in my hand, I turned to Piper and told her about Nathan waiting for me outside the bakery this morning.

"Hmm, Nathan Sundry. Very interesting, Boo. He's hot. Even in high school, when he was the quiet, broody football player, he was still super-hot. He could be fun. You know what I mean by fun. He's never really dated anyone seriously. He's one of those locals who only likes to hook up with tourists. I can't remember the last time I saw him with a girlfriend. He's the perfect guy to get under if you know what I mean." Piper chuckled and raised her eyebrows up and down.

I waved my hands back and forth, "No way, Piper. I don't think Nathan even looks at me that way for one thing and for another; my life just epically blew up. I'm not looking for a new man. As a matter of fact, I may be done with men forever."

Piper just rolled her eyes at me and laughed. "Okay, Gracie girl. Whatever you say." I knew Piper was dropping the subject to appease me, but I couldn't help but think about what she said. I had always had a little crush on Nathan. He had been so cute in high school, but now he was devastatingly handsome. I would be a fool to think he wanted more than friendship with me. Wouldn't I?

******

I adjusted my notes, smoothing the pages against the table for what seemed like the hundredth time. Nathan was late again. I told myself it didn't matter—this wasn't a date or anything—just tutoring. I was helping him pass the biology test so he wouldn't fail, so he wouldn't have to repeat junior year.

The door to the library creaked open, and there he was, all easy charm and slightly rumpled jeans. "Sorry, Gracie," he said, flashing that grin as he dropped his backpack onto the chair beside me. "Got held up. You ready to help me save my grade?"

I forced myself to roll my eyes instead of smiling back. "If by 'save your grade' you mean drag it kicking and screaming out of the gutter, then yeah."

Nathan laughed, leaning closer to see my notes. I caught a whiff of his scent—fresh ocean breeze mixed with cedar and citrus- and it made my heart do an embarrassing flip. Focus, I told myself. "Okay, mitochondria," I began, pointing to my carefully labeled diagram. "What's it called?"

"The… powerhouse of the cell?" he guessed, his voice hesitant.

"Right!" I said, maybe a little too enthusiastically. His eyes lit up, and I felt my cheeks go hot. Stupid. "Now, what does it actually do?"

Nathan blinked at me blankly, and I sighed, unable to hide a small smile. "Okay, let's try this again."

I walked him through the basics for the next hour, trying not to notice how he fidgeted with his pen or leaned closer when I spoke. It was just tutoring. I was just helping. And if my heart raced every time he said my name, he didn't need to know that.

Chapter 2

Nathan

Driving away, I silently cursed myself for stopping by Beach Buns. What the hell had gotten into me? Michael was my friend. Maybe the friendship had its share of ups and downs, but, Jesus, there is a guy code, after all. How was I sitting in front of her bakery, flirting with Gracie? Sure, I'd had a crush on Gracie in high school. How could I not? She was funny and sweet with her share of hidden snarkiness. Those whiskey brown eyes always looking directly into my soul. There were so many times over the years I'd been jealous of Michael. Jealous that he had the girl I had always wanted. So many times, I didn't want to cover for him when he cheated over and over—finding out now that Gracie had always known what Michael was doing and my part in it broke my heart. God, I need to snap of this. I can't be anything but a friend to Gracie. No matter what Michael has done, he doesn't deserve his friend to betray him.

For the past couple of months, I've hung back watching Gracie. Beach Buns had become my favorite spot for a quick treat between work. When she and Michael ended, I thought that was my chance. Finally, I could go after Gracie, but she had been crushed and embarrassed. When you live in a town the size of Moonrise Bay, everyone knows your business and thinks they're entitled to their opinion on your life. I've been on the receiving end of those opinions time and again.

Here we are, and nothing changes. Michael is still fucking things up with Gracie. Letting Madison send that "save the date." I knew Madison could be a petty bitch, but Michael had at least loved Gracie at some point. At least, I thought he did. I can't imagine how Gracie felt getting that card in the mail. It makes me sick in the pit of my stomach.

I decide to turn on the radio; the last few lines of the Zach Bryan song play. Heading towards the newest house I'm building, I glance out the window of my truck. The winds have picked up, and the skies were beginning to darken. It looked like a storm was rolling off the coast. I change to the weather station and hear what I was afraid of. A tropical storm is heading toward the North Carolina coast. This time of year is usually notorious for the worst storms, even though the end of hurricane season is just around the corner. The unusually warm weather seems to be fueling the ocean's fury as if it is seeking revenge on the coastline.

My primary concern is getting to the job site to protect the frame my team just finished. In the back of my mind, I'm also worried about my home and Gracie. I hope the storm will hold off a few days so I can board up my house and protect it from the storm. Once I secure both the job site and my house, maybe I'll head inland to my parents' house to ride out the storm. Or maybe before heading out, I'd stop by and check on Gracie.

*****

I could hear the music in the street as I approached Gracie's townhouse. The thumping bass and melodic tunes grew louder with every step I took toward the front of the house. The vibrant rhythm of the music pulsated through the air, creating a palpable energy that filled the neighborhood. As I neared the front door, I couldn't help but smile. I could see the source of the energy through the front window. There she was, all wavy hair and smokey laughter, dancing the night away with her best friend, Piper Jackson. I froze at the sight of the two women, their silhouettes dancing to the beat of Taylor Swift's "Are You Ready for It?" Their slightly slurred voices carried the lyrics as they danced with unbridled enthusiasm. The unmistakable scent of bourbon hung in the air, and my eyes widened as I noticed the near-empty bottle on the nearby table. It was evident that they had indulged in quite a few drinks, and I couldn't help but feel a mix of surprise and curiosity as I watched them enjoy their impromptu party.

As the song's final notes faded away, Piper and Gracie both jumped in surprise at the sound of my clearing throat. With her heart still racing from the unexpected interruption, Piper blurted out "Lord love a duck, Nathan Sundry. Make a girl pee her pants, why don't you?"

I couldn't help but chuckle at Piper's reaction.   "Sorry about that," I said with a sheepish grin. "I didn't mean to startle you. Looks like you two are having quite the party for two here."

Gracie, slightly flushed and still swaying to the music, grinned and replied, "You have no idea, Nathan. We decided on an impromptu tropical storm party. There's plenty of booze and storm snacks. Get on in here and join us for some dancing and drinking!!"

I stood there for a moment, my thoughts a whirlwind of uncertainty. I questioned whether I should be here in this situation with Gracie or if I was just overthinking things. It was just a dance and drinks, right? But I couldn't ignore the undeniable feelings I had for her. Man, she look absolutely gorgeous. Swaying to the music, completely uninhibited. She danced like she didn't have a care in the world.

As I pondered the situation, thoughts of my friendship with Michael weighed on my mind. I knew Michael had royally fucked things up with Gracie, but he was still my friend. Did I want to jeopardize that? With a deep breath and a wry smile, I walked towards Gracie, just for tonight. I would drink and dance without worrying about what it meant.

Surprised, Gracie shouted, "Woohoo, Nathan Sundry, you dirty sneak. Let's turn things up a notch and pour another round of shots." Gracie's excitement was infectious, and I couldn't help but get caught up in the moment.

"Alright, Gracie," I said with a grin, "let's grab those shots." As we moved to the makeshift bar, I decided to set aside my doubts and live in the moment. Having a few drinks with Gracie didn't mean anything. After all, I'd known her just as long as I'd known Michael. We'd all been friends for years. No, for now, I'd go with the flow and see where the night would take me.

Chapter 3

Gracie

I couldn't believe I was standing here in my living room taking shots with Nathan Sundry. When was the last time we had hung out like this without Michael? Grad night, maybe. Damn did this man fill out a Henley shirt and a pair of blue jeans. I could swear Nathan's biceps were trying to escape the sleeves of his shirt. Great, now I was picturing Nathan without his shirt on. Phew, was it getting hot in here? As if Nathan could feel my eyes on him, he looked down at me with a devilish grin across his face.

"You alright there, Gracie," Nathan said wryly. "See something you like?" Nathan winked and wandered over to Piper with drinks in hand.

A blush crept up my cheeks as Nathan walked away, chuckling. Good Lord, did I love to watch him walk away. Jesus, what has gotten into me tonight? Was it the old fashioneds that Piper had been mixing all night or the shots? Or was it the smokin' hot man singing along to Tyler Childers's "I Swear to God" in my living room? I wasn't sure what was happening. I could feel a zing all through my body when Nathan snuck glances my way. I had to remind myself that my relationship had just epically exploded. Not to mention, Nathan was Michael's best friend. Even if Michael and Madison didn't respect those boundaries, I sure as shit did. Didn't I?

As I walked over to Nathan and Piper, I couldn't help but notice the intensity of their conversation about the impending storm.

"What do you think the chances are this storm will blow past Moonrise?" Piper asked Nathan.

"Well," Nathan began, "I've been following the it, and even though it's only Tuesday, it seems like there's a good chance the storm may blow past Moonrise. But you know how unpredictable these things can be." He glanced my way, and it seemed his attention was momentarily divided between the storm and staring into my face.

I gave a warm, if not slightly tipsy smile, "From your lips to Mother Nature's ears." I said softly, my voice carrying a hint of concern and intoxication.

Piper, swaying a bit, glanced between me and Nathan and abruptly announced, "Okay, kids, I'm drunk, it's late, and I have to open the library tomorrow, assuming the town doesn't close down. I'm taking my happy ass up to the guestroom and calling it a night."

Nathan and I exchanged a knowing look, amused by Piper's announcement. Nathan chuckled and softly said, "Thanks for letting me crash your party tonight, Piper; sleep well."

I nod my agreement, my smile reflecting Piper's infectious spirit. "Thanks for always being one text away, girl. Love you Pipes."

Blowing me a kiss and playful wink, Piper headed up the stairs, making her way to the guestroom. As she disappeared from view, Nathan and I were left alone. The wind had begun to gust a bit outside, but a sense of warmth and connection filled the room. We sank into the comfort of the plush sofa, the silence between us speaking volumes. The sound of rain tapping against the windows and the occasional rumble of thunder filled the air, creating a cozy atmosphere. We both seemed lost in our thoughts and the unspoken connection we shared.

Finally, after what felt like forever, Nathan broke the silence, "It's been quite a night," he said softly, his gaze turning towards me.

I turned towards him, a hint of a smile playing on my lips. "It has," I replied, my voice equally gentle. "Sometimes the best moments are the ones where nothing needs to be said."

Nathan and I sat in companionable silence for a while, just listening to the rain. I could feel my eyelids growing heavier and couldn't fight them much longer. Out of habit, I rested my head on Nathan's shoulder. I'd just close my eyes for a few minutes. I'd had so much to drink and was so exhausted from the stresses of the past months. God, had it only been a couple of months since my life had exploded? It seemed like a lifetime ago. As I drifted to sleep, I felt a sense of safety and warmth in Nathan's presence.

****

I didn't remember falling asleep, let alone falling asleep on the very rock-solid body of one Nathan Sundry. As soon as I realized that it was Nathan's arms wrapped around me this morning, I carefully extracted myself from the sofa situation and made my way upstairs to my bedroom.

Glancing in the bathroom mirror, I was horrified by the image staring back at me. Since

I had more or less passed out last night, I had makeup smudges under my eyes, and my caramel brown locks were sticking out in all directions. Lord have mercy; it might take a miracle to make this presentable. I quickly brushed my teeth and ran a brush through my untamable hair. Deciding to just give up and throw my hair up in a top knot, I made a quick pass over my face with a warm washcloth and headed downstairs to get the coffee pot going. Remembering I was supposed to meet with Louisa and Miquel, I texted them that I was running behind and I probably wouldn't be there when they opened at 8 am.

Me: *So sorry, guys. I may have had a bit too much to drink last night…. Running late.*

Louisa: *No worries lady!!! If anyone deserves to blow off some steam, it's you. Don't worry about the bakery; Miquel and I've got you.*

Miquel: *Yeah, boss, we got you, and if that shitbag ex of yours comes anywhere near the bakery, he'll*

be very sorry.

Me: *Aww, you guys really are the best crew!!!*

I couldn't help but smile after putting my phone down. I was so lucky to have people like Louisa and Miquel working for me. I threw on my Beach Bun's sweatshirt and favorite pair of yoga pants and headed to the kitchen.

Passing the living room on the way to make coffee, a quiet laught escaped me at the sounds of Nathan snoring. He sure did look cute, snoozing away on my couch.

I headed into the kitchen and pressed start on the coffeemaker. Remembering I had a batch of the bakery's signature cinnamon sugar cruffins in the freezer, I decided to grab a few and throw them in the oven to warm up. I smiled, thinking how they were Nathan's favorite.

Piper slowly entered the kitchen, holding her head and looking a little like death warmed over.

"Ugh, remind me again why I thought drinking an entire bottle of bourbon would be a good idea." She slumped down in one of the barstools around the island and threw her head down.

I laughed and asked, "Do you need coffee Pipes?"

Piper looked up at me with one eye open and replied, "Can you just shoot some straight in my veins? I have no idea how I will face the kindergartners we have coming into the library this morning."

I tried to hide the smile on my face as I handed Piper her steaming cup of coffee. I couldn't figure out why I wasn't feeling as hungover as Piper looked, but I felt almost energized this morning. Was it because I had woken up spooning on the couch with the deliciously handsome Nathan Sundry? I could still smell him on my me. The scent of cedar and the sea with a hint of citrus. I took a deep breath, inhaling that glorious scent. I tried not to read too much into those thoughts. For goodness sake, I'd just broken up with Michael not more than two months ago. I definitely should not be having lusty feelings for Nathan.

Piper's head whipped around to the living room. She heard Nathan stirring on the couch, and then she shot me a devilish smile.

"Gracie Ann Henderson, you sneaky, sneaky bitch. Did you and Nathan sleep together last night?" Piper asked while wiggling her eyebrows. "You know they say the best way to get over someone is to get under someone new."

I had to keep from spitting my coffee across the room as I whispered angrily, "Keep your voice down, Piper, and no, nothing happened between me and Nathan. We just fell asleep on the sofa after too many drinks. For goodness sake, I've barely been single. I'm definitely not ready to mingle."

Piper moved from the stool she was sitting on and crossed to where I was standing.

Wrapping her arms around me, she said, "Simmer down, Gracie, and don't get your undies in a bunch. I was just teasing you. But...I would be thrilled at the idea of you and Nathan Sundry. Girl, the man is a walking Calvin Klein billboard, for Christ's sake. He's so hot you could probably fry an egg on his rock-hard stomach. I'm not saying you need to act on anything right now; I'm just saying, don't shut out thoughts of something happening in the future." She smacked a loud kiss on my face and turned to walk down the hallway towards the front door. "Wish me luck today, babes. I'm gonna need it."

I smiled, thinking about hungover Piper trying to corral a bunch of five-year-olds. I loved that girl with a fierceness and counted my lucky stars that Piper and I were still friends after all these years. Without Piper, I would never have had the courage to open the bakery, and I certainly wouldn't have been able to climb out of bed after the disaster my relationship with Michael turned out to be.

I stopped in my tracks at the noise coming from the living room. The floor betrayed Nathan's stealthy approach with a loud creak, startling me. My eyes widened as I turned toward the source of the noise. Damn, Nathan looked hot first thing in the morning with his sleep-mussed air and disheveled appearance. He was frozen, realizing he had been less discreet than he'd intended. I think my surprised look must have mirrored what Nathan was feeling as he said, "Oh, sorry. I didn't mean to startle you," he stammered, embarrassed that he'd been caught gawking at me.

I recovered quickly, offering a warm but mischievous smile. "No worries, Nathan. I'm jumpy before my first cup of coffee in the morning," I teased, easing the tension in the room. "Did you want to join me for a cup, or do you just want to lurk in the shadows? I've got your favorite cruffins warming in the oven."

Nathan chuckled, his cheeks turning slightly pink. "Well, I can't say no to one of your famous cruffins, can I?" I motioned for him to come closer, handing him a cup of coffee. Nathan stepped towards me and smiled. "Now, what's this I hear about a Calvin Klein model?"

I nervously tucked a loose strand of hair behind my ear, "Oh, you heard that, did you? Not spying on us girls, were you?"

Nathan leaned down close enough that I could feel his warm breath kissing my neck, and I steadied myself at the invasion of my space. His lips were so close to brushing my ear as he said in a husky voice, "Gracie, a man can't help but eavesdrop when he hears two beautiful women talking about him."

I could feel my face redden as Nathan

took a few steps back and leaned against the refrigerator, smiling like the Cheshire Cat. I was stunned silent until the oven timer dinged.

"Hmm, saved by the bell," Nathan replied, "Thanks for breakfast, Gracie, and for last night." Nathan pushed off the fridge and leaned in towards my face. I was glued in my spot as Nathan's warm lips gently pressed against my cheek. It was the lightest of kisses, but the jolt of heat that zinged through my body made my mind reel. My brain screamed at me, "This is wrong; this is Nathan," but I couldn't push him away.

Nathan smiled, grabbed his to-go cup of coffee and warm cruffin, and started walking towards the front door. Just before leaving the kitchen, he turned and said, "Hope we can do this again, Gracie," and walked down the hallway and out the door.

I just stood there in a state of WTF. Like seriously, what the hell just happened? I blew out a deep breath and tried to get my shit together.

Was Nathan Sundry seriously flirting with me? In my kitchen, no less? Jesus, what a way to start the day. First, I'd woken up spooning him on my couch, and now this...whatever the hell this little interaction was. God, when he leaned in to whisper in my ear, I thought I would turn into a puddle of goo on the floor. Even thinking about it now made my heart skip a beat.

No, no, this was ridiculous. I had been single for all of a hot minute; I had no business picturing Nathan naked, hands roaming my body. Ugh, I needed to get out of here and distract myself with work—no more impure thoughts. Grabbing my keys and coffee, I ran out the door, hoping I would be able to keep my mind off Mr. Nathan Sundry.

Chapter 4

Gracie

Well, that didn't last long.

Chapter 5

Nathan

I kept busy the rest of the week getting both the job site and my house ready for the coming storm. Thankfully, by Thursday, the storm had been downgraded to a tropical depression, and it just amounted to a few days' worth of rain and some wind. The downside to working construction during lousy weather was that when it rained like this, there was no work. I hated getting behind on a deadline. That would mean double the time for my crew and me so we could finish this house on time. This house was part of a development Michael's father was working on, and I was happy to have the job. I didn't go to college like the rest of my friends after high school. Instead, I stayed in Moonrise Bay and went to work for my Uncle Jay's construction company. About five years in, he made me his partner, and we have been the main construction crew in the Bay Area ever since.

It was Friday morning, and I was the first

to arrive at the job site. I was in my trailer looking over the designs when the trailer door opened, and Michael walked in. He had a scowl on his face.

"Hey man, can we talk a minute?" He sat down and looked a bit uncomfortable.

"Sure, what's up, Mike?

"This is awkward, especially given my current situation, but I heard something the other day, and I just wanted to check with you and see if it was true."

Shit, shit, shit. He must have heard about me leaving Gracie's house Tuesday morning. I fell asleep on the couch after drinking too much with her and Piper. Nothing had happened. Well, nothing but waking up with Gracie in my arms. I had woken up with her backside pushed flush against my crotch. That certainly did not help with my morning wood situation. Staring down at her sleeping face, I felt helpless; full of conflicting emotions. I had always had this attraction for Gracie, but she was also my friend's girlfriend. Well, technically, not anymore, but there was a bro code to consider.

"Okay...just tell me what's on your mind, Mike." I was dreading what he was going to say next. While we hadn't been as close as we were in high school, I still considered him a friend. I didn't want to ruin our friendship.

"Did you spend the night with Gracie Monday night? Come on, man, the body isn't even cold yet."

"It wasn't like that, Mike. With the tropical storm warning, I was worried about her, and I stopped by to check in on my way home. She and Piper were drunk and invited me in for a drink. I was too drunk to drive myself home, so I slept on her couch. I promise nothing happened."

"Oh man, that's a relief. I know I don't have much room to say anything, but it freaked me out thinking of you and Gracie together."

I didn't know why, but that pissed me off. I know that I shouldn't get involved with Gracie. I know that goes against "bro code," but what about what Mike and Madison had done to Gracie? What about all the other times he had cheated on her? What about all the awkward positions he put in me in covering up his indiscretions? Was I only now seeing Michael for the selfish bastard he was? Was I guilty of being just as naïve as Gracie had been all these years? I didn't know the answers, but I didn't like how I was feeling looking at my friend, so I decided it was time to confront him.

"Jesus, Mike, don't you think that's a little hypocritical of you? You're currently screwing one of Gracie's friends, and you're marrying her in a couple of months. Are you worried about whether something happened between Gracie and me? Frankly, I think you lost the right to know who's in her bed the minute you put your dick in Madison Burke."

The stupefied look on his face said it all. I had never said anything like that to him in his life. Just like everybody else around him, I'd let Michael always get away with whatever shit he'd tried to pull. Not anymore.

"What the hell, Nathan? Look, I know what Madison and I did was wrong, but we fell in love. We didn't intend for it to happen. You've always had a thing for Gracie, going back to high school. So what, I end things with her, and now you're swooping in?"

"Whoa, whoa, whoa, dude. Let's get a few things straight. First, she literally caught you with your pants down. Second, I haven't "swooped" anywhere. She's my friend too. Lastly, you knew I had a thing for Gracie in high school and asked her out anyway? That makes you a shitty friend for going after her in the first place."

Fuck this guy, I thought to myself. He knew I liked Gracie in high school and had asked her out anyway. Thinking back on the day I finally worked up the courage to ask her out, it all made sense.

I walked into English class with the usual mix of boredom and dread. Senior year was grinding on, and Mr. Henson's lectures on symbolism weren't exactly lighting anyone's fire. As I slid into my seat near the back, I glanced around the room—and there she was. Gracie. She was sitting at her desk near the window, the sunlight catching her caramel brown hair in a way that made it look like a fiery halo. She laughed at something Piper whispered to her, the sound so effortless and genuine that it seemed to pull all the air from the room. I had always thought she was beautiful, but it hit me differently today.

Maybe it was the way her eyes crinkled at the corners when she smiled or how she absentmindedly twirled her pen in her fingers. Or maybe it was the growing realization that I was tired of sitting back and admiring her from a distance.

I'd been holding back for months, convincing myself it wasn't the right time, that she didn't feel the same, or that our friendship would complicate things. But as I sat there, watching her laugh like she didn't have a care in the world, I knew I couldn't wait any longer.

This was the moment. I was going to ask her out.

The bell rang, and Mr. Henson began droning

about the significance of some river in Huckleberry Finn, *but I barely heard a word. My heart was pounding in my chest, and my palms were clammy. I couldn't stop glancing at Gracie. I pictured how I'd say it—casual but confident. "Hey, Gracie, do you want to go out sometime?" Simple.*

It was perfect in my head, but the bubble of anticipation popped when I overheard Piper's voice behind me.

"Oh my gosh, I can't believe Michael Garrett asked you out," Piper said, her voice brimming with excitement.

I froze, my pen suspended mid-note.

Gracie's response was quieter, almost shy. "I know. I didn't see it coming, but... yeah. He's really sweet."

My chest tightened, and a cold, bitter feeling spread through me. I turned slightly in my seat, catching the way Gracie's cheeks turned pink as she smiled.

Michael.

My best friend.

I gripped my pen so tightly that I thought it might snap. Michael knew. We'd spent countless late-night gaming sessions where I had confessed how much I liked Gracie. How I couldn't get her laugh out of my head or stop thinking about how her handwriting was just as neat and thoughtful as she was. Michael had teased me, sure, but he'd never once hinted at liking her too.

And now Michael had swooped in, acting like none of that mattered.

I barely heard the rest of the class. My stomach churned with a mix of anger and betrayal. I avoided looking at Gracie, afraid I might say something stupid—or worse, let her see how much it hurt.

I grabbed my books and bolted for the door when the bell finally rang. I needed air. More than that, I needed to figure out how I was supposed to face either of them.

******

I watched Michael storm out of the trailer and realized how little he cared about anything but himself. I'm done. Done with Michael and his bullshit. Done tiptoeing around Michael's feelings. It was time for me to shoot my shot with Gracie Henderson finally. Michael Garrett wouldn't get in my way this time. I pulled out my phone and sent a quick text to Gracie.

Me: *Hey, Gracie. Holding down the fort over there? No more bourbon parties?*

Gracie: *You mean my super-secret bourbon parties? Wouldn't you like to know?*

Me: *So, how does one get invited to a super-secret bourbon party?*

Gracie: If I told you that, it wouldn't be super-secret, now would it? *laughing face emoji*

Me: You're trouble, aren't you, Gracie Girl?

Gracie: And don't you forget it, Nathan

Me: Goodnight Gracie Girl

Gracie: Goodnight Nathan.

Chapter 6

Gracie

It had been a quiet couple of weeks at the bakery. Even though it was later downgraded, the impending storm had driven many vacationers home early, making our tiny beach community quiet again. The slow week had allowed me to get caught up on paperwork and schedule custom orders. Even though Moonrise Bay was a small town, the bakery was still busy during the holiday season. With Halloween right around the corner, I had a ton of custom cake and treat orders. Thankfully, I had been so busy the past couple of weeks that I hadn't really had time to think about Michael. Nathan, on the other hand…I couldn't get him off my mind. Thank God for the upcoming holidays.

This was my favorite time of year. From Halloween to New Year's Eve, I considered this my awards season. Not to toot my own horn, but I am a very talented baker. Being an art major in school had helped with cake design and I had become the area's premier wedding cake designer.

The last customer had just walked out the door when Miquel whooshed past me with the mop.

"Thank Fuck, Mama!!! I thought this day would never end." He kept mopping while I walked over and turned the open sign off.

"Jesus, I know what you mean. Thanks to that damn storm, it was even slower than it usually is in the off-season. Hopefully, with Halloween coming up in a couple of weeks, things will pick back up. We do have a bunch of new custom orders, so it should be a busy weekend."

Miquel just rolled his eyes and continued mopping "Girl when are you going to get back up on the horse and show that asshole Michael just what he let go? You work so much; you're never going to meet anyone. Hey, my cousin Ramon just moved back to town. Want me to hook you guys up?"

It was all I could do not to laugh. Miquel's cousin Ramon was 330lb, balding and maybe 5ft 7. Not exactly my type. Not that looks are the only thing I look for in a man, but I'm not really interested in a large, balding short man if you know what I mean. I just smiled and said, "No thanks Miquel. It's really too soon for me to even think about going on a date. I'm just not ready to meet someone."

"Ok girl, but you might want to tell that to fine piece of man sitting in his pickup truck parked out front." I jumped at Lousia's stealthiness. I hadn't even heard her step up behind me.

Laughing I turned to Louisa "Jesus woman, you about gave me heart attack. I didn't even know you were standing there. What guy parked out front?"

Louisa just shrugged and said "Nathan Sundry. I know that man loves our cinnamon sugar cruffins, but he also knows it's closing time. Something tells me he's not here for your muffin" she smiled devilishly and said, "Or is he?"

I could feel my cheeks getting warm and knew I had a slight blush blooming. Looking out the window and trying not to be noticed, I wondered why Nathan was sitting in his truck. He had been so sweet to check on me the night of the storm warning. One day, he'd even stopped by and picked up the rest of Michael's things from the back patio. I smiled at the memory of leaving them in the pouring rain. I know that wasn't fair to Nathan, but I didn't give a shit if it pissed Michael off.

Other than that day, I hadn't seen Nathan since the morning I woke up spooning him on the sofa. As awkward as that moment was, all I could think about was how good it had felt to have Nathan's arms around me. I kept telling myself, that's just the hurt talking. Yes, in high school, I had a little crush on Nathan, but I had loved Michael. These warm feelings growing between my legs when I thought about Nathan were only because I felt so betrayed by Michael. I was not, under any circumstances, going to revenge fuck Micheal's friend. The image that just flashed through my mind had me clinching my thighs together. Nathan, naked and thrusting. Woo was it getting hot in here? Fuck, I need to get home and get my vibrator out.

Louisa patted me on the back, leaned in, and said, "Honey, just go out there and talk to him. Nobody ever got in trouble for just talking." That said, she turned and walked to the back of the bakery. Miquel was nowhere in sight. I guessed that he was waiting by his locker for Louisa. Maybe she was right. Nobody did get in trouble for just talking. I didn't know why I was being so silly. It was just Nathan, after all.

Walking out the front door, I saw him sitting in his truck. Ballcap pulled down over his eyes, the seat moved all the way back, and his legs propped up on the dash. Damn, was he a beautiful man? I hated to disturb what looked like a nice nap, but I decided to tap on his window anyway.

Jolted by the knock on his window, Nathan pulled the ballcap up and turned to face me. He smiled as he rolled his window down.

"Hey Gracie, sorry, I didn't even realize I'd fallen asleep." The sheepish look on his face made my heart pitter-patter.

"Hey Nathan, can't get enough of our cruffins, can you?" I winked and smiled at him.

"I don't know Gracie. I guess you just can't get too much of a good thing." The smile he gave me in return was the most panty-melting smile I've ever seen on anyone's face. How did he keep doing that? I knew he could see the blush creeping up on my face. I wasn't ready for Nathan to know how much he affected me, though.

Putting my hands on my hips, I replied, "Well, maybe we'll just have to see about that, won't we." If looks could make a girl wet, then the look this man was shooting my way was about to cause a flood. God, it felt good to flirt again. It felt good to feel light and sexy.

"Have dinner with me tonight, Gracie, and maybe we'll find out."

Phew, knock a girl over with a feather because I did not have Nathan Sundry asking me out to dinner on my bingo card. I just stood there gawking awkwardly before I even tried to respond. Honestly, I didn't know what to do. I wish Piper were here. She'd tell me exactly what to do. I could almost hear her voice saying *if you don't go out with Nathan Sundry, I'll never speak to you again.* Maybe it was time for me to stop thinking and start doing. It was just dinner, for crying out loud, not a marriage proposal.

Before I could change my mind, I said, "Dinner sounds fun, Nathan. I need to finish closing the bakery, but I'd be happy to meet you somewhere. Have a place in mind?"

He smiled, and his eyes did that crinkling in-the-corners thing that I love, and he replied, "Oh, I have a place in mind. Why don't you come to my house, and I'll grill some steaks for us? You bring dessert and wine. How's seven sound to you?"

Before I could chicken out, I nodded and said, "I have the perfect treat."

Nathan laughed a low, rumbling laugh and began to roll up his window.

"You're trouble, aren't you, Gracie Henderson?" he said as he began backing out of his parking spot. I didn't have a chance to respond before he pulled out of the lot. What have I gotten myself into? Dinner with Nathan

Sundry. Oh God, what was I going to wear? Shit, I needed to finish closing so I could get home to shower and call Piper. I needed emergency fashion help ASAP.

****

Immediately after walking through my front door, I fired off a text to Piper.

Me: *Pipes, HELP!!!! Nathan asked over to his house for dinner—no clue what to wear.*

Piper: *OMG!!!! It's happening. Ok, do not panic. You need to play it totally causal. Wear your super cute boyfriend jeans, tight tank, and pink cardigan. Pair it with those cute pink, strappy sandals you have. Hair up in a top knot with a few wisps of hair framing your face and light makeup. Definitely wear that luscious pink lip gloss. It totally makes your lips look kissable.*

Me: *Do I want to make my lips look kissable? Am I ready for that???*

Piper: *YESSSSS. Babes, relax. Have a nice dinner and some good wine. Enjoy yourself, and stop overthinking.*

Me: *Kk, I'll try. Thanks for always talking me off a ledge, Pipes.*

Piper: *Love you, boo boo.*

Me: *Love you, mean it, Pipes.*

Okay, fashion crisis averted, now it was

shower time. I followed Piper's advice to a tee and grabbed my favorite bottle of pinot noir to take to Nathan's. Shit, I'd almost forgotten my triple chocolate brownies. These were a customer favorite, and I brought a freshly baked batch home from the bakery. I took a deep breath and gathered up my courage. I kept reminding myself it was just dinner. It's not like Nathan had said, "Hey, Gracie, wanna come over to my place and bang one out." That's not the type of guy Nathan was. No, this was simply two friends getting together to have a nice dinner and hang out. Sure, we hadn't hung out in a while, and come to think of it, I don't think Nathan and I had ever really hung out, just the two of us. Maybe back in high school, but I think that was technically me tutoring Nathan in science. I don't really think you could call that hanging out. Ok, Gracie, you're spiraling; get it together.

I grabbed my bag and my keys and jumped in my Scout. It was a beautiful night out. The sky was lit up with beautiful hues of pinks, oranges and purple. No clouds in the sky, and it was a perfect night for dinner on the patio.

Pulling into Nathan's driveway, I'm struck by how lovely his house is. Maybe I shouldn't be, given the fact that Nathan is a contractor. I guess I'm stereotyping him with men in general, but he has the cutest farmhouse-style home. A gorgeous white two-story house with black shudders and a wraparound porch. Perched on the side of the front door are the most adorable rocking chairs. Standing there, I could envision Nathan and me sipping iced tea, sitting on the porch while we watch our kids running around the front yard.

Wait, what? Where the hell did that come from? I really need to get it together, or I'm never going to make it through this dinner. Jesus, why am I so nervous? Ok, it was now or never.

Here goes nothing. I lift my hand and knock on the front door. As the door opened, I held my breath at the vision in front of me. Nathan Sundry...hottest man I've ever seen and tonight all his attention would be on me.

Chapter 7

Nathan

Opening the front door, Gracie almost takes my breath away. My God, she's a beautiful woman. Standing on my front porch in loose-fitting jeans; with a tank top that makes her tits look like they're trying to escape. Whoa. And don't even get me started on her damn pink lip gloss. Jesus, I hope she doesn't sneak a peek at the bulge in my pants. I'm sure I've got the makings of a righteous hard-on started and I don't know if I'll be able to explain that away.

"Hey Gracie, let me take your bags. Mmm, what smells so good?" I say as I grab what's in her hands and usher her inside.

I can see her blush a little bit as she says, "Oh, thanks, Nathan. It must be my triple chocolate brownies. I figured you can't go wrong with red wine and chocolate, right?"

Damnit, she's so cute. I'm a goner, for sure.

"Come on back, and we can open that wine, or would you rather start with a cocktail? I make a pretty mean old-fashioned."

"Well, I won't say no to an old-fashioned," she says with the cutest smile. "Nathan, your house is gorgeous. Did you do all the work yourself?"

I felt a swelling of pride when she complimented my house. My uncle and I did most of the design work, and I'm pretty damn proud of what we built. It's nothing too fancy, but it's all mine. I lead her into the kitchen, which is a more masculine kitchen than most houses—deep walnut cabinetry with a grey marble backsplash and concrete countertops. The ceiling, with its exposed wood beams, opens to a skylight, allowing natural light into the space.

Handing her a drink, I say, "Thanks, Gracie. My uncle and I did most of the work ourselves. The guys on my crew pitched in, too. I guess you could say it was a labor of love."

"Well, your kitchen is fabulous and that view off the deck is stunning. It's almost as nice as mine," she says with a little wink. "And you weren't lying. You do make a pretty mean old-fashioned."

"Cheers to that." We clink glasses, and I grab the steaks and salad makings out of the fridge along with a small charcuterie board I've put together. Don't laugh. Even guys can assemble charcuterie.

"Wow, charcuterie. You are impressive, Nathan Sundry." Gracie gives me her sweetest smile, and my heart clinches. It's all I can do to not trip over my words when I talk to her.

"I do aim to please. Why don't you make yourself at home while I go out and fire up the grill? I'm keeping it simple tonight. Grilled steaks and a wedge salad. I hope that's ok with you?"

"Sounds perfect, Nathan. Thanks again for dinner. I'm still getting used to being alone in the townhouse. It's nice to get out." She smiles, but the smile doesn't quite reach her eyes. I can see she's still sad over what Michael did to her, and it makes me even angrier with him. I'm really starting to question why I've been friends with him for as long as I have. It takes a special kind of asshole to break Gracie Henderson's heart.

I walk over and squeeze her hand. "I'm glad to have you. Truth is, I don't really have too much company these days. I'm so busy with work that I usually come home, fix a quick dinner, watch a little TV, and head to bed. It's nice to share a meal with someone."

I smile and walk out to turn the grill on.

Watching Gracie through the window, I'm struck by how much I really like this girl. It's not just a sexual attraction, because believe me, that's there too, but I really admire her. She could've wallowed in her heartbreak, but she didn't. She's strong, and that's so damn attractive. In my mind, I know it's too soon to start anything with her, but my heart has a different opinion. One that I know is going to get me in a lot of trouble.

It's a nice night, so we decide to have dinner out on the deck overlooking the water. We talk about work, and she told me about all the custom orders she has to work on this weekend. I tell her about all the progress my crew is making on the new housing project we've been working on. After we finish dinner, I light a fire in the fire pit; we bring our wine and pull the Adirondack chairs around the fire.

"How are your parents doing, Nathan? They moved out of Moonrise Bay, right?"

"Yeah, Mom and Dad moved up to Chapel Hill a few years back. Dad is a professor at UNC now. They really love it. I'm surprised since they love the coast so much, but I guess they were tired of hurricanes. Living in Chapel Hill, they don't have to worry about that as much." I shrug my shoulders and ask, "How's your mom doing? Is she still in the house you grew up in?"

Her face gets sad again as she says, "Yeah,

mom couldn't bring herself to sell after dad died. You know I moved back in with them when he first got sick. I knew Mom needed my help, so I gave up this internship I had with a gallery in Asheville and moved back home. That's how I got my start baking."

I remembered her dad. He was one of those men who was larger than life, and when he got cancer, the illness took all that life away. My heart breaks for Gracie and her mom. My dad and I are more best friends than father and son most of the time. I can't imagine what it would be like if something happened to him.

"What do you mean, that's how you got your start in baking?" I ask, my curiosity getting the better of me.

"Oh well, you know I went to UNC Asheville, and I was sure I was majoring in chemistry, but that all changed after taking my first art class. I changed majors and got a coveted gallery internship at one of the most sought-after galleries in Asheville. Then Dad got sick, and I knew Mom needed my help. Moonrise Bay isn't exactly known for its art scene, if you know what I mean. I've always loved baking and the science behind it, so I started baking and decorating cakes. I could put my art skills to the test, so to speak. My custom cake business took off, and after Dad died, I took the money he left me and invested it into Beach Buns, and here I am. I am twenty-eight years old and the owner of my own business. I have dad to thank for all of it."

She wipes the tears that have formed in the corners of her eyes and stares at the fire. I reach for her hand and entwine her fingers with mine. We sit there for what feels like hours, just holding hands, listening to the lapping waves of the Intracostal. I've never been so comfortable with anyone in my life. With her hand wrapped in mine, I have to fight the urge to lean over and kiss her. I knew that it would spoil the moment and tonight had been pretty perfect.

We sit there by the fire for a few more minutes before Gracie turns to me, blows out a breath and says "Well Nathan, tonight has been just lovely. I don't know what I was expecting but I really have had a wonderful time and you're a perfect host" looking at her watch she continues, "It's getting late though, and I've got a lot of work tomorrow. I think it's time, I pack my things and head home."

Not quite ready for the night to end, I say "But wait, we didn't even get a chance to try those fabulous smelling brownies. Are you sure you can't stay for one?"

"I'll tell you what, I'll leave the brownies with you, and you can drop the plate by my house when you're finished. No worries, Nathan, but I really should go. I've got to get up at the ass crack of dawn tomorrow. I've got a wedding cake to deliver plus a few other custom orders to finish up. Thanks again for a wonderful evening."

Not wanting to push her, I grab our wine glasses and walk her to the door. Fuck, I want to grab her in my arms and kiss her. That mouth of hers looks delicious. Resisting the urge, I take her hand in mine and trace circles on her palm. Gracie looks up at me with parted lips and my self-control snaps. I trace her jawline with my finger and tip her chin towards me. I take it as a sign that she hasn't moved away or asked me to stop. Leaning in, I place the lightest of kisses on her soft lips. Gracie gasps as she deepens the kiss. She places her hands on my chest but doesn't push me away and we continue kissing in the moonlight. Fuck, she feels so good. I could feel her mouth open for me and I dip my tongue in, slowly exploring her warm mouth. This feels right. Holding Gracie Henderson, her lips on mine, this is where I belong.

Our kiss slowed and Gracie began to gently push me away. She looked at me with slightly swollen lips and her face flushed.

"Phew, Nathan, I wasn't expecting that. Honestly, I don't know if I'm ready to jump in with anyone else right now. I'm spinning a bit. I really need to get home." She turned and quickly headed to her truck. I didn't even get a chance to call after her.

Great, now I've probably scared her off, but she was right there with me. I know she enjoyed that kiss as much as I had. I heard her tiny moan when my tongue slipped between her lips. I blew out a deep breath and walked back inside hoping I hadn't just ruined what had been a perfect night.

Chapter 8

Gracie

Me: Pipes, holy shit. Nathan Sundry kissed me tonight and it was so hot!!

Piper: WHAT???? Details babes, details.

Me: I don't even know how to describe it, certainly not in a text. Stop by the bakery in the morning and I'll share everything.

Piper: Ugh, fine. I guess I can wait. I just have one question, are you okay?

Me: Yeah, I may have panicked a bit but Pipes, it was the best kiss I've ever had. I think that's what freaked me out so much. Is it too soon?

Piper: Oh babes, I don't know. There isn't a formula for how long you have to wait out a heartache. Only you'll know when you're ready. Don't let anyone, not even hot as fuck Nathan Sundry, talk you into anything you aren't ready for.

Me: Thanks Pipes. You always know just what to say. Love you girl.

Piper: *Love you more babes.*

Holy shit, did that really just happen? Did Nathan Sundry just kiss me goodnight? My lady parts had been buzzing the whole ride home from his house. I'm for sure pulling my vibrator friend out and taking care of business. Never in my life has a kiss felt so magical. I don't know if I'm ready for this. I know it's just a kiss, but it was just a little over a month ago that I was engaged. At least in my mind, I was engaged. I guess in reality, that wedding was never going to happen. Maybe if I think about my situation that way, it's really no big deal that I had the hottest kiss of my life with Nathan Sundry tonight.

****

The next few days were whirlwind. I had a wedding cake to deliver in Wilmington and several birthday parties to cater various treats. Louisa and I spent all of Saturday traveling around the Wilmington and Moonrise Bay area. I barely had time to even think about Nathan let alone that delicious kiss.

By mid-week, things had begun to slow down, and the bakery was back to its usual off-season traffic of regulars. I even had time to work on my costume for The Pirate's Chest's annual Halloween contest. Usually, Michael and

I would do a couple's costume, but of course, that wouldn't be happening this year. Thankfully I had Piper for that now. We had decided to go as Tinkerbell and Vida. We had both loved the Tinkerbell movies when we were younger so it was only natural that we would go as them. It didn't hurt that both could be sexy outfits and that's exactly what I planned on making. A little part of me couldn't wait to see the look on Michael's face when he saw me in my Vida costume. I was working on my maroon fairy dress when I heard my phone ding. I looked down at the screen and my heart did a flip.

Nathan: *Hey, how would you feel about hanging out later? I hear there's a good band playing down at The Crystal Boat tonight.*

Me: *Hmm, I don't know, that all depends....*

Nathan: *Depends on what? You've piqued my interest.*

Me: *Well, a girl's gotta eat dinner. Why don't you let me return the favor from the other night and I'll cook for you this time.*

Nathan: *Now I'm not going to turn down a homecooked meal. Especially if you're one the doing the cooking. I finished the last of the brownies this morning and those were the best brownies I've ever eaten.*

Oh my god, I couldn't believe I had just invited Nathan to dinner at my house tonight.

Who am I? I've never been this bold in my life. Even in my relationship with Michael, I was usually the passive one and he made all our plans. Who was this person I was becoming around Nathan? I kind of liked her.

Me: *Aww, poor Nathan. I'll just have to up my dessert game, I guess.*

Nathan: *Now I'm definitely intrigued. The band goes on at nine, how about I come to your place around seven, does that work for you?*

Me: *It's a date*

Nathan: *It most certainly is.*

I felt like I was sweating now. Nathan was coming to my place for dinner. Shit, what the hell was I going to make. I knew I was going to take home my gooey pumpkin bars for dessert. They were a new addition to the bakery menu, and they had been flying off the shelves ever since I added them. Maybe I could cut out early. We were slow after all. The rest of this paperwork could wait until morning. I needed to head to the grocery store and pick up something for dinner. I'm thinking, I'll make my gnocchi alla vodka. You can't go wrong with gnocchi. I'll pair it with an arugula salad, crusty bread and nice bottle wine. I know that Nathan likes bourbon, so I'm going to pop by the liquor store and see if they have any interesting bourbons on the shelf. I'm not going to overthink tonight. I'm just going to go with the flow and enjoy myself. Maybe there will be more kissing in my future. Shit, I sure hope so. I've never been kissed so deliciously in my life. I had butterflies in my stomach just thinking about it. I packed up my stuff and locked the bakery doors. I had just enough time to grab groceries and shower before Nathan showed up.

Nathan arrived right on time. Thankfully I had given myself plenty of time to get home, shower and change clothes after running my errands. Instead of my usual work outfit, I was now in a soft pumpkin colored V-neck sweater that fell off the shoulder slightly. I paired it with my favorite distressed jeans and camel-colored booties. I had beach waves flowing through my hair and had just a light smattering of makeup on my face. When I opened the front door, Nathan was standing there in all his gorgeous glory. He had the perfect amount of stubble lining his perfectly chiseled jawline. The ice blue Henley he wore made his stormy blue-gray eyes stand out even more than usual. The way his dark blue jeans hugged his ass, made me clinch my thighs together a little tighter. God, was I going to survive the night?

"Hey Nathan, right on time. Come on back. Do you want a drink? I have beer, wine and of course bourbon."

"Well, I'm not one to turn down a

bourbon." He shot me another one of his panty melting smiles. We walked to the kitchen, and I fixed him a drink.

Nathan stopped and inhaled deeply. "Mmm, what smells so good?"

"Hmm, it's probably my vodka sauce. I hope you like gnocchi alla vodka."

"I don't think I've ever had it but sounds delicious." He smiled and my heart swooned. This man and his smiles might just be the death of me.

I poured myself a glass of wine and grabbed my focaccia bread from the oven. Ooh, it smelled and looked divine. I threw together the makings of an arugula and parmesan salad and started to plate our pasta dish. I could feel Nathan's eyes on me the entire time. To avoid those beautiful eyes, I grabbed dishes and began taking them to the table. Nathan reached over to help, and his hands brushed against mine. When I tell you there was a zap of electricity shooting through my whole body...man oh man, I just know I'm in trouble here.

We sat down to dinner and had a great time. Nathan was funnier than I remembered, and I laughed so hard I almost snorted wine out of my nose. Now that wouldn't have been remotely embarrassing.

He helped clear the table and even helped

me clean up the kitchen after dinner. "You cooked, the least I can do is help clean up" he'd said as he cleared plates from the table.

I don't think Michael ever helped with any housework the entirety of our relationship. He was always too tired or stressed from work. I know I shouldn't compare the two. I know in my heart it's not really fair. Michael was just a boy when we started dating and Nathan is a grown man. I'm sure he was just as immature as the guys his age when he was teenager. The problem with Michael is he never really grew up. Sure, he has a great job and provides very well for himself, but he's always been very self-involved. I can't remember a time that our dinner conversations started with something about me that Michael would turn around and make it about himself. He was never really a good listener. Honestly, I don't know why I stayed with him as long as I did. I sure as hell don't know why I said yes to his marriage proposal. I guess it was the security in the familiarity.

Being here in my kitchen with Nathan, I'm beginning to wonder if I really did love Michael all these years later. None of this remotely excuses Michael's and Madison's affair but I'm starting to understand how Michael could have felt trapped. Ugh, I'm getting so confused by all these feelings.

With the last plate rinsed and put in the

dishwasher, Nathan turns me, smiles sweetly and says,

"Are you ready to head out? The band should be getting started soon and I want to grab us a good seat."

My tummy gets butterflies, I try to not let it show and say, "Yup. I'm ready whenever you are Nathan. Just let me grab my bag."

He laces his fingers with mine and I'm suddenly very aware that I no longer care if we make it to the bar at all tonight.

Chapter 9

Nathan

The Crystal Boat is packed when we arrive, but I find a table not too far from the stage and point Gracie in that direction. She looks absolutely stunning tonight. From the bit of shoulder that's peeking out her sweater to the way her ass looks in her jeans. I have to adjust myself as we head towards our seats. I have a feeling I'm in for an uncomfortable night if you know what I mean. Gracie and I get seated and the band starts up. They're pretty good and the set list is full of various country covers. I can't help but sneak little glances at Gracie throughout the night. It's as if she's put a spell on me.

She turns to me during the bands cover of Chris Stapleton's "White Horse" and shouts, "Oh man, I love this song!! This band is so good."

I smile and nod, unable to come up with anything to say. I tell her I'm going to grab us another round and head to the bar.

Like a lot of places in Moonrise Bay, The Crystal Boat is pirate themed. Rumors are, Moonrise Bay was one of Blackbeard's hideouts and supposedly there is buried treasure somewhere on the island. The bar at the Crystal Boat is littered with hanging "pirate booty." By that, I mean over the years, women have left their bras to be hung from the ceiling of the bar. The bar itself is a deep mahogany color full of knicks and scratches showcasing the good times that have been had here over the years. The Crystal Boat is one of those peanuts on the floor kind of places. Just a place where you can grab a drink, listen to a good band and maybe get into a little trouble along the way.

I grab us both a couple of beers and am stopped dead in my tracks when I see who walks through the front door. Holy shit. It's Michael and Madison. I mean I knew there was always a chance we might see them here tonight, but I was hoping they would wind up at one of the other bars in town. This was definitely going to throw water on my night with Gracie. I avoid being spotted by them and head back to where Gracie is dancing to the music.

I put the beers on our table and walk to Gracie wrapping my arms around her. She glances over her shoulder smiling at first but then the look on her face changes as she sees them. Her face changes from nervousness to anger in just a few seconds.

"Oh my God Nathan.   Michael and Madison are over at the bar. What do we do if they see us?"

"I know. I saw them walk in when I was grabbing our drinks. I don't know about you, but I don't really give a shit if they see us together. Gracie, we've done nothing wrong. You and I have been friends for a long time and there's nothing wrong with two friends hanging out, having a few drinks and listening to good music together."

Gracie narrows her eyes at me as she says, "Two friends who've happened to share two dinners together and one kiss. I don't know about you Nathan, but I don't typically go around kissing my friends the way I kissed you the other night."

I gotta admit, I like how she says that. Like I gave her the best kiss of her life. I know that's what it felt like for me.

I try to feign bashfulness as I say, "I certainly hope you're not kissing your friends the way you kissed me the other night."

She slaps my shoulder and laughs. "Nathan, you kissed me first."

Yes I did and I'm damn proud of that fact.

I'm hoping to kiss her again if the appearances of Michael and Madison don't mess things up for us.

Gracie stops laughing abruptly and I know that Michael is standing behind me. I can see her demeanor change and it's as if the air has been sucked out of the room.

It's Madison who says something first, "Well, well. What a surprise seeing you two here...together."

Gracie pulls herself together. I can tell she's dying to say something bitchy to Madison, but she takes the high road instead.

"Hello Madison, hi Michael." She turns back to me and says, "Nathan, I think I'm ready to head home. This place just got a little too crowded for me." She downs her beer in one chug, grabs her bag and my hand and we head to the door.

"Wow Gracie, you're such a hypocrite. How long have you been sleeping with Nathan?" Madison turns her venom towards me and shouts, "I thought you and Michael were friends, Nathan. Whatever happened to bro code?"

Before I can even respond to Madison's stupidity, Gracie whirls around and unleashes holy hell.

"What the fuck Madison? Guilty conscious much? I'm not even going to sink to your slimy level, you troll. As for friends moving in on other friend's ex's, you're one to talk. You didn't even wait for me to become Michael's ex before moving in. Oh, and I know you totally made the first move. Don't worry I know you share the blame for the affair with Michael, but I know you well Madison. Anytime I've had something you wanted; you took it. I mean shit, you even took my wedding date not to mention my groom. I don't know why it took you so long to make your move. Maybe you couldn't stand the idea of me getting married before you. That fear that no man would want you for more than a warm body. I just know that Michael is too stupid to see you for who you really are. Enjoy each other because I can guarantee that whatever this is, it won't last long."

Gracie stalks towards the door and I stand there in awe of her. That was fucking awesome. I've never seen anyone speak to Madison Burke that way. I can almost see fire shooting from her eyes. She's pissed because deep down she knows Gracie's right and it's killing her.

I turn to both her and Michael, blow out a deep breath and laugh, "Well that was... awkward. Have a good night you two. The band is awesome."

As I'm heading towards Gracie, I hear Michael sneer "Yeah Nate, have a nice night too. Enjoy my sloppy seconds bro." I hear him and

Madison start laughing, and I see nothing but red. Gracie shakes her head at me as if to say, they're not worth it.

I rush towards him, fists clinching at my sides "Dude, if anyone's the sloppy the second, it's you. Don't you ever talk about Gracie that way again."

I walk to where Gracie is waiting for me at the door, grab her hand and take her to the car. I don't give a shit what anybody thinks, I'm going to make Gracie Henderson my girl if it's the last thing I do.

*****

The ride back to Gracie's house is tense and quiet. Neither one of us has the energy to talk. Things were going so well until those two assholes walked through the door. This was not where I thought this night would go when I asked Gracie out tonight. I was hoping to get another kiss out of her. Maybe that would be pushing things. I know she just got out of a long-term relationship, but I feel like I've waited a lifetime for her. I blew my shot in high school and Michael swooped in and got the girl.

I steal a look at Gracie and her whole demeanor has changed. Earlier in night she was lighter and maybe even a little freer. After the run-in with Michael and Madison, it's as if she's just shut down. Of course, I don't want to rush her into anything. I'm not an asshole. I just hate seeing her like this. Seeing her knock Madison down a peg tonight had been incredible if not a little bit of a turn on. Honestly, I have never understood why Gracie and Piper were friends with Madison in the first place. There was nothing good about Madison Burke and never had been in my opinion. She was just evil, plain and simple.

We pull up to Gracie's place and she gets out the truck. I take a deep breath and follow her up to her front door. I have no expectations as to where the rest of the night is going. As she reaches for the door, Gracie turns to me and says, "I don't really want to be alone right now. Will you come in for a drink? Maybe watch a movie?" Her eyes look so sad, there's no way I could tell her no.

I slowly put my hand under chin and lean down to place a gentle kiss on her forehead.

"There's nowhere else I'd rather be Gracie" I say to her, and I mean it. I was hoping she would invite me in. I didn't want that bar confrontation to be the way our night ended. She smiles and reaches for my hand and leads me inside.

After grabbing a beer and a glass of wine,

we settle on the couch to watch a movie and eat the absolutely delicious pumpkin bars Gracie had made for dessert. I feel like the luckiest guy in the world right now. Honestly, I couldn't even tell you what we watched that night. All I could focus on was the fact that Gracie was snuggled up against my side. I spent the entire movie rubbing small circles on her back and inhaling her scent. She smelled like vanilla and warm spices. She fucking smelled delicious.

The movie ends and neither one of makes a move to get up from the couch. Gracie just lifts her face to look up into mine. My heart stops. There is so much happening in that one look. She doesn't even have to say anything to me. Before I know it, my hand is caressing her cheek and my lips are pressed to hers. My tongue parts her lips ever so gently and explores the warmth of her mouth. The moan from Gracie has my dick stirring in my pants. God, this woman is all I've ever wanted. I deepen the kiss and our tongues become a tangle of heat and desire. My other hand slides down Gracie's back and slips underneath her sweater. Her smooth skin feels so good under my rough hands. Gracie runs her hands up and down my chest and she eventually grips my shirt with both hands. I don't think I've ever experienced a kiss like this in my life. The feeling of Gracie's lips on mine and the warmth of her mouth.

The kiss begins to wind down and Gracie slowly pulls away, but her eyes remain locked with mine. The desire in her eyes stirs something in me. I want to say something but I'm struggling to find the words.

"Gracie, that was...wow. I don't even..."

"Yeah, I don't know where that came from. I don't know that I've ever been kissed like that in my life. Jesus Nathan, what are you doing to me?" She gives me that sexy smile of hers and I know in that moment, my heart and soul are hers.

"I can tell you there's a lot more I'd like to be doing to you" I say with a chuckle.

Gracie blushes as she replies "Oh, Nathan. I don't know that I'm ready for more than just kissing right now. I don't want to give you the wrong idea. I love kissing you and I do mean I love kissing you. That was honestly the hottest kiss I've ever had. I'm just not ready to take this thing between us further than that."

I cup her face with my hands, rubbing her jawline with my thumb. I can't imagine not being able to touch her now that I've my hands on her soft skin. She's all I've wanted for so long.

"Gracie I will never push you to do anything you're not ready to do. I've wanted to kiss you ever since I was a stupid high school boy. I can tell you that the real thing is so much better than anything I could have ever dreamed."

She looks stunned by my confession. Honestly, I'm pretty stunned myself. I can't believe I just admitted to having a crush on her since high school. I can feel myself getting panicky and I'm hoping she can't see the dismay written all over my face.

Gracie takes a deep breath before she's able to speak. I can tell she's digesting everything I've just admitted.

"Wow, Nathan. I don't know what to say. I can't even imagine you having a crush on me when we were in high school. I was such a science nerd. I really thought it was a joke when Michael asked me out. I can't even imagine what I would have thought if you had asked me too."

I pause for a moment, still cupping her face. I don't know how to react. How does she not understand how utterly beautiful she is. Not only her outer beauty but the beauty of the person she is. I've never known anyone like Gracie before. She's kind-hearted, giving, smart, and funny. Truly the whole package wrapped up in one person.

"How can you not see yourself Gracie? You're everything. Did you never wonder why Michael and I weren't as close after everyone went away to school? I hated how he treated you and I hated how I covered for him. I eventually pulled away from our friendship and threw myself into work. He and I didn't become friends again until he moved back home and started working with his dad at the real estate firm. These last few years, it's really been more of a business relationship than a true friendship. He always knew how I felt about you and he didn't give a shit. Then to treat you like dirt on top of it..."

I could see the tears slowly falling down her cheek and I brushed them away as they fell. My heart ached for this woman. I pulled her against my chest and rested my head on top of hers. We sat there, silent except for the sounds of our breathing.

When she finally looked into my face, she said the words I longed to hear from her for what had felt like a lifetime.

"Will you stay with me tonight, Nathan? Stay with me and hold me? I don't know that I can promise anything more than that, but I don't know if I can stand to watch you walk out that door."

"Gracie, I would love nothing more than to wrap you in my arms and sleep next you to all night."

And I meant that.

Chapter 10

Gracie

I woke up with the most peaceful feeling. Nathan's arm was draped over my side and my back was tucked firmly against his front. I couldn't believe he had agreed to stay the night and just hold me all night. Who was this guy? Was he even real? And can we talk about what he confessed last night. He's had a crush on me since high school. What the hell? I wish I had known that way back when. If Nathan had made his move, I never would have given Michael the time of day.

Reality hit, and I realized I really needed to pee. I knew I needed to extricate myself from Nathan's sturdy arms, but it was so cozy here snuggled in my bed. Carefully, I rolled out from under Nathan and made my way to bathroom. It was still pretty early, and the sun had barely woken up the day. Watching the sun rise over the water is one of the biggest reasons I bought a townhome on the water in the first place. The various pinks and oranges waking up the sky, showcasing the steam rising off the water; it looked like it was going to be a beautiful, crisp fall day here in Moonrise Bay.

I love fall, especially fall in Moonrise Bay. The way downtown decorated with tons of pumpkins and haybales. Driving past the beautifully decorated fall porches on my way to work was my favorite part of my day. This town really embraces fall every year. From the pumpkin patches and fall festivals, it's a great place to be.

As the delicious aroma of coffee wafted its way, I finished my morning routine and decided to head down for a cup on the back deck. I didn't have to get to the bakery until ten, so thankfully I could have a leisurely morning. That was a luxury for a bakery owner.

Stepping out of the bathroom, I was immediately greeted by the site of Nathan's bare chest. My God, he was built like a sculpture. All chiseled abs and pecks. He was a gorgeous specimen of man. I couldn't tear my eyes away. His eyes met mine and he smiled. He walked to where I was standing in the bathroom doorway. Tipping my chin up with his hand, Nathan placed the sweetest kiss on my lips.

"Morning beautiful. How'd you sleep?"

"I'm pretty sure that was the best night's sleep

I've had in a while. I don't think I moved all night. How about you? Did you sleep ok? I hope I wasn't a bed hog."

Nathan looked at me and I wanted to grab him and toss him on the bed. I wanted to devour this man. What is wrong with me? I'm never like this. At least, I'd never felt this way with Michael. Don't get me wrong, the sex with Michael wasn't bad but I didn't have anything to compare it to either. Michael is the only man I've ever slept with.

"I slept great but how could I not with someone as beautiful as you to wake up to in the morning?" He stared straight into my eyes and I kid you not, I felt my knees weaken.

"Tell you what gorgeous, how about I make us some breakfast? I don't know about you but I can't function without my coffee in the morning." Nathan winked at me and pulled his shirt over his head.

"Wow, someone making me breakfast for a change. How can a girl say no."

"Great, let me just hit the bathroom and I'll meet you downstairs. You don't happen to have a spare toothbrush. I didn't, umm, plan for a sleepover." Nathan gave me a sheepish grin and I chuckled.

"Oh yeah, sorry about that. Let me get one for you. I keep my guest bath stocked with stuff like for nights that Piper has had one too many and needs to stay the night." I quickly walked down the hall to the guest bath and grabbed a toothbrush, toothpaste and a few other things in case Nathan needed them. Our hands grazed each other as I handed him the items and I couldn't help but smile at the zing that shot through my body. The things just a touch from this man did to me. Lord have mercy, I could only imagine what would happen if we got naked together. Great now I was blushing again because I was picturing Nathan naked again.

"Where'd you go just then Gracie? You're mind seemed to wander."

"I suppose that's for me to know and you find out. How about you finish up in the bathroom and I'll head downstairs and get out the breakfast fixings." I needed to get a bit of distance from this man before I turned into a puddle on the floor.

"Deal. I'll be quick."

Downstairs, I get to work finding everything I thought Nathan would need to make breakfast. My tummy is full of butterflies. I can't remember the last I felt this jittery over someone. Sure, when Michael and I started dating, I felt giddy and excited but over the years, he and I had settled into a comfortable companionship. At least I thought we had.

Maybe that was the problem. Maybe I had overlooked the fact that Michael and I had really become more friends than lovers over the past couple of years. Turning a blind eye to all of Michael's indiscretions, focusing on getting the bakery going, I really lost track of myself and what I needed. These budding feelings for Nathan have opened my eyes to what has been missing. I wonder if I really was in love with Michael or I just thought he and I were supposed to be endgame. Damn, it's way too early to have an existential crisis.

Breakfast was delicious and the view wasn't half bad either. Let me tell you, there is nothing more sexy than a gorgeous man, standing in the kitchen, making food for you. Seeing Nathan, in his tight henley and low-slung jeans , baseball hat turned backwards, cooking eggs and bacon on my stove erased most of the memory of finding Micheal and Madison screwing each other on my island. Lord have mercy, what it is about a man with his hat turned backwards that really gets a girl going.

Spending time with Nathan like this makes me wonder why I never saw him in this light before. Nathan and I have such an easy rapport. Conversation seems to flow naturally between the two of us.

"Hey Gracie, the bakery closes early on Sundays right? I was thinking of taking the boat one final time before the weather turns too cold. Why don't you come with me? One last trek down the Intracostal before winter gets here."

That smile Nathan had gleaming across his face. How could I resist that smile? What was happening to me? Just a few months ago I was engaged to be married. Nathan and I were just friends. For crying out loud, he was Michael's best friend. Now, when I look at Nathan I see anything but a friend and that scares the shit out me. I feel like I should put the brakes on whatever this is but this magnetic pull I feel for Nathan is something I can't resist. I know I should say no to a day on the boat. I know I should spend less time with Nathan and try and focus on me. But that's not what I want. I want a day on the boat and I sure as hell want that day on the boat to be with Nathan.

"That sounds amazing Nathan. I would love to take one last boat ride for the season with you. I close up the bakery at noon on Sunday's. Meet me here after close. I'll bring the snacks."

Nathan leaned down and placed the sweetest of kisses on my lips.

"Sounds perfect Gracie girl."

A girl could get used to this. Nathan's lips so soft and the gentle caress of his hands on my cheek. His intoxicating scent of cedar and ocean breeze made my head swim.

Nathan and I cleaned up our breakfast mess and he headed out to his truck. I watched him drive away; my fingertips pressed against my lips. Trying to hold onto the memory of his kiss. Nathan Sundry was trouble with a capital T but he was the kind of trouble I wanted to get into.

*****

True to his word, Nathan was waiting for me after I closed the bakery. I packed a picnic lunch of sandwiches and some cookies and grabbed some bottled water from the bakery's cooler. As I walked outside towards Nathan's truck, I was struck by how truly handsome he was. Well over six feet, body full of muscles and the perfect amount of scruff dotting his jawline. Eyes the color of a stormy sea, he almost took my breath away.

"Get yourself together Gracie", I whispered to as Nathan got out of the truck.

"Here, let me help with that Gracie. I brought you a sweatshirt too in case it gets chilly out on the water. I thought we could take the boat down to the bay itself and hang out on Mariner's Island. If we're lucky, we might get to see the wild horses."

One of my favorite things about living on the coast of North Carolina are the wild horses that roam our shores. These horses have called the beaches of the Outer Banks and Crystal Coast home for over 500 years

"Oh I hope we can see them. I don't know what it is about seeing those horses running free. It's peaceful, almost magical I suppose. It's really one of my favorite things about living here."

"Well come on Gracie girl. Let's pile this stuff in the truck and head to the boat. I can't promise magic but I can promise you a good time." Nathan grabbed my cooler and my bag from my shoulder and winked as he headed to the back of his truck. God, I think I'm goner for Nathan for sure and I don't know what I'm going to do about it.

Our afternoon on the boat was one of the best days I've had in a long time. I can't remember the last time I took a Sunday afternoon not focused on the bakery. I realized today that I've been neglecting my personal life some. Running my own business, I don't really take enough time to focus on me. Maybe that was part of the problem in my relationship with Michael. I know I'm not the reason he cheated but maybe I focused too much on my business and not enough on what was happening in my life. Maybe if I had paid more attention, I would have seen that I wasn't happy with Michael. Maybe I would have noticed that he was a shit head, liar and a cheat. I guess I knew he was a liar and cheat since I looked the other way when we were in college but maybe if I had taken the time to focus more on myself, I would have left him before saying yes to marrying him. God, when I look at it that way, I really was such an idiot. For some reason, I was willing to settle for a liar and cheater instead putting my needs first. If being on the boat with Nathan taught me anything today, it's that I deserve a hell of lot more than Michael ever had to give.

Leaning back against the passenger seat headrest of Nathan's truck, eyes closed, Zach Bryan playing on the radio, I felt completely at peace. For the first time in months, I felt happy. I didn't need to look in the rearview anymore.

A ping from my phone, alerting me to a text message, brought me out of that feeling.

Miquel: *Girl.....you need to get downtown ASAP. Some serious shit just went down and it effects all of us.*

Me: *WTF!!! I'll head that way now. Was out on the water with Nathan but he's bringing me back to the bakery to grab my truck. I'll be there soon.*

My stomach immediately began to groan and I scrubbed my hands down my face. What the hell was going on now?

"You good Gracie?" Nathan asked, concern crossing his face.

"Yeah, I just need to get back to the bakery so I guess it's a good thing we're heading that way. Miquel just texted that some shit just happened and I need to get there ASAP."

"Did he say what happened?"

"No but it can't be good if he's asking me to come in on our afternoon off."

Nathan squeezed my hand and we drove the rest of the way in silence, me hoping that whatever happened would be an easy fix. I really didn't know how much more drama in my life I could take.

Pulling up to the bakery, Miquel and his boyfriend Alan were standing outside waiting for us. Alan is usually a very calm person but today he looked anything but. It takes a lot to ruffle his feathers but today I could tell something was really bothering him.

Standing at 6'3 tall, Alan is a very handsome man. His salt and pepper hair is matched only by his periwinkle blue eyes. He's greying prematurely which makes him look a bit older than his 32 years, but he has one of the kindest faces. The fact that something has him so angry that he's turning a bright shade of red has me concerned.

I get out of Nathan's truck and approach the two of them gingerly.

"Hey you guys. What's so urgent that I'm rushing down to the bakery on a Sunday afternoon?"

Both Alan and Miquel stop their conversation and take deep breaths. They take a moment to look at each other before answering. Finally, Alan, with a tinge of sadness in his eyes, turns to me and says,

"Oh sweetie, I don't even know how to tell you this so I'm just going to rip the band aid so to speak. A bunch of the businesses on this side of the street had notices slipped under our doors this afternoon. It seems like that asshat ex of yours and his new "friend" have decided they want to sell the buildings they own. Of course, they're hoping that won't affect the businesses in those buildings, but they can't make any guarantees." He rolled his eyes and looked at me sympathetically.

"Yeah Mama, we had one of those notices under our door when I checked after Alan got his. I can't believe that dumb shit is really doing this. First, he screws your supposed best friend and now he's trying to screw you out of your livelihood."

Exasperated, I throw my hands in the air and blow out a deep breath.

"Well, ain't this a nice pile of shit. Here I thought, my day started off perfectly. I spent the day on the boat with Nathan; we even got to see the horses on Mariner's Island but now I find out that no, the universe isn't giving me a reward for my fuckwit ex cheating on me. Nope, the universe is laughing at me again. Jesus, just when I thought things were turning around..."

Miquel just looked at me with is jaw hanging open and his chocolate brown eyes wide.

"Damn girl, you mean to tell me you spent time with hunky Nathan without his shirt on. Good for you Mama."

I blushed a little at Miquel's reaction as Nathan chuckled. "Well, usually when you're out on the water, you do it in your bathing suit. I hate to disappoint you Miquel but it was a little too chilly for anyone to be shirtless. Ugh, why is Michael doing this? Do you think that asshole is seeking some kind of stupid revenge on me for going out with his friend? No, it can't be that. He can't really be that petty can he?"

I stood there looking up and down the street. All of these beautiful storefronts, decorated for Halloween. These people were my friends. Most of them, I've known since I was a little girl. Most of these shops and restaurants have been in Moonrise Bay for as long as I can remember and were family-owned businesses. I just can't believe Michael and Madison would do this.

Alan walked towards me and grabbed both my hands in his. His eyes were sad but there was a sort of comfort in them.

"Sweet girl, this is in no way, shape or form you're fault. In the end, that dipshit of an ex of yours is a businessman and all businessmen care about is money. Maybe just thank your lucky stars that things ended between the two of you. Now, I've been talking to some of the other business owners and we're planning a meeting for tomorrow night to discuss strategy. It will be at the town hall around 7:30. Be there or be square babers." He kissed my cheek and walked back towards his shop.

Alan was right. All Michael and Madison did care about was money. They didn't care about this town or the business owners. The people who had put their heart and souls into these shops. I hadn't grown up wanting to run a small-town bakery, but over the years, I've come to love my job. I love interacting with the locals and the vacationers. I treasure my friendships with Miquel and Louisa. I knew what I had to do. I was going to fight for my shop one way or another. I'd find the money to buy the building outright if I had to. No matter what, I wouldn't lose my business.

Me: Pipes, you free to stop the bakery tonight? I'll supply an early dinner

Piper: Yeah girl, I can pop by for some free grub.

Me: I've got something to tell you and you're not going to believe it.

Piper: Ooh, I'm intrigued. See you around five babes.

******

After relaying the events of the afternoon to Piper, we had a serious brainstorming session. It was all I could do to keep her from heading over to Michael's office and punching him straight in the face.

Piper turned to Nathan. "Nathan, you've got to have some contacts in the real estate world. You being a contractor and all. At the very least, you must know some finance people."

"I don't know Pipes. Don't you think that's asking too much of him?" I say shaking my head. I didn't want to put my problems on Nathan's plate. It's not like we were a couple. So far we had shared a couple of dates and two incredible kisses. I don't know if it's appropriate to ask for his help or get him involved.

I turned to Nathan and said "You don't have to get involved Nathan. I know Michael's your friend. I don't want to make things more awkward than they already are between the two of you."

Piper rolled her eyes before saying, "Girl, that man would do anything for you. Don't you remember all the time he spent helping you get ready for the tropical storm. Come on Gracie. We've all been friends forever. He would drop everything for you."

Nathan blushed. Honest to God blushed.

"She's right Gracie, I'll do anything I can to help you. Let me reach out to a few contacts I know and see what the deal is." Nathan reached across the table where we were all sitting and grabbed my hand; twining his fingers with mine.

"Thanks Nathan. Ugh, I just don't understand why Michael is doing this. He knows how much this bakery means to me."

Piper reached out and grabbed my and Nathan's hands. I knew what she was going to say, and I knew she was right. Michael had never been the person I'd thought he was. I was only just now seeing how much he and I had really grown apart over the years. I just can't believe how much I overlooked.

"Babe, Michael is not that boy we knew in high school, just like you're not that girl. You both want different things out of life then what you thought you did all those years ago. You've outgrown him and it's just taken this situation for you to realize how much."

I knew Piper was right and I knew it was time I faced up to it. As much as I want to blame Michael for everything that went wrong in our relationship, I know I bear a little bit of the responsibility. Did I deserve to be cheated on, hell no. But I did turn a blind eye to a lot of our problems because staying with Michael was comfortable.

Chapter 11

Nathan

I could see the frustration on Gracie's face. Betrayed again by people she thought had cared for her. I was still holding her hands and began rubbing my hands up and down her arm as I spoke.

"You're not going to lose the bakery, Gracie. No one is going to lose their shops. I have a lot of contacts in the real estate world. I'll reach out to some people and see what I can do. In the meantime, you and the rest of the owners need to band together. Get the word out to the town. Moonrise Bay is a close-knit community. They won't like the idea of some big-name retailers opening stores downtown that no one can afford to shop in."

I could see relief wash over Gracie's face and could feel my heart squeeze. I knew just the guy I was going to reach out to. He had deep pockets and was always looking for a good investment. He would blow whatever plans Michael and Madison had right out of the water. Piper walked towards me and clapped on me on the back.

"See Gracie, I told you Nathan was the man for the job. You're a good egg Nathan Sundry. I say let's all have a drink, get ready for the tenants meeting, then drink some more. It feels like a good occasion to make poor decisions."

The group of us laughed and cheered at Piper's suggestion. Gracie grabbed a bottle of bourbon from the kitchen as well glasses for everyone. We toasted to the ruination of Michael and Madison and to saving downtown Moonrise Bay.

***

The town hall was packed with angry business owners as well as angry citizens. Their harsh voices ricocheting off the walls. It wasn't hard to understand their frustration. Most of the businesses had been in these buildings since I was a kid. The majority of them being family-owned. What the hell were Michael and Madison thinking. Were they so money hungry that they've forgotten the heart of Moonrise Bay? Do they even care about the town they've grown up in? Gracie sat near the front next to Alan and Miquel ringing her hands with worry. I hated to see her like this. It made my stomach twist in knots.

"Beach Buns is my whole life", she said her voice quivering, "What happens if I lose it?"

I reached over and laced her fingers with mine. "You're not going to lose this bakery Gracie. I promise."

She looked up with a smile that barely reached her eyes. "Thanks for being here Nathan. It really means a lot to me."

Brushing her hair off her face I tell her, "Nowhere I'd rather be Gracie girl."

The mayor steps up to the podium as someone shouts from the back "Down with Garret Realty" and another yells, "Save the heart of Moonrise Bay."

The mayor holds up his hands trying to quiet the crowd. After about five minutes, everyone seemed to be quiet and ready to hear what the mayor had to say.

"As most of you here are aware, Garret Realty, the owners of the downtown buildings, have now decided to sell off their holdings. I know everyone here is concerned what that means for you businesses. I have been assured that Garret Realty is looking for a buyer who will keep our downtown intact and not push any business owners out of their businesses."

The crowd noise grew louder. Clearly the mayor's statement didn't ease the tension in the room.

Alan stood up to address the mayor. "That's all well and good mayor, but how can we trust what they say? Are they putting that in the buyers agreement? How can we be assured that the new owners won't price us out of our leases? Will Garret Realty allow us to purchase our buildings at a fair price? We have questions mayor that unfortunately I don't think you're prepared to answer. We need a representative from Garrett Realty here to answer them."

The crowd applauded and cheered Alan. Clearly everyone was agreement.

"People, people. I understand your concerns" the mayor said trying to calm the room down "I'm worried about the sale as well. I don't want anything to change with our little town but I promise you, I believe Mr. Garret when he says nothing will change once ownership changes hands."

The meeting continued on for another thirty minutes with the mayor trying to appease the group to little avail. The consensus of the crowd was they were going to do whatever it took to save Moonrise Bay. It frightened me a little bit to be honest. Put this group of people together and you never know what could happen.

After the shop owners' meeting and a few more drinks, Gracie and I said our goodbyes to the group and walked down to the waterfront. With our hands twined, we strolled in companionable silence. Stopping once we reached the boardwalk that followed along the water, staring into the moonlight.

"I'm sorry you're having to deal with more of Michael's bullshit, Gracie. I just don't know what the hell he's thinking these days." Gracie turned her face up to look at me and she smiled that perfect smile of hers.

"You know Nathan, this mess has made me realize that Michael and I must have never really loved each other as adults. As teenagers, sure but we'd outgrown each other over the years. I stopped being honest with myself after my dad died, I think. I couldn't take any more change, so I didn't want to see what was right in front of my face. I don't think I've been in love with Michael since we were in college. I think I just stayed with him because it was easy and comfortable. I'm not excusing his cheating by any means, but I'm just realizing the part I played in the demise of our relationship."

She let out a deep breath and turned back towards the water. I placed my hand under her chin turning her face towards mine. I stood there for a moment, hand under her chin, staring into her whiskey brown eyes. Gracie's tongue slid across her lower lip, and I felt a stirring in my stomach. It might sound silly, but hell I don't care. This girl gives me God damned butterflies.

I move my hand to caress her jawline and lower my lips to hers. So fucking soft. Deeper I delve into her mouth, gently opening her lips with my tongue. Gracie's arms wound their way around my neck as she stepped further into the kiss. Warmth filled my entire body and what started as a chaste kiss quickly became intense.

My hands wound their way into Gracie's caramel waves, gently tugging her hair. Lips met lips and tongues tangled with tongues over and over again. Gracie's hands had moved from around my neck and were now firmly gripping my ass. This woman, who I've dreamed about since I was a teenage boy. She was more than I could have ever dreamed of. As the kiss began to slow, I pulled my face away keeping my hands in Gracie's hair. Jesus, I hoped she let me take her home tonight. I wanted nothing more than to wake up to her face in the morning and all the mornings after that. Nothing more than to feel her body wrapped around mine. Her soft touch, smell her sweet scent of cinnamon and vanilla. Wake up and get lost in her deep brown eyes. I wanted everything with her.

Gracie placed her fingertips to her lips

tracing the swollen memory of our kiss.

"Nathan, will you come home with me, stay with me?" I felt that plea deep in my soul and it took everything I had not to fall to my knees. It was as if she had read my mind, my heart, my everything.

"There's nowhere else I'd rather be right be tonight, Gracie."

I took her hand in mine and guided her back towards downtown. I knew in my heart that Gracie was the end of the line for me. There was no turning back now, this girl was mine. I know it's crazy. We've never been anything more than friends, but I know deep down that there will never be a woman who makes me feel what I feel when I'm with her. It's an ease, a comfort, a quietness. It's as if when we're together, no one and nothing exists around us.

As we approached my truck, I pushed Gracie against the passenger side door and with her hands fisted in my coat, press my lips to hers again. The heat from our kiss created a steam around us; bracing against the cold night air. To show her just how much she unraveled me, I pressed my hardness against her thigh. A deep moan escaped her throat, and I deepened my kiss. Gracie began fumbling for the door handle with one hand while pulling me with the other.

"Nathan, I need you now." Gracie

moaned.

I felt a deep growl beginning low in my throat. I wanted Gracie but not this way. I broke the kiss before saying to her, "Gracie, I'm not going to fuck you for the first time in the back of my truck. I'm going to take my time and worship your body. Now, we just need to decide are we going back to your place or mine?"

I felt her knees buckle and grabbed her to keep her steady. Reaching behind her, I opened the truck door and helped her inside. I'd decided we'd head back to her place. I wanted this night to be perfect for her. As we drove towards her house, I kept her hand in mine. I needed to keep constant contact with her body. I craved every bit of her.

As soon as we walked through the front door, we're on each other. Lips, hands, touching, tugging and pulling. Feverishly pulling off coats and tangling our lips together. I grabbed Gracie's hand and guided her upstairs to her bedroom. The only light in the room was the light from the bathroom leaking through a crack under the door. I pushed Gracie towards the bed and began pulling her shirt over her head. I could feel her shaking a bit with nerves.

"You don't have to do anything you're not ready for, Gracie." I whisper into her ear.

She looked into my eyes, and I could see

nothing but desire. Gracie ran her hands down my chest and began to pull at the hem of my shirt.

"Nathan, this is exactly what I want. There's nowhere else on earth I want to be than in this room with you." She slowly tugs my shirt over my head and begins running her soft, nimble fingers over my chest and stomach, curling her fingers in my chest hair. God, it's like heaven and I can't help but groan at her touch. Slowly reaching again for her shirt, I tug it over her head. Putting my hands in the waistband of her yoga pants, I slide them down her legs. Gracie steps out of them and stands there enshrined by the moonlight. I can only stare at her, the curves of her body. She's simply breathtaking.

Gracie starts to cross her arms over herself out of self-consciousness, but I reach out and grab her hands before she can.

"Don't Gracie. Don't cover yourself up. Let me look at you. Do you not know how absolutely stunning you are? This, this moment right here. This is what I've been dreaming of for as long as I can remember. I just want to take it all in and sear it in my memory. I need to hold unto this moment forever Gracie."

With her hands in mine, I gently pull Gracie towards me. Slowly, I pull the straps of her bra down her shoulders, placing a kiss on each one as I go. I unclasp her bra and let it fall to floor.

Patience isn't usually one of my strengths, but I finally have Gracie Henderson in all her naked glory before me, I'm damn sure taking my time with her. Lowering myself to my knees, I begin pulling down her panties. Kissing every one of her curves along the way. I wasn't kidding when I said I was going to worship her body. I've waited a lifetime for tonight and I plan on savoring every moment. I take my time kissing, touching Gracie on each inch of her. I kiss the tops of her feet, massaging up her legs until I reach that spot I've been yearning for between her thighs. She gasps as I kiss her inner thigh, my hands finding the warmth of what I've been craving. She moans as my hands trace every place I've just kissed and licked.

"Look at me Gracie" I growl as I rub my hands up her smooth body. Her eyes heavy with lust, lock with mine. I thrust my fingers into her warm center, and she moves her body in rhythm with them.

"Damn baby you're so wet for me."

More moans.

Not taking my eyes off her, my tongue slips through her wet folds, rubbing and stroking her swollen clit. I'm rewarded with a series of sounds that get increasingly louder the more I torment her with my tongue. All the while, my fingers are deftly exploring her pussy, looking for that perfect spot.

"Nathan, oh my God" Gracie moans as her eyes roll back. I can feel her knees buckle; I grab her before she falls and lay her softly on her bed. Stopping for a moment just to bask in her glory. Naked and spread before me.

"Fuck, you're beautiful Gracie." I say as I again work my way down her luscious body. She's spectacular. My tongue spreads her wet folds and I taste her. She's so fucking craveable. I lick and suck, probing her pussy with my fingers. My other hand grabbing her breast, flicking and pinching her hard nipple. I can't wait to get my mouth around them. They're so perfect. Gracie's hips move up and down rubbing her clit in time with my tongue while she's fucking my face.

"Fuck, Nathan. Don't stop... oh my God. What are you doing to me?"

"No baby, no stopping now." I say as I continue to feast on her glorious pussy all the while my fingers are rubbing that bundle of nerves deep inside her. I can feel her walls begin to shudder around my fingers while her legs quiver. I know she's close. I lick and suck harder, grabbing her nipples and tugging as I focus all my attention on her swollen clit. Then it happens. Gracie comes undone.

"Nathan, I'm coming!!!" She moans and I feel the damn break. Her pussy walls clinching around my fingers as she comes on my face. She's fucking perfect.

Chapter 12

Gracie

BEST FUCKING ORGASM EVER!!!!

I can't believe Nathan Sundry is face deep between my legs and just gave me the most explosive, mind-blowing orgasm of my life. Like, I had no clue an orgasm could feel that way and I'm mad at myself that I was going to settle for what Michael thought passed for them. Jesus, this is what I've been missing.

"Damn baby, I can't wait to feel you come on my dick. You taste so fucking sweet and I just can't get enough of you."

I can feel myself blush before I say "Oh my God Nathan, I've never felt anything like that in my life. It felt like fireworks were shooting off. Jesus, the way you work your tongue…."

He gives me the sexiest smile and I'm unwell and undone. This man is a fucking God. Why the hell did I waste so many years with stupid Michael. He couldn't find a g-spot with a map and x marking the spot.

Slowly, Nathan drags himself up the length of my body. He's so fucking sexy; I don't know what to do with myself. He wraps his lips around one of my breasts and begins to suck while kneading the other with his hand. God, he's good with his hands. Nathan releases my breast with a popping sound and stares into my eyes.

"Gracie, your body is perfection. I could lay here, sucking and exploring for days on end." I reach out and run my fingers through his hair. This man. What a beautiful surprise he's turned out to be.

Nathan takes my mouth in his. Tongues tangling, I taste myself on his lips and can I just say, that's a fucking turn on. Michael never really enjoyed oral, unless he was the one getting it, so I never really enjoyed it either. Now that I've had a taste (literally) of how it's supposed to be, I know I'll never be able to get enough.

Moving my hands slowly down Nathan's body, I caress the plains of his chest and abdomen. When I say this man is built, I mean built. He doesn't just have a six pack; it feels like he has double that. I reach down to take off his jeans and begin pulling at the button. Nathan puts his hand over mine before saying,

"Gracie, we don't have to go any further tonight." With those words, I swear this man has won my heart. I can literally feel how much he wants to go further on my inner thigh, so the fact that he's willing to leave me with the best orgasm in history...

With my hand unbuttoning his jeans, I purr "Nathan, I'm not done until I feel you coming inside me." I swear I could see fire light in his eyes at my words. He rips his jeans off and his boxer briefs go with them. He's fucking naked in front of me, and his dick is glorious. So hard and his tip is glistening with the wetness of precum. I reach down and stroke his cock from tip to balls paying close attention to the wetness. I lick the precum off my fingers and Nathan growls. He actually fucking growls. I want to please him the way he pleased me. I need him to feel the way I feel right in this moment. Licking my palm, I begin stroking his dick while Nathan moans and pumps his shaft in my hand. I can feel every vein and ridge.

With my wet hand, I keep pumping and stroking. Nathan can't take his eyes off me, and I can feel the want emanating from his body. His hand grasps mine and we're stroking his dick together. So fucking hot.

"Baby, if I'm not inside you in the next few minutes, this night is going to end before it even gets started", Nathan groans as he grabs my hand and places his body between my thighs.

"Condom?" He asks. I bite my lip at his request. I've been on the pill since college and after my discovery of Michael and Madison, I had myself tested. I know I'm clean. Something inside wants to feel Nathan bare. Nothing between us but flesh. When he comes inside me, I want to feel every hot spurt he has to give.

I look Nathan deep in his eyes. "I'm on birth control and I was tested after the breakup. I'm clean. I want to feel you Nathan. I don't want anything between us." I don't even know how to describe the look he gives me. Pure desire. Carnal heat. His lips crush mine as he primes his dick for me.

"Are you sure Gracie? I'm clean. I haven't been with anyone without a condom."

"I'm sure Nathan. I need to feel you", I plead.

"Fuck Gracie, you're perfect. There's nothing I want more in this world than to feel your pussy wrapped bare around my dick." With that confession, I'm undone. I grab his face and we're a tangling of lips and tongues. I can feel Nathan line the tip of his cock with my center. He gives me a look as if he's saying, "last chance to back out" but I just spread my legs wider in acknowledgement. He enters me and it's as if the world explodes around me. He fills me slowly, spreading my lips wider than they've ever been spread. I gasp at the fullness.

"Are you ok? I'm not hurting you am I?"

I take my hands and caress Nathan's face. "That was a gasp of happiness. Nathan, nothing has ever felt this good before. Nothing." He rests his forehead against mine and begins gently pumping inside me. We stay there like that for what feels eternity. This feeling is deeper than any feeling I had with Michael. The connection between Nathan and me...his forehead resting against mine, hips moving between my thighs, dick thrusting between my folds.

"Kiss me" I beg and Nathan crushes his lips to mine. He grazes his teeth over my bottom lip, and I suck in a gasp. His movements begin to hypnotize me. I run my hands up the length of his back, feeling each and every muscle as he pumps deeper inside me. With each thrust, I dig my nails deep into his flesh.

"Put your tit in my mouth" he commands. I do what he asks and as he begins to suck, my eyes roll back in my head and I'm moaning again. Nathan is fucking me and licking and sucking my breast and I swear to god, I'm going to come all over again. I wrap my legs around him, using my feet to pull him in deeper. I need him deeper, harder, all of him.

"Nathan, Jesus. Harder, fuck me harder." Arching my back, my breathing becomes heavy.

I look down between us and can see his dick moving in and out.

Nathan flips us over, never losing connection. I'm now straddling his lap and riding is dick. I take him deeper and deeper. I can't get enough of him. Placing my hands firmly on his chest, I begin to ride. My hips pumping up and down. Nathan grabs my ass, kneading and massaging. Pulling me harder onto his dick.

"More Nathan, I need more" I scream.

He begins pumping faster and harder. I can feel his grunts and groans as he thrusts inside me. My pussy walls suck him in and clinch tighter around his hard dick.

"Jesus Gracie, your pussy is a fucking miracle. So wet and so delicious. Those lips sucking my dick so hard."

His words only make my pussy wetter, and I can feel myself clinch harder around his cock, diving further inside me.

His hand moves down, and his thumb is rubbing that sweet bundle of nerves again. Dear God, I feel like I'm breaking apart into a million pieces. With one hand Nathan is tugging and pinching my hard nipples between his fingertips and with the other he's stroking my clit. I throw my hands up, gripping the headboard. Holding on for dear life. Riding him faster and harder.

His hands gripping my hips as he guides me up and down his shaft. I'm seeing stars. I see actual fucking stars. I can't believe it, but this man is giving me another incredible orgasm. WTF, that's never happened in my life.

"That's it baby. Yes, I can feel you pulling my dick in deeper. Let go baby, let me feel you come."

And just like that... "Fuck, I'm coming again." My walls are tightening around his dick and I feel that jolt of an orgasm moving though my body. It's like Christmas and my birthday all rolled into one. It's a fucking dream. My whole body is on fire and trembling at the same time. My toes curl and my eyes roll back in my head. I can't even catch my breath before Nathan's body tenses, dick hardening and he's riding out my orgasm with one of his own.

We come together in whirlwind of sparks and stars. Grunts and groans. Our sweaty bodies colliding together in something that can only be described as spectacularly perfect.

I collapse on his chest. Our bodies a sweaty tangle of legs and arms. Both us breathing heavily as if there's no air left in the room.

"Oh my God Nathan. I never knew it could be like that. Never knew it could feel like that." I just stare up at him from where I'm laying across his chest. My fingers curling through his smattering of chest hair. Nathan just smiles a crooked smile and gently presses a kiss to the top of my head.

"Honestly Gracie, I've never experienced anything like that in my life. You're... I don't even know how to describe what happened. Fucking amazing."

As I begin to snuggle into his body, I feel his dick stir against my stomach. Jesus, he can't already want to go again.

I smile and raise my eyebrow as I say, "You can't possibly be ready to go again."

He flips me onto my back before saying "Won't it be fun finding out."

****

We spend our night as a tangle of bodies. Not much sleeping going on for the two of us. If I even lightly brush up against him, his arms wrap around me, grabbing breasts.

Fondling.

Sucking.

Stroking.

Licking.

To say we were obsessed with each other would be an understatement. One moment, we were taking our time. Moving slowly, worshipping each other. Soft touches, gentle movements. But it was as if we couldn't get enough of each other's bodies. Tangling limbs and crushing lips. Slick bodies moving together becoming one.

Now the sun is just beginning to seep through a crack in the blinds and I open my eyes. There he is. His dirty blonde hair, rumpled from a night of rolling around in the sheets. I can smell him all over me. That distinct smell of cedar and the ocean breeze. I just want to melt into my sheets. I turn over and start to crawl out of bed. Before I can even put my feet on the ground, I feel strong hands pull me back down.

"Mmm, you're not going anywhere baby." Nathan purrs as he pulls me on top of him. How can this man possibly be ready to go again?

I chuckle and gently stroke his chest hair.

"Oh my goodness Nathan, you can't possibly be able to go again. I think we've slept maybe an hour the whole night."

"Well, I'm making up for lost time Gracie." He winks and places the sweetest of kisses on my forehead.

God this man is just perfect.

"You might be able to go again but I think I'm going to need a gallon of Gatorade and ice pack for my lady parts. She's never seen so much action and I was in a relationship for ten years if that tells you anything."

Nathan laughs and rubs his hands up and down my arms.

"You were with a boy all those years Gracie. He didn't know what to do with you."

That makes me laugh so hard I almost fall out bed. He's not wrong though. I've only ever been Michael so of course I didn't know that there was more to sex. I know I shouldn't be comparing the two, but I just can't help myself. When it comes to Nathan Sundry, he's all man. There is nothing boyish about him. You would think that Madison was someone who knows what they're doing bed, so why she's settling for Michael, I have no clue. Maybe the next time I see here, I'll thank her. If it weren't for her, I never would have had this glorious night with Nathan and let me tell you I'm so grateful for this night.

"Oh my God Nathan, you don't know how right you are. But let's stop talking about that jackass." I crawl up Nathan's chest, kiss him and quickly get away before he can tempt me to stay in bed. It's Halloween week and I have a ton of orders I need to finish plus Piper and I need to get our costumes together for the Pirate's Chest costume contest. As much as I would love to stay in bed with a naked Nathan, I've got to drag my ass to the shower.

I scream as Nathan chases me to the shower. Let's just say it was a longer shower than I planned on taking and may have been cold by the time we finished. I manage to get dressed and get my morning coffee. On the way to bakery, Nathan holds my hand. I'm grateful for the touch because I'm not ready to let go of the connection.

"So Gracie, what's your plan for the day? Busy day for the bakery?" Nathan asks as he traces circles with his thumb in the palm of my hand.

"Well, we have a few Halloween orders to finish for a couple of customers but not too busy. I really need to get with Piper so we can get our costumes together for the contest tomorrow night. She's the other half of my couple this year." I blush and give a sheepish grin.

"Oh yeah, I guess you and Michael always did the couples contest at Pirate's. So what's the plan for this year? Sexy baker, sexy librarian?" He laughs and I shoot him the dirtiest look.

"Come on Nathan. Give us more credit than that. We're so much more than a sexy baker or a sexy librarian. Nope, we're going back to our childhood and she's Tinkerbell and I'm Vidia."

Nathan has the most confused look on his face as if I've sprouted horns from my head. I guess he wasn't a Tinkerbell and Friends fan as kid. Go figure.

"I guess you never watched a lot of Tinkerbell and Friends as kid" I say and start laughing hysterically. I crack myself up with the image of Nathan as a kid sitting around the house watching a Tinkerbell movie. I know he has a younger sister, but I doubt they sat around watching TV together.

"Ha, ha, ha. Um, no I was too busy playing football outside with my friends. But I'll bet you'll look hot. I can't wait to see you in your costume." He says as he wiggles his eyebrows at me.

Lord love a duck; this man is something else and I just don't know what I'm going to do with myself.

We pull up in front of the bakery and I just sit in Nathan's truck. Neither one of us ready to make any kind of move to get out. We sit with our hands twined together. I turn and look into his ocean blue eyes, and I get lost. I don't want to say goodbye. I just want to turn the truck around and go back to bed but I know I have too much work to do.

"Well Gracie girl, I hope I can see you later. Why don't I come over after work and bring some takeout for you and Piper? That way you don't have to worry about dinner and you two can just work on costumes. Maybe I'll get an advance viewing."

"Oh Nathan, that would be great. Let's make it simple, just grab a pizza and big salad from Sal's. I'll provide the wine. Does that work for you?"

Nathan leans over and places the softest kiss on my lips. So soft my stomach is doing flips. He gently caresses my cheek and says "Sounds perfect Gracie. I wish it were already tonight." And with that, he opens his truck door and jogs around to the passenger side. He opens my door and helps me out.

I run my hands up his chest and step up on my tip toes. God his chest should be considered one of the wonders of the world. I still can't believe I had that chest all over me last night (and this morning).

"Goodbye Nathan. Last night was..." I let out a deep sigh, unable to put into words just how much I needed last night. All I can do is put my lips on his and kiss him deeply.

Tongues dancing together.

Arms wrapping around one another.

"See you later Gracie." Nathan says as he gets back in his truck and drives off. I just stand there staring after him. Not really knowing what to do next. Fuck, I'm in so much trouble.

***

Me: *Girl, you're never going to believe what, or should I say who, I did last night.*

Piper: *WHAT????? OMG, did you sleep with Nathan and when I say sleep I mean sexy times you know.*

Me: *Yes girl. I spent the whole night, naked and tumbling in my bed, on the floor and in the shower with THE Nathan Sundry. And can I just say, Oh. My. God. I missed out all those years I wasted with dumb fuck.*

Piper: *Ok, I'm meeting you at the bakery for lunch. I need full details in person.*

Me: *You got it, Pipes. I'll have Louisa make your favorite sandwich for you.*

Piper: ***thumbs up emoji***

Me: ***eggplant emoji, peach emoji, water drops emoji***

Piper: *FUUUCKKKKK*

Chapter 13

Nathan

I can't wipe the shit eating grin from my face. I spent the whole night inside Gracie Henderson. Yup, the whole night. Whenever one of us moved in the middle of the night, we wound up tangled in each other. Bodies pressed together.

Moving.

Groaning.

Licking.

Sucking.

It was freaking amazing. Everything I'd always imagined and more. She's fucking perfect and she's mine. I made her mine last night (and this morning btw) and she made me hers. I don't know how I'm supposed to get any work done. I know I'm going to spend the entire day doing nothing but thinking about Gracie, naked. Spread open for me, moaning for me, coming for me. Ugh, great and now I'm hard.

I'm sitting at my desk, stack of papers in front of me, with a hard dick. Calm down Nathan. Think about payroll and the inspector coming later today. DO NOT think about Gracie. Too late, an image from this morning of her naked body, pumping up and down on my cock, caramel brown hair curtaining down around her face, her perfect tits slamming against my mouth, pops in my mind. I'm a goner for sure.

Just then the trailer door pops open, and my Uncle Jay walks in.

"Hey kid, how are things shaking out down here."

"Hey Uncle Jay. Job seems to be going smoothly so far. Waiting on the electrical inspection before we move on, so it's a quiet day today. How about you? Enjoying semi-retirement."

He rubs his reddish-grey beard and chuckles. Jay is big guy. 6ft 6 and probably close to 300lbs. He played college ball until he blew his knee out. That's what put him in the contracting business. My Aunt Kim has been asking him for the past couple of years to take it easy.

"Well, if your aunt had her way, it would be full retirement. I don't think she realizes just how crazy I would drive her if I wasn't working part-time. We already snipe at each other as is, I can't imagine what will happen when it's time to fully retire."

"Yeah, the whole bay area may have to evacuate. Sometimes your fights are as bad as a hurricane."

"Just you wait Nathan. Once you meet that girl who changes everything. I tell you, there's nothing like making up after a fight." He shoots me the biggest grin and wiggles his eyebrows. I can't help but feel a mixture of horror and excitement at the same time. Obviously, I don't want to think about how my aunt and uncle make up after a fight, but my mind can't help but drift to thoughts of Gracie.

"What's that smile for buddy boy? You got a girl you've been keeping secret from Ol' Uncle Jay?" I laugh at that because Uncle Jay is anything but old. Being the youngest of my dad's siblings, he's only 49 years old. The only reason my aunt keeps asking him to slow down is because of his years playing football and working in construction have taken a toll on his body. Honestly I don't really see Uncle Jay slowing down much more than he has. That man will work in some capacity until the day he dies.

"Not keeping her a secret. Things just happened before I really had a chance to tell anyone." I answer, obviously not wanting to go into the details. I get his curiosity. I've never been the serious relationship kind of guy. It's not like I've lived my life like a monk. I'm definitely no virgin. I've just never found anyone I wanted to spend more than a few nights with. That's the bonus to living in a tourist town. In the past I'd been happy to pick up a tourist girl from the bar and spend a few nights with her. That was until Gracie.

Uncle Jay puts his hands in mock surrender, "Ok, ok Nathan. I can take the hint. I think I know who the girl is based on the small-town rumor mill. All I'm going to say is, be careful. Michael Garrett is an arrogant son of bitch, but he was also your friend at one point in time. Just make sure you know what you're doing."

I roll my eyes and blow out a deep breath. This is how things have always been in the town when it comes to Michael. *Be careful. Don't rock the boat. He and his dad hold the cards to a whole lot of business in Moonrise Bay, we want don't to piss them off.* I've heard all these things most of my adult life and honest to God, I'm sick of it. I'm sick of walking on eggshells because Michael is a baby who gets his feelings hurt easily. I hate that I've had to worry he'll run to daddy complaining and that might cost us business. He's the idiot who fucked things up with Gracie. He's the one who knew how I felt about her and went after her anyway. I've sat back all these years and practically let him get away with murder, but I'll be damned if I'm giving up my shot with Gracie this time.

"I know what I'm doing Uncle Jay; you don't have to worry about anything." I reply with a slight edge to my voice.

"Alright, don't get pissed at me for caring. I just don't want to see you get hurt. I love you kid, like you're my own." He claps me on the back and starts to walk away before turning back and saying "I've always got your back Nathan. Don't ever forget that."

"Thanks Uncle Jay. That means a lot."

With a wave, he walks out the door and I turn back to work.

***

The day felt excruciatingly long. The electrical inspector had been a no show and without that inspection, we can't really move further on the job. I couldn't keep Gracie out of my mind either. Every time I tried to focus on paperwork, her beautiful face would pop in my head. I could still feel her lips against mine, her body pressed against me. I had a constant hard on all day and it was starting to get uncomfortable. Thank God I'd been in the office by myself today. So many times I had to stop myself from picking up the phone to call her. I just wanted to hear her voice, but I didn't want to push or crowd her. I know I'm in a fragile place with her. We've been friends for so long and she just ended a very long relationship. I don't want to scare her with the enormity of my feelings for her. I know deep down that I'm in love with her. If I'm honest with myself, I've always been in love with Gracie. I know she felt it last night. Felt our connection but I know she's not ready for this to be more than what it is for right now. I can wait. She's worth waiting a lifetime for.

Glancing down at my phone, it's finally after five and the workday is finally over. I decide to shoot off a text to Gracie and see what flavor pizza she and Piper are in the mood for.

Me: Hey Gracie, it's quitting time. Getting ready to stop by Sal's and grab a couple pies. What are you and Piper in the mood for?

Gracie: Hmmm, I don't know if I like you asking what Piper is in the mood for...

This girl is killing me!!!

Me: I don't think what you're in the mood for is on Sal's menu, but I think I can help you out with that later.

Gracie: **flame emoji** Ok, ok, before my phone bursts into flames, how about a pepperoni/jalapeno and large chopped salad. I've got plenty of wine and you know I've always got some kind of treat in my *kitchen.*

Me*: **thumbs up emoji** Sounds good. See you guys in a bit.*

Gracie*: Can't wait Nathan **kissy face emoji***

*****

Pizza and salad in hand, I opened the door to Gracie's house to snorts and giggles. It totally threw me back to 10th grade English class. Just as they are now, Gracie and Piper were a dynamic duo. I never understood how they could be friends with a girl like Madison. It always seemed like she dimmed their shine whenever she was around. I don't mean because she was prettier or funnier. No, it was the opposite. It was her meanness and controlling ways that made Gracie and Piper less noticeable. Listening to the two of them now, it's so easy to see why they are still best friends.

Rounding the corner towards the kitchen, the tail end of their conversation catches my attention.

"That big!!! Girl, how are you walking today?" Piper asked with snorts of laughter.

"Umm, I may have needed to ice my lady parts at one point in the day today." Gracie responded while blowing out a deep breath.

I decided I better make some kind of noise

to announce my arrival instead of eavesdropping on their conversation (as much as I was enjoying listening in).

I cleared my throat as I announced "Hey ladies, pizza's here. Who's ready to grub?"

Cheers and hoots roared from the living room where I peered in to see a mess of fabric and craft items strewn on every surface of the room.

"Jeez you two, it looks like a craft store threw up in your living room. What the hell happened in here?" I chuckled as I placed the pizza boxes on the kitchen island. I smirked a little, remembering what Gracie and I had done in the kitchen in the middle of the night when we both needed water.

"Pay no attention to that madness. Genius will arise out of the craziness I promise you. This year Gracie and I will reign victorious in The Pirate's Chest costume contest. Mark my words. That trash ass bitch, Madison, will rue the day she came for my girl. Now, point me in the direction of that pizza. Momma's been working hard and she's hungry."

"Pepperoni and jalapeno as requested, and I added a bacon and onion pie. Help yourself Piper. I don't want to get in the way of a hangry woman." I flipped both pizza boxes open as Gracie grabbed plates from the cabinets. I grabbed a beer from the fridge while noticing the look Piper was shooting me over her slice of pizza.

"Ooh, look at you Nathan, making yourself at home here in Gracie's kitchen. If I didn't know any better, I'd think you two had jumped a few steps in this *relationship* developing between you guys."

Gracie, almost on choking on her own slice, replied, "Jesus Piper, he only grabbed a beer from the fridge. It's not like he dropped his pants at the front door. Give the guy a break."

"Alright, alright. Whatever you say. I'm just teasing anyway. I feel like a toast is in order. Nathan, honest to God, I haven't seen my girl this happy in...well shit, I don't think I've seen her this happy. Just keep doing what you're doing buddy, and we have no problems here." Piper sidled up to me and bumped me on the shoulder before finishing "but if you do anything to hurt my Gracie girl, I'll have your nuts in a vise so fast, you'll think you see Jesus."

"Gah, Piper, simmer down for Christ's sake." Gracie said while rolling her eyes, "Can we not just eat in peace instead of you threatening poor Nathan here."

"Trust me Piper, you don't wait all the years I've waited for a girl like Gracie and fuck it up." I turned and looked into those whiskey brown eyes that owned my soul and said "This is it for me. Gracie is the type of girl you treasure."

I smiled at Gracie's deep inhale. I knew right then and there that she understood what I was saying. That I was in this thing for the long haul. Nothing was scaring me off and I hope she was feeling the same way.

Chapter 14

Gracie

Piper and I had spent the past couple of days working on our Halloween costumes while I've spent my nights working on Nathan Sundry, if you know what I mean. I don't know if I've ever been happier or, let's face it, more satisfied in my life. This man and how he already knows exactly how to work my body. It's absolute perfection.

His touch.

His kiss.

His everything.

Knowing that he's going to be at the big Halloween party tonight has my lady parts singing hallelujah. What I'm dreading is running into Michael. I know he and Madison will be there. I've come to terms with seeing them as a couple. I just don't want to deal with his reaction when he sees me with Nathan. I know he'll see the happiness written all over my face and I'm worried about how that will affect Nathan. I could give a shit less what Michael thinks of me. I'm more concerned about how this is going to affect whatever relationship he and Nathan have left. I know their friendship was somewhat fractured before Nathan and I got together but they have known each other since we were all kids. They interact regularly because of their jobs. I know how Michael is when he gets his feelings hurt. He can turn into a petulant child and become spiteful. I would hate for Michael to mess with Nathan's business because he's pissed that Nathan and I are seeing each other.

The doorbell rings and my heart flutters. Even though we're not entering the contest as a couple, Nathan said he would pick me up for the party tonight and we'd grab Piper along the way. I head down the hallway towards the door, pausing to take a look in the mirror. I've got my dark hair up in a high ponytail with a bit of a bump to it. Soft makeup to accentuate my brown eyes. My outfit is a skimpy purple sleeveless dress with a feathered skirt and deep V-neck that makes my boobs look fucking hot. There's no way Piper and I don't win this contest. I take a deep breath, run my hands down my body, smoothing out my dress before reaching the door.

As the door opens, I can see Nathan's reaction to my outfit immediately. This is the first time he's seen the whole thing put together and he looks as if he wishes we could just stay in, and he could rip this dress right off me. If I'm being honest, I'm kind of wishing the same thing.

"Damn, Gracie. You're fucking sexy as hell. I don't know if I want to share you with the rest of the bar." His arm wraps around my waist as he drags me towards his body. He leans down and gently kisses my lips.

"I wouldn't want to mess up your makeup before the contest but you can be sure we'll be messing it up later." He says with a wink and I can feel my whole-body light up with excitement.

"Well Nathan, I see you really went out on a limb with your costume there." I say with a hint of sarcasm. It seems that Nathan decided to keep it easy with his outfit tonight. Don't get me wrong. The man looks hot. He's in dingy, skintight jeans, a white t-shirt, yellow construction vest and a hard hat. He fills out his jeans nicely.

Nathan chuckles and rubs his hands over the scruff on his chin. "I'm not really that into dressing up for Halloween anymore but I figured I couldn't accompany the most beautiful girl in Moonrise Bay without being in some kind of costume. You gotta use what you've got, right?"

"I'm just teasing you Nathan. I appreciate

the effort. I know you've never been into the Halloween festivities at The Pirate's Chest. I'm so happy you decided to come with me and Piper tonight. I think we're going to have a lot of fun."

"Are you at all worried about running into Michael and Madison?"

"I'm really not. Does it bother me to see the two of them together? I would be lying if I said no. Sure it bothers me but not for the reasons you'd think. I've reflected a lot since my breakup with Michael and I really think we held onto that relationship for all the wrong reasons. I should just have ended things when I found out about the first girl he cheated on me with but I was too scared to be on own. I was scared that no one would want me the way Michael did. I stayed with him because it was comfortable. I think I always knew we wouldn't last."

"Do you mind if I ask why you said he yes to marrying him?"

"No I don't mind. That's part of what I've been reflecting on. I think it goes back to comfort. Probably some naiveté on my part. My mom told me all the time, that I shouldn't saddle myself to one man for the rest of life. That I was too young. I'm not super comfortable with change and honestly I really thought I was in love with Michael but I know now, I hadn't been in love with him for a very long time."

Nathan reaches for my hand and intertwines our fingers together and just stares at me for a moment before saying anything.

"I'm sorry Gracie. I didn't mean to bring up bad memories. Let's get out of here, grab Piper and win you that costume contest."

******

The Pirate Chest is packed when we get there. Halloween is the biggest night of the year for the bar. Just about everyone in Moonrise Bay shows up all decked out in various forms of costume. I glanced around the bar, taking in all the different costume pairings, looking for a table. My eyes land on one with a group of the guys that Nathan works with. I guess they all decided to stick with what they know since it's a table full of, you guessed it, construction workers.

Nathan nudges me and Piper and says "You two have this in the bag. No one else's costumes can even compare."

"Damn straight, we got this in the bag." Piper declares before heading to the bar.

I point to the table where Nathan's crew is sitting and shout to Piper to meet there after she grabs drinks.

Nathan places his hand on the small of my

back as he guides me towards the table. I can feel eyes on me as we're walking and I know Madison and Michael must be here somewhere. That's the downside to living in a small town. Everyone knows your business whether you want them to or not and I know everyone here is wondering what's going to happen when Michael spots me with Nathan and his buddies. Lord knows, this town does love a good scandal to gossip about.

We reach the table and Nathan introduces me to his crew. Of course, I know most of them. They come into the shop most mornings for coffee and breakfast sandwiches. They're a good group of guys and welcome me into their group right away. Cheers erupt at the table when Piper shows up with a couple pitchers of beer, followed by a waiter carrying mugs and several baskets of chips and salsa.

"Ok boys and girl...have at it. First round is on me."

"Thanks Piper. If you keep this up, you can hang out with our crew anytime." Pete, one of the guys on the crew says as he reaches for the pitcher.

There's a face at the table I don't recognize. He's not one of Nathan's crew and he seems to be paying close attention to Piper. She *is* smoking hot in her Tinkerbell costume. Skintight, green velvet dress with a deep v neckline. Her blonde hair is pulled back into a French twist and the makeup she chose, makes her green eyes pop. This guy just can't take his eyes off her and I'm curious who he is.

I stick my hand out to him and introduce myself. "I don't think I've seen you around town before. I'm Gracie Henderson."

He shakes my hand and smiles. He's a good-looking guy with his dark brown eyes and almost black hair.

"Hi, I'm Levi Anderson and no I'm not from around here. I'm a friend of Nathan's. I'm in town for a few days and he invited me tonight."

"Oh, he didn't mention he had a friend in town. Where are you visiting us from Levi?"

"I'm from New York. I was in Wilmington doing some business and Nathan asked me to stop by Moonrise Bay before I headed back to the city. Said he had a business opportunity he wanted to discuss with me and I was intrigued to say the least." He eyes turn back to Piper before he finishes, "it seems Moonrise Bay has a lot to offer."

"Welcome to Moonrise Bay Levi, it's very nice to meet you" I say before pointing to Piper, "This is Piper Anderson. She's my best friend and partner in crime." I say with a wink. "She's also our local librarian."

At hearing someone talking about her, Piper turns towards Levi, hands on hips, holds out her hand to him and says, "The pleasure is all yours, I'm sure."

The whole table erupts into peel of laughter but Levi just holds Piper's gaze and shakes her hand.

"I bet you're you trouble with a capital "T"" he replies with a smirk.

"Oh you have no idea. Now boys, it's Halloween night. Drink up. Lots of mischief to be had tonight."

Our table is a little rowdy but that's what makes it fun. My typical Halloween night used to include hanging out with Michael and his stuffy friends. Where I would always want to make Halloween night fun and a little wild, Michael used it to schmooze his friends and woo business associates. Tonight is how it should have always been. Just a group of friends, dressed up in silly costumes, having a good time.

The band starts up. Playing a Lumineers cover. Nathan comes to stand behind me and wraps his arms around my waist. This feels so right. Like this is where I'm supposed to have always been. Standing here with Nathan. Surrounded by Piper and Nathan's friends. I lean back into the comfort of Nathan's chest.

We stand there, arms wrapped around

each other, swaying to the music. Almost in our own little world.

"Well, well isn't this cozy. Just look at the two of you. You didn't waste any time did you now, Nathan." At the sound of Madison's voice, I feel my spine immediately stiffen. Before I could even turn around, Piper stepped in Madison's path.

"Jealous much Madison. Don't tell me you're new man isn't satisfying you. Are you here begging for scraps like the dog you are?"

Our whole table goes silent. Waiting for Madison to strike. I pull myself out Nathan's arms and stand next to Piper.

"Isn't this getting a little old Madison. You got what you wanted. You have Michael and no need to worry about me wanting him back. I don't want to fight. I just want to move on from all of this. Honestly, I've got much bigger things to worry about than what you and Michael are doing all over town."

Madison turns her viciousness my way. "Ha, that's laughable Gracie. As if I'm remotely worried about Michael wanting you back. Trust me, my man is sat-tis-fied. More so than he ever was with you. Oh and I know all about your other troubles. Who's idea do you think it was for Garrett Realty to sell off their holdings in downtown Moonrise?" She smirks as if she's offering some sort of revelation. Madison has never been known for her brains.

"Oh, poor Madison. Did you think I hadn't already figured out why Michael's father suddenly wanted to sell the buildings he owns downtown? I'm not as stupid as you look." Piper laughs so hard at that she spits her drink straight in Madison's face. Our table again erupts in laughter and Madison seethes with rage.

"You bitch. You did that on purpose." She yells at Piper as she approaches with her hand clenched in a fist. I step in her path and grab her hand before she can punch Piper in the face. Nathan is close behind and surprisingly Levi has put himself by Piper's side.

"I'd suggest you find somewhere else to be Madison or I'll help you find it. You are done here."

Madison pulls her hand from my grasp and gets right in my face.

"You haven't won anything Gracie. You're nothing and no one. You always have been nothing and you'll always be no one."

She flips her hair and spits on the floor like the "lady" she is and walks back to her side of the bar. Because the music in the bar has been so loud, no one but the people at our table witnessed the altercation with Madison. Typical. This is who Madison has always been. I think I always knew she didn't care about anyone but herself. Reminds of another time Madison showed her true colors.

Madison twirled her straw in her iced coffee, the ice clinking loudly as she watched me with a smile that didn't quite reach her eyes. "So," she said, her tone sugary sweet, "you and Michael, huh?"

I nodded, trying to ignore the flutter in my chest at the mention of his name. "Yeah. He asked me out after class yesterday. We're going to that new Italian place on Friday."

"Wow," Madison said, drawing the word out like taffy. "That's... unexpected."

I frowned. "Unexpected?"

"Well," she said, shrugging as if she didn't have a care in the world, "I mean, Michael's great and all, but I always thought he had a type, you know? Like sporty or more, I don't know, flirty?" She sipped her coffee, her eyes darting to mine over the rim of her cup.

My stomach twisted, but I forced myself to laugh it off. "Well, I guess he's mixing it up," I said, trying to sound casual. "He asked me, and I said yes. No big deal."

"No big deal?" Madison leaned forward, her voice dropping conspiratorially. "This is Michael Garrett" the quarterback of the football team. No

big deal????"

Her words felt more like a jab than encouragement, but I nodded. "Yeah, I guess it kind of is."

Madison's smile tightened. "Good for you," she said, her tone making it clear she didn't mean it. "I mean, I thought for sure he was going to ask me out after we spent all that time together planning prom committee stuff, but hey, you win some, you lose some, right?"

I blinked at her, unsure of what to say. "Uh… right."

Madison leaned back in her chair, crossing her arms. "Well, I hope it works out. For both of you."

The way she said it made it sound like she hoped the opposite

A whistle rings out across the table drawing me out of the memory as Pete says "Woo wee, that woman is a snake. It almost makes feel sorry for Michael Garrett."

"Her bite is definitely worse than her bark but don't worry about Michael. He got what he deserved." I say before I turn back to Nathan.

"Come on Nathan. Let's not let that witch spoil our night. Join me out on the dance floor."

I grab his hand and pull him towards the band. I look to the left and see Piper and Levi involved in quite an intense-looking conversation. Hmm... maybe Piper won't be going home alone tonight.

Out on the dance floor, Nathan puts his hand under my chin and lifts my face to his. He leans down and places a gentle kiss on my lips.

"You doing ok Gracie?" he asks sweetly.

I breathe out a deep sigh. "I'm fine Nathan. I'm used to Madison and her antics. The best way to handle her is not to give her what she wants. She's the typical bully. If you show her that what she does isn't bothering you, she eventually gets bored and moves on to her next target. I've learned from being her target off and on over the years. Mark my words, she'll get bored soon and move onto the next sucker."

The night passes without any more trouble. I guess Madison and Michael left early because when Piper and I are announced the winners of the costume contest, they are nowhere to be seen. As Nathan and I begin to say our goodbyes to our tablemates, Piper pulls me aside with a sly grin on her face.

"No need to take me home tonight Gracie. I think Levi and I are going to hang around the bar for a bit longer. He's promised to get me home."

"Are you sure Pipes? You've just met him."

Piper laughs off my worry. "I'm a big girl Gracie and just because I'm letting him drive me home doesn't mean I'm letting come home with me. Besides, he's a friend of Nathan's. I doubt he would do anything to piss Nathan off."

"I guess you're right. Nathan wouldn't have brought him to town if he didn't trust him. Just be careful Piper. Love you babes."

"I love you too babers." She places a kiss on my cheek and heads towards the bar. I head over to where Nathan is standing with Levi. The two seem to be in an intense conversation.

"I don't mean to interrupt you guys but Nathan I need to be getting home. I've got an early morning at the bakery tomorrow."

"Sure thing Gracie." Nathan says before turning back to Levi, "Thanks for coming tonight man. I hope you've been able to get a sense of what Moonrise Bay has to offer."

"I've explored a little a bit of the town and I like what I've seen so far." I can't help but follow his gaze towards the bar and Piper. I bet he likes what he's seen. "Gracie, I was hoping I could stop into your shop tomorrow. Maybe get a little sense for the downtown area and hopefully meet some of the other store owners."

"Oh, well sure. I mean I don't know about the others, but of course you're welcome in the bakery. I'm happy to show you around Levi."

"Great, I hear good things about your cinnamon sugar cronuts. Being from New York, I'm curious to see how yours fair against the original."

It's Nathan who responds when he says "Well my friend, I can tell you they are out of this world delicious. In my opinion, no others can even compare."

I smile and blush a little at Nathan's declaration. He wraps his arms around my waist and shakes hands with Levi before we make our way out of the bar. I turn to face him as we approach his truck.

"Tonight was fun Nathan. Thanks for putting up with me and Piper and the costume contest. I hope it wasn't too goofy for you."

"Babe, all I could think about all night was you in that costume, splayed on your bed for me to feast upon. Definitely nothing goofy about it."

My whole-body heats at his words and it's all I can do to not wrap myself around this man, right here, right now in the street. Just his words can get my blood racing.

"Well, I guess we better get home before we wind up in the back of your truck with that kind of talk."

The delicious look on Nathan's face has me thinking that's just what he had planned. He helps me into the passenger side of the truck before getting behind the wheel himself. And it's full speed ahead back to the townhouse and hopefully a sleepless night.

Chapter 15

Nathan

I woke with a start to the sound of pots and pans clanging around in the kitchen. The smell of something wonderful cooking wafted up into the bedroom and I thought how sweet it was that Gracie was making breakfast even though she had to get into the bakery this morning. I slowly came to the realization that it wasn't Gracie down in the kitchen because she was still in bed with me, naked, curled against my side. I didn't even have time to appreciate how beautiful her naked body was as I realized someone was in Gracie's house and they were cooking breakfast for us. Weird. Could it be Piper? Maybe she was here to talk about what happened between her and Levi last night. Gently, I nudged Gracie awake to let her know that we weren't alone in the house.

"Babe, babe. Wake up. Someone's downstairs cooking in your kitchen."

Gracie groggily began to wake up. Damn is she

cute in the morning.

"Unh… what do you mean someone's in my house?" She jumped as she heard movement downstairs and the sound of another pan banging in the kitchen.

"What the hell? Who's in my kitchen? Nathan, why are you so calm about all this?"

"Well I figured they don't want to kill us since they're making breakfast. I thought it might be Piper, here to talk about what happened after we left the bar last night." I say, wiggling my eyebrows.

"Piper does not make anything in the kitchen. She's a master at ordering takeout, Nathan."

Just as it hit me that it couldn't be Piper downstairs, a voice came calling up to us.

"Yoo-hoo, Gracie. Wake up sweet pea. It's your mother. Remember me? The one who gave you life. I've got your favorite breakfast down here. If you're not down in thirty seconds, I'm heading up."

"Oh my God, Nathan, we have to get you out of here. Maybe we can hide you in the closet until I can get my mom out of the house. Shit, shit, shit."

I chuckle as I watch Gracie panic while trying to get dressed. She's so damn cute it's killing me.

"Gracie, why are you hiding me from your mother? Ashamed of me?"

"What?? No, God no. It's not you Nathan, it's her." She says as she throws my clothes at me. "Look, I love my mom and we've gotten super close since my dad died but she's a little kooky. If she finds you in here, she won't let you leave until she has your life story. Please, please, just hide in the bathroom until she leaves."

Too late. Before I can even respond, I see Gracie's mom standing in the doorway.

"Well, well, well, Gracie. Who is this handsome, half-naked man standing in my daughter's bedroom?"

Fuuuckkk. This is not the way I wanted to meet Gracie's mom. Sure I remember her a little bit from our high school days but I doubt she remembers me.

"Ugh, mom, why are you here so early and why didn't you call first?"

"Hmm, why didn't I call first? Well my sweet daughter, I've been calling you for several days and you haven't responded to a single call or text. I was worried about you so I figured I'd pop across the bridge and come make you breakfast. I didn't know you were.... entertaining a gentleman."

"Jesus mom, this isn't the antebellum south. I lived with a man for several years. You don't have to act shocked to find me in my own bedroom with a half-naked man." I can tell Gracie is beginning to get irritated with her mother's teasing. Her cheeks are turning red and she's clenching and unclenching her hands by her side.

Her mom must notice this too because she replies "Oh Gracie, I'm just teasing. I just wasn't expecting to find you not home alone. Especially since you haven't told me you're seeing someone. I was just surprised, that's all."

Gracie's mom then turns to me and offers her hand, "Alice Henderson and you are?"

I awkwardly hold out my hand before saying "Nathan Sundry, it's, um, nice to meet you Mrs. Henderson."

"Nonsense call me Alice. Hmm...Nathan Sundry. Not the same the same Nathan Sundry who was best friends with Michael Garrett in high school?"

Gracie smacks her hand to her forehead and yells "MOM!!!"

I give her a reassuring glance and then say "Yes ma'am. One in the same. Michael and I were best friends in high school, but we kind of grew apart after he went off to college. We're still acquaintances. Mainly work acquaintances but...um, not as close as we used to be."

Gracie's mom just stands there for a moment. She seems to be absorbing what I've just said. Alice Henderson isn't a tall woman. I guess that makes sense Gracie is only 5'4. But what she lacks in height, she makes up with intimidating looks. She looks to be a few years older than my Uncle Jay. She's almost the spitting image of Gracie. Her brown hair is streaked with gray and her eyes are more amber brown than Gracie's but they have the same smile and mannerisms.

"Well Nathan, it's nice to meet. I wasn't your English teacher in high school was I?"

"No ma'am. I wasn't lucky enough to get you as a teacher." See what I did there. Trying to butter up my girl's mom. Who said I was a dummy?

"Aren't you just a charmer. I can certainly see why Gracie likes you." I watch her eyes trail down my bare chest. Hmm...checked out by my girl's mom. That's gotta be a first for me.

"Mom, stop making Nathan feel weird and let us finish getting dressed. We'll be down in a minute for

breakfast."

Her mom throws her hands up in surrender. "Okay, okay. I know where I'm not welcome. I'll just go get breakfast plated up and pour a cup of coffee for everyone. You two look like you could each use a cup." She smirks as she walks away. I swear, I hear her laughing as she's walking downstairs.

"Nathan, I'm so sorry. That's not how I expected our morning to go."

I throw my shirt over my head and walk over to Gracie. I grab her into a hug and rub circles on her back.

"Definitely not the way I planned on meeting your mom, but certainly a fun story to tell later on." I feel her chuckle as she wraps her arms tighter around me. "So tell me more about how you expected our morning to start out?"

*****

The week passes without too many issues. For some reason, our electrical inspection keeps getting pushed. Whenever I or Uncle Jay call the permit office, we get the run around as to why our inspection has been moved. Same old story. Too many jobs, not enough workers. The city guys are behind on their inspections. They'll get to us soon. I sure hope they do because the job is kind of at a standstill. We have a few things we can do to work around the electrical but that means I can't have my whole crew here. I know some of them have picked up side work here and there over in Wilmington. Hopefully that won't effect this job once that inspection does finally come through. I'm starting to worry that maybe my Uncle Jay was right about Michael. Especially since I haven't heard from or seen Michael in a while. Maybe he is my problem at the permit office. I guess at some point, I'm going to have to get to the bottom of things and see where Michael and I stand now. I'm not giving Gracie up and I'm not going to let Michael ruin my business. That's part of the reason I brought Levi to town. He's a big-time real estate investor from New York and I'm hoping he'll want to invest in Moonrise Bay. He's told me in the past that he wanted to get out of the city and invest in something waterfront. I think Moonrise Bay is the perfect place for Levi to sink his money into. The added bonus will be when he shows Michael just how little Michael understands about the housing market. Levi is a shark when it comes to business and he'll eat Michael for breakfast, lunch and dinner. I know I shouldn't root for my friend's failure but after everything he has done to Gracie, I'm done protecting him.

It's been a long, slow day, and I'm ready to get out of the office, get cleaned up and meet Gracie at her place for a little date night. I'm just stepping out the door when my office phone starts ringing. I hesitate to answer it. I really just want to get home and meet up with Gracie but something in my gut tells me I need to take this phone call.

"Sundry Construction, how can help you?"

"Is this Nathan Sundry?" The voice on the other end asks in a hushed tone.

"It is, who am I speaking with?"

"No names, I'm just calling to let you know that someone is messing with your permits and causing your inspections to be delayed. I shouldn't be telling you this but Michael Garret is trying to get all the permits pulled on your job. I just thought you should know."

I sit there for a moment. Unable to say anything. I knew this was a possibility but there was always a part me that was hoping it wouldn't be true.

"Are you still there?" The voice asks nervously.

"Yeah, yeah, I'm here. Just shocked. Uh, thanks for the heads up. Thanks for taking a risk with this with call."

"Just do me a favor, and when you try to fix things, don't tell anyone you got this call." The caller hangs up before I have a chance to respond. I slam the phone down and slump into my office chair. That petty asshole. After everything I've done for him in the past. All the covering up I've done for him. Making him look good to his father. He's going to mess my family's business. I don't think so. I need to talk to Levi and see if he can help with more than just the downtown issue. Maybe I can get him to buy out Garrett Realty on this housing development. I don't know how much capital he has available but maybe he can get me in touch with other investors. I need to do something and do it fast. I can't lose my crew to the bigger companies in Wilmington. These are my guys and they're a great group. I can't expect them to wait forever for these inspection and permit issues to work out. I know they all have bills to pay and some have families to support. Fuck, this is not the way I envisioned the night going. Gracie and I were going to cook a little dinner, maybe watch a movie and definitely spend the night naked. Now, all I'm going to be able to think about is saving my job and my business.

I decide to call Levi and see if he can meet tomorrow for breakfast and give me some advice. One thing's for sure; I'm not going down without a fight.

"Yo, Nathan. How's it hanging?"

"What's going on Levi. Hope I'm not interrupting anything."

Levi laughs on the other end of the call

"Nah man, I'm just sitting in my rental. Going over some paperwork. Daydreaming about a certain librarian. What can I do for you?"

"So something did happen between you and Piper. Interesting, very interesting."

"A gentleman never kisses and tells Nathan."

"Ha, like you're a gentleman." We both laugh knowing neither one of us has ever been accused of being a gentleman. "So Levi, I need some business advice. I've got a problem with some of my inspections being delayed purposefully. I was wondering if you have time to meet for breakfast tomorrow so I can pick your brain."

"Damn Nathan, someone out to get you or what? Sure man, I can meet for breakfast. You want to meet at Beach Buns?"

"I was thinking we'd meet at the diner. I'm not ready for Gracie to hear about this yet. It looks like it's her ex who's causing the issue and I don't want her to think any of this is her fault."

"Gotcha man. Alright, I'll meet you at the diner at 8am. I'll see what kind of information I can dig up in the meantime."

"Thanks man. I appreciate the help. I'm glad you're in town Levi."

"Don't worry man. This asshat won't

know who's coming for him."

After hanging up with Levi, I feel a little bit better. I didn't want Gracie to find out what's going on yet because I knew she'd blame herself. That's just what Michael wants. He's punishing us because we're happy and because Gracie isn't sitting around, miserable without him. I won't let him do that to her.

Chapter 16

Gracie

Nathan is unusually quiet as he sits at the kitchen island while I get dinner started for the two of us. I can tell something is weighing heavily on his mind but I'm not sure how to approach the subject. It must be something work related. I know that his current job has been put on hold waiting for some kind of inspection. Honestly, I feel like I've been so wrapped up in my own issues with the downtown buildings being sold that I haven't really paid much attention to what's happening with Nathan. That's kind of shitty of me. After all, it was Nathan who brought Levi down here to help with the whole downtown situation. Levi had some really interesting ideas on what he sees as the future for downtown Moonrise Bay and to say I was intrigued would be the least of it. But I'm getting away from myself again. I need to focus on Nathan right now. Something is bothering him and I can tell he doesn't want to worry me with it. That must mean Michael or Madison has something to do with it.

I'm quietly chopping vegetables for the salad, when I glance over at Nathan. He's staring out the back window that faces the water, beer bottle resting against his lips.

"Hey Nathan, what's wrong? You've been quiet since you got here. Did something happen at work today?" I feel him tense a little at my question and I see his inner debate about whether he's going to tell me or not. That makes me a little sad. I want Nathan to feel like he can trust me with whatever is going on. I've let him in on everything that has happened to me recently and I really want him to feel like he can do the same with me. I need him to know that he can trust me and I would want to help him with whatever he's going through.

Nathan puts his beer down and rubs the back of his neck. I can tell he's struggling with how he's going to answer. "Ugh, I'm sorry Gracie. It was just a shitty day at work. We're still being stonewalled on the electrical inspection and my guys have had to take other work in the meantime. I'm starting to worry that once this inspection finally comes through, I won't have enough of a crew to finish the job. I'm sorry I'm bringing our night down. Maybe I should just head home and sulk on my own."

I put my knife down and move around the island so I'm standing directly in front of Nathan. I put both hands on either side of his face and look deeply into in eyes.

"Don't you dare apologize to me Nathan and don't you dare you leave. You've ruined nothing. How many times have you listened to me bitch and moan about my day or me worrying about the fate of the bakery? You're allowed to share your life with me, Nathan. If you have a bad day, tell me. This relationship is a two-way street. I don't want it to always be about you taking care of me. That's what I had with Michael. It was always about him and I won't do that to you. I care about you Nathan. Talk to me, don't just sulk. And if all you need to say is *I don't want to talk it about right now,* then I'll understand that too. I just want you to know, that I'm here." I stroke his five o'clock shadow and lean down, placing the lightest kiss on his lips.

He smiles at me and whispers "What did I ever do to deserve you?" He places his forehead against mine and continues "I don't really want to talk about it anymore tonight. I just want to salvage our night and be here with you. I promise, when I have more to talk about, I'll tell you everything. Now let's get this salad finished and get to our dinner. It smells glorious."

He takes my hand and kisses my palm

before getting up from his barstool. Electricity shoots through my body and I just hope we actually get through dinner before I rip this man's clothes off. I smile at Nathan and head back to finish salad. Nathan grabs the bottle of wine and heads to living room where we plan on eating dinner tonight. I grab our plates of chicken piccata and the salad and make my way to the couch.

"Ok Gracie girl, what are we watching tonight?"

"Come on Nathan, are you kidding me? It's Thursday Night Football and I've got a few players from my fantasy league playing tonight. We're watching the game of course."

"God, could you be any more perfect?" Nathan reaches over, grabs my waist, kissing me deeply. His hands begin sliding under my t-shirt as he deepens the kiss.

"Whoa there guy. You keep kissing me like that and we won't be watching the game."

Nathan gives me a devilish grin before saying "Would that be such a bad thing Gracie girl."

"Dinner first Nathan and I promise if you're a good boy with a clean plate, you'll get dessert."

"Promise" Nathans asks as he wiggles his

eyebrows.

I smack him on the arm and turn the game on. "Promise you idiot. Now eat your dinner."

"Watch out Gracie, those are fighting words." Nathan shoves a forkful of chicken piccata in his mouth and I desperately try not to laugh at him. This casual type of evening is what I realize I had been missing from life for a long time. Even with Nathan in a shit mood, he put aside those feelings and we salvaged our evening. Something Michael was never able to do.

Nathan and I settle onto the couch with our dinner. We watch the game, rooting for my fantasy players. Unfortunately, my players aren't doing well but I did promise Nathan there would be dessert if he cleaned his plate.

I move over and straddle Nathan's lap. I can feel his immediate excitement as I rub against his hardened length.

"Mmm, Gracie girl. You feel so good." Our lips meet and heat shoots through my core. This man is sex on a stick and I can't get enough of him.

His touch.

His mouth.

His everything.

I want him every waking minute of the day.

Nathan deepens our kiss. Tongue surging in, tangling with my own. Lips crushing lips. Kissing each other like this is our last. His hands roam up my back and slide underneath my t-shirt. I feel instant wetness pool between my legs. He pulls my shirt over my head. "Fuck Gracie. I can never get enough you. Your tits are fucking amazing." He tugs the cups of my bra down and sucks and tugs on my nipples until they harden in his mouth.

"Oh my God, Nathan...please don't stop." Nathan lifts me underneath my ass and flips me down to the sofa until I'm lying on my back.

He pulls the waistband of my sweatpants down and I lift my hips to help him gets my pants off. Lying here in nothing but my black lace bra and panty set, I feel so vulnerable. I know that Nathan has seen me naked many times in the weeks that we've been seeing each other, but something about the way he's looking at me right now; my heart melts for him.

"Fuck Gracie, I don't think I'll ever get enough of you. You're so fucking sexy, so fucking beautiful. I still can't believe you're mine." Nathan runs his hands from my throat to the edge of my black panties. Slowly running his finger under the band, while his tongue traces his path. I can't help but moan. The way this man treasures my body. It's something I've never experienced before. He takes his time, almost teasing me until I'm about to break apart.

"Mmm Nathan, if I don't get you inside me soon, I'm going to come from you just teasing me. I don't think I can take it much longer."

"You go ahead and come for me baby. It will just be the first one of the night." Nathan gently pulls my panties down and my whole-body thrums with heat. I widen my legs for him as he begins rubbing slow circles over my clit.

"So wet for me Gracie. Such a pretty pussy." Nathan down on his knees, head between my legs, licks my slit. Tongue circling my clit as I squirm in pleasure.

"You taste so sweet baby. I can't get enough of you. I crave you every minute of the day." Licking up and down my swollen clit, he sticks two fingers in my pussy. I almost jump off the sofa from the pleasure coursing through me.

"Does that feel good, baby. Tell me what you want Gracie?"

"I-I, oh my god. I want your dick Nathan. I want to come all over you rock hard dick."

"Fuck, I can never hear that enough baby but first I want to feel you break apart on my tongue." He starts licking, sucking, tugging my clit harder and harder. All the while, he's fucking me harder with his fingers until he reaches that magic spot inside my pussy. I can feel the first waves of my orgasm breaking like a wave deep in the ocean.

"That's it, baby. Come for me." And just like that, I break apart. Coming so hard, I feel like I might blackout from the sheer pleasure. I look up and see Nathan standing over me, pulling his clothes off as quickly as he can. I reach up and help him as he gets down to his boxer briefs. I graze my teeth on my bottom lip as I see the tip of his cock sticking out of his waistband. I get up on my knees, lick my palm, take his length in my hand and begin pumping up and down on his hard cock. I take his cock and bring the tip to my lips. I lick him from tip to balls.

"Fuck Gracie...that feels...fuck" Nathan pushes my head down on his cock and I begin sucking him. Taking him deep in my mouth. Nathan thrusts his hips, fucking my mouth harder and harder. I take him deep until I can feel his tip hit the back of my throat, rubbing his balls as I'm sucking and licking. He moans, growls as I graze my teeth up his length.

"God don't stop Gracie. Baby, you're going to make come." I don't stop. I just moan deeply, the sound vibrating on his cock. Nathan reaches down and pulls me off his cock.

"Baby, I don't want to come in your mouth. I want to come in your pussy. Now turn over." He flips me over unto my stomach, lifting my hips and pulling my ass back against his dick.

He rubs he palm over my ass "Fuck, I love this ass. So beautiful." He smacks me, leaving a slight sting on my ass cheek. I jolt at the pleasure.

"You like that baby?"

"Y-yes Nathan. So much."

Nathan lines his dick up with my pussy and enters me hard.

"Gracie, I can't fuck you softly. It's got to be rough." Nathan begins pounding into me. Thrust after thrust. I feel sweat from his body dripping on my back. He reaches around and begins rubbing my clit again and that is my undoing. I can feel the walls of my pussy begin to grab his dick as my orgasm unravels.

"Oh fuck Gracie, I'm fucking coming so hard baby." I can feel Nathan's dick harden within my pussy walls before he's unloading his own orgasm inside me. With his final thrust, Nathan rubs his hand from the base of my neck, down my ass crack.

We both roll to floor, completely spent.

I look over at Nathan with the slightest smile on my face. "I did promise you dessert if you cleaned your plate."

Nathan tosses his head back and laughs, pulling me to his side. "Baby if that's dessert, I'll clean my plate every fucking time. So fucking worth it."

After cleaning up ourselves and our dinner mess, Nathan takes me upstairs where he makes love to me slowly before we fall asleep tangled in each other's arms. Feeling the safety of Nathan's arms wrapped around my naked body, I know I'm exactly where I'm supposed to be.

*****

Me: *I miss my best friend. Drinks later?*

Me: *Piper, since when don't you answer my texts?*

Me: *Okay, now I'm getting worried. What's going on? Where are you? If you don't answer soon, I'm using my emergency key and busting in your house.*

Piper: *Whoa, whoa, whoa. Cool your jets Gracie Boo. All's good, I've just been super busy.*

Me: *Super busy unh. This wouldn't have anything to do with a certain friend of Nathan's would it?*

Piper: **blushing emoji* Maybe, a lady never tells.*

Me: *Bullshit Pipes. You've made me tell you every detail about me and Nathan.*

Piper: *Buy a girl a drink and I might be convinced to change my mind *smiley face emoji**

Me: Meet me at The Pirate's Chest babes. I could really use some hot gossip.

Piper: Deal babes. Meet you there in an hour.

I'm sitting at the bar with two old fashioneds when Piper breezes in. No shit, but she looks like a girl that has been getting some on the regular. Speaking from experience of course.

"Hey girl, I can't wait to hear the explanation for this spectacular glow. You look like a woman who's been properly fucked."

Piper's eyes widen in shock and she lets out a boisterous laugh. "Damn Gracie, warn a girl before you hit her with "properly fucked". Speaking from experience are we?"

I smile and grab Piper for a hug. Damn, I've missed hanging out with her. Between figuring out how to save the bakery, keeping up with work and spending time with Nathan, I feel like I've neglected our friendship.

"I have no complaints in the man department, that's for sure Pipes. It's the rest of my life that has become an epic shitshow. But I don't want to talk about that tonight. I want to hear what's new with you. Tell me what's going on with you and Levi."

She blushes, actually blushes. Man, she must really be into this guy because as long as

I've known Piper Jackson, she has never had this reaction over a man. I don't know if I've ever seen her in a serious relationship with anyone.

"We're just enjoying each other Gracie. He's only here for a few more days so it's nothing serious. I'm just going to have fun while he's here and let me tell you girl, he's a lot of fun. I've never had so much "fun" in my life. Sorry I kind of checked out on you Gracie. I know you've got a lot on your plate right now."

"Don't you dare apologize to me Piper. You've been there for me from the minute I found out about Michael. You deserve some fun and I'm glad you're finally taking some time just for you. Whatever that man is doing you must be good. Your skin has never looked better and that grin you currently sporting tells me everything I need to know."

"I'll toast to that Gracie boo." We toast to our men and spend the night talking and laughing about all things Levi and Nathan. It feels good to be here with Piper. It reminds to not to take her for granted again. Piper has always dropped whatever was going on in her life to help me.

"Ok Pipes, I'm definitely a bit tipsy. I think it's time to call it night. I think I'm going to text Nathan and see if he can take me home."

"Ooh girl, that sounds like a good idea. I

think I might booty text Levi too. It's not like he knows that many people in Moonrise Bay, so I know he'll be free." We both laugh and pull out our phones when Madison and couple of the mean girls we went to high school with walk through the door.

I see the look on Piper's face and turn to see them walking towards where we're sitting at the bar. I groan and roll my eyes. What the fuck does this bitch want? She's got Michael and she's already told me she was responsible for the selling off of the downtown buildings. What more does she want to do to me? What more can she do me and why does she care so much?

"Gracie, here without your guard dog or should I say lap dog?" She's so fucking smug and her little minions giggle thinking she's hit her mark with her little dig at Nathan.

"Keep moving Madison and take your little gaggle with you. We're not buying whatever your selling." Madison turns on Piper with such venom it almost makes me recoil.

"Was I talking to you Piper? Why don't you go stack some books. God, you have got to be the most boring person with the most boring job."

"Unh, you might think I have a boring job but I least I didn't have to fuck the boss' son to get work. Now run along before I decide to take out the trash."

Madison's minions hiss, actually make hisses sounds.   Honestly this is getting ridiculous and I'm putting it to end tonight.

"Madison, just keep moving. Grab your drinks and move along. I don't give a shit what you think about me and Nathan. You did me a favor by sleeping with Michael. It opened my eyes that I haven't been in love with him for a very a long time. I was only holding onto the memories but there was nothing left between us anymore. I'm in a good place. So maybe I should thank you. I don't know, but I'm done with this pissing match you try to start up whenever we're in public." I look at her and can see she's angry she hasn't been able to get to me. I smirk and finish what's left in my glass. "Hope you guys have a great night. Come on Pipes, let's meet Nathan and Levi at The Crystal Boat. I'm not wild about the vibe in here tonight."

Piper and I link arms and walk out into the cool night. Laughing and leaving all that angst behind us.

Chapter 17

Nathan

Gracie: *Grab Levi and meet Piper and me at The Crystal Boat*

Me: *Sure thing baby.*

Gracie: *We're a few cocktails ahead of you guys. We got started a little early.*

Me: *Should I be worried? I'm not so sure about the combination of you and Piper and day drinking.*

Gracie: *I don't know about how worried you should be. You should be wondering what you're going to do with me later. I'm feeling a warm and tingly in all right places.*

Me: *Tell me more Gracie*

Gracie: *I'm not wearing any panties Nathan.*

Me: *Fuuuckkk*

The week went by in blur. After my breakfast with Levi, he decided to use his connections in the permit office and see what Michael was doing to hold up our inspection.

Oddly enough, after his snooping, the inspector showed up, finished the inspection and we were back in business. Needless to say, it did nothing to alleviate my suspicions that Michael was trying to mess with my business. I tried to push it aside for now and just focus on work. This house my crew is working on now is the last one in the development and I could not wait to get it finished up. Now that the electrical passed inspection, we just had the finishing touches left. Our paint crew was hard at work getting the exterior painted as well as the landscaping crew. Once all of that was done, I could turn the houses over to Garrett Realty and free myself of Michael for good.

I was closing down the office for the night when my cell phone dinged. I looked down and saw a message from Levi.

Levi: *Hey man, just wanted to give you a heads up. It seems my poking around the permit office has people nervous. Keep your eyes and ears open. I don't trust Michael Garrett. If I were you man, I'd stay as far away from that guy as I could.*

Me: *Thanks for the heads-up man. We're just putting the finishing touches on this last house and then I'm handing things off to Garrett Realty. I'm so happy to be done with Michael and his family.*

Levi: *Don't blame you one bit man. Look, I'm hoping to get back down there after the holidays.*

I've got a few things to close out here in the city, and then I'm going to try and make Moonrise Bay more permanent.

Me: **winking* I bet I know a certain librarian who will like the sound of that. It will be good to have you down here man.*

Levi: **laughs* I hope you're right man.*

I grabbed my phone and locked up the trailer. Gracie was working late at the bakery tonight trying to get a start on the Thanksgiving rush. Even though it was the off season for tourism, holidays were still her busiest time of year. People even came in from Wilmington to get their holidays treats from Gracie. I was so proud of my girl. She had taken a hit when Madison came up with the idea for Garrett Realty to get rid of their downtown holdings. One of those being the building Gracie's bakery is in. Even with that hit, Gracie kept her head held high and just kept working. Our little community was proud of our downtown area. Those businesses were a big reason people came back year after year to Moonrise Bay. I know the town is going to band together and make sure that those businesses don't go anywhere.

Driving through the streets of Moonrise Bay, the amount of love the community had for downtown was evident everywhere. The townspeople had posted sign after sign asking to "Save Our Downtown". These people were not going to let Madison and Garrett Realty get away with bringing in some stranger to change things up around here. That's part of the charm of living in a small town. Sure everyone knew your business but they also cared deeply about the people and businesses that are a part of the community.

As I pull into my driveway, my phone pings with a text message. I see it's my sister Landon. Interesting… I haven't heard from her in a few weeks.

Landon: *You're in so much trouble Nate *laughy face emoji*. Mom is pissed that she heard through Moonrise gossip that you're dating Gracie.*

Fuck, I knew I should've taken the time to call my parents but I had just been so wrapped up in everything that I just forgot to call them. Between work and Gracie, I just let everything else in my life get away from me.

Me: *Shit, how mad is she. I've been meaning to call her but life just got away from me here.*

Landon: *I tried running interference with her the best I could, but you know how mom gets. Plus she knows how long you've been pining away for Gracie.*

Me: *Jesus, I have not been pining away for Gracie. Yes, I had a crush on her in high school, but I put that aside when she and Michael started dating. I* *have dated other women Landon. It's not like I've lived my life as a monk.*

Landon: **rolls eyes* Ok Nathan, you only had a crush on Gracie in high school. Sure, sure. Whatever you need to tell yourself. Just call mom. I can't hold her off much longer.*

Me: *You're lucky you don't live close by... I'd make you pay for that. I promise I'll call mom as soon as I get inside. Thanks Stinker. Love you!!!*

Landon: **angry face emoji* Ugh, don't call me that Nathan. Love you too loser!*

I knew I needed to call my mom. I'm sure she's gotten an earful from Uncle Jay. Honestly I don't know why I've been putting this off. It's like Landon said, it's not like it was a secret in the family how I'd felt about Gracie in high school. I walked through my front door and headed for my back deck. Even though it was November, North Carolina weather had a way of being unpredictable. Tonight felt like a late summer night. The air was still a bit warm with a slight breeze blowing across the bay. I plopped down in one of the Adirondack chairs and dialed my mom's number.

"Well it's about time Nathan. I've been wondering when you were finally going to call your mother." Man was she good with a guilt trip.

"Hi Mom. You know phone calls work

both way. You could've called me too you know."
There. Guilt trips could work both ways.

"Fine, fine, Nathan. I suppose we're both
to blame. Now instead of trying to make your
poor old mama feel bad, tell me all the details
of you and Gracie Henderson finally becoming a
couple."

"Jesus mom. You make me sound like
some poor schlep who's been pining after a girl
for most of his life. I'll have you know; I've dated
plenty of women over the years. I've been pining
for no one."

"Nathan, I'm perfectly aware of your
dating prowess. I also know about the crush you
had on Gracie in high school before that jackass
of friend of yours started dating her. I'm happy
for you Nathan and excited too."

This is what I love about my mom. She's
a straight shooter and we've always had a close
relationship. I have a great relationship with
both my parents but my mom and I have always
been especially close. I know it hurts that I've
taken so long to tell her about me and Gracie.

"Thanks Mom. She's great and I'm very
happy.   Things started as a friendship after
she and Michael ended and then escalated from
there. I don't really know what else to say. I'm
just really happy."

"Oh Nathan, I'm so happy for you. Maybe

I'm not getting any younger you know."

"Good grief mom. You're only 54 years old. You have plenty of time left to be a grandma. Besides, Gracie and I just started seeing each other. We haven't discussed anything close to marriage. Can't we just date for a little while before you rush us down the aisle."

"Yeah, yeah, yeah. Clocks ticking Nathan."

"Okay mom, gotcha. On that note, I've gotta go. I'm meeting my crew at Sal's for pizza and beer. Celebrating the end of the job. I promise to call later in the week."

"Fine, break your mother's heart. I'm going to hold you to that promise Nathan. I love you sweet boy and I am really happy you've found some bliss."

"Love you too Ma. I promise to keep my promise."

*****

I met the guys at Sal's and we grabbed a table, several pies and a quite a few pitchers of beer. I realized it'd been awhile since I'd hung out with this crew. Let me tell you, they didn't let me forget it.

As soon as I walked through the doors, there was a chorus of whistles and cheers and quite a few claps.

"Well look what the cat dragged in. Is that Nathan Sundry? No Gracie tonight? That's a site I thought I'd never see" Pete yelled across the room as I walked towards the group.

I threw my hands up in surrender and laughed. I loved these guys. We had been a tight-knit crew for a long time now and the business wouldn't be what it is now, without them.

"Well, Gracie is a lot better looking than your ugly mug Pete. You can't blame a guy for spending all his time with her." The rest of the guys at the table laughed as Pete tossed a balled-up napkin my way. I sat down and poured myself a beer. I could feel the rest of the guys of the studying me.

I lifted my glass in a toast "To finally finishing this sub-division. You guys kicked ass as usual. There's no other group of guys I'd rather work with." The whole table erupted in cheers and table banging. These really were the best the group of guys and I considered myself lucky to have them on my crew. I knew they'd always have my back.

"SOOO, did you ever figure out what the holdup was with the electrical inspection? As long as I've been working with you, I don't think it has ever taken that long to get somebody out for an inspection. I was worried for a minute I was going to have to start looking for a new gig." Pete was a good guy. Probably one of my best friends. He hadn't grown up around here but he's lived in Moonrise Bay for the past five years. Once he joined my crew, we had become fast friends.

"Yeah, I had my friend Levi do some digging. He has connections with various city officials and looked into it for me. Turns out, Michael was sabotaging the job. I don't know if it's because he's pissed I've started seeing Gracie or if he wanted to tank the job but he apparently was paying off the inspector's office to not send any inspectors show up. I guess once he heard that someone like Levi was sniffing around, he decided to stop holding up the job."

"What a dick. This is the guy who cheats on his fiancé with her so-called best friend and he's pissed because she's moved on with someone bigger and better? Makes me what to punch him straight in the nuts." Pete took a giant swig of beer as the rest of the guys nodded in agreement.

"Yeah, he's just a daddy's boy who's not used to being told no. I've never been happier to finish the job before."

"Okay, okay. Now that we've wrapped up

this development, let's talk about how the guys and I never see you anymore. At least not without your beautiful baker by your side." I knew this was coming. I knew Pete and the guys weren't going to let how much time I'd been spending with Gracie slide.

"Come on Pete. How long has it been since our boy was getting some on the regular. You've got to admit it sure has made working for this asshole a lot easier." Jimmy, my drywall guy, elbowed me in the stomach and chuckled.

"Yeah, yeah. I'm just giving him a hard time. But seriously Nathan, I'm happy for you. She's a sweet girl and you really have seemed a hell of lot happier since you guys started messing around."

"No messing around here Pete. This girl is the real deal. She's got my heart and I don't think she's giving it back anytime soon." All the guys put their hands over their hearts and made kissy face noises. I knew I should've kept that bit of information to myself.

"You pussy faced motherfucker. You're done for, for sure." Pete clapped me on the back and the night continued on with more of the same. We ate, we drank and they teased me like all good guy friends do. I couldn't help but think about my Gracie the whole the night and hoped she was having just as good a night as I was but I sure did miss my girl.

Chapter 18

Gracie

It had been a really long day at the bakery and I was exhausted. Thanksgiving wasn't far off and the custom order requests had begun to pile in. I was up to my eyeballs in all things pie. With the craziness of the day, I let Miquel and Louisa head home early and decided to finish closing up the shop by myself. I had just finished cleaning all the equipment and was sitting down with a cup of ginger tea and my paperwork, when I heard the door open. Realizing I had forgotten to lock it, I looked up to see Michael, of all people, walking in. I'm sure my shock was written over my face. Maybe a little bit of anger too. What the hell could he possibly want.

"Hey Gracie. Surprised to see me I suppose?" Michael at least had the decency to look somewhat contrite, not sure I actually believed he was.

"What do you want Michael. I just finished closing up the bakery and was getting ready to head home. I'm not in the mood for a confrontation and honestly I don't really know what we have to say to each other." I could barely contain the exhaustion lacing my voice.

"Home to Nathan?"

"Don't start Michael. I don't owe you any explanation about my private life and I have the "save the date" card to prove it. You are the one who betrayed me. In my own house for fuck's sake. You lost the right to know anything about my life the minute you put your dick in Madison."

Michael winced as if my words had physically slapped him across his face. Then he put his hands up in mock surrender.

"Ok, ok Gracie. Sorry. You're right, I shouldn't have asked you about Nathan." Michael dragged his hands through his hair and blew out a deep breath. "I fucked up Gracie. I royally fucked up. I don't know what I was thinking; messing around with Madison, but I'm miserable. I miss you Gracie, I miss us."

I just stood there, opening and closing my mouth like a fish gasping for air. For a moment it was as if my mind had frozen. Completely unable to form words. I could slowly feel the rage building in the pit of my stomach. The audacity of this man standing before me. The absolute nerve of the person who had burned my world to the ground. First, the cheating, then the scheme to sell off the downtown properties including my bakery. Now he was here, telling me he was miserable without me. No, he wasn't doing this to me again. I wasn't falling for his bullshit anymore.

"No, Michael. Just stop. You don't miss me. You may think you do but you just miss the way I made your life so easy. For ten years, I took care of you. I always made sure you had everything you needed. You cheated me time and time again but I just turned a blind eye to it. That's what you miss. The carpet to wipe your feet on. Because that's all I was to you. I've grown a backbone since we broke up and it feels good. If Madison isn't enough for you or if she's too much for you, that's not my problem. Talk to her but leave me the hell alone. I'm happy for the first time in a long while. I don't miss my old life or you. I don't wish you any ill will Michael, but I also don't want you in my life anymore."

"You can't mean that Gracie. Fuck, we were together for ten years. We grew up together for Christ's sake."

"How many of those ten years were you truly faithful to me Michael. Yes, we grew up together but we also grew apart. I'm not the same girl I was when we first started dating. When my dad died, my priorities changed. I don't feel the need to experience city life. I'm happy with my life here in Moonrise Bay. That will never be you Michael. You will always be looking for the next best thing. I can't live life like that."

"I'm not giving up on us Gracie. You'll see. Nathan isn't what you want. You'll get bored with his simple life and you'll come crawling back to me."

I laughed so hard; I thought I was going to pee my pants. Who did he think he was? I almost didn't recognize the man standing before me but then I realized what was happening here. I was telling Michael he couldn't have something he wanted. He never took it well when someone said no to him.

"You're absolutely delusional Michael. Keep living in that little dream world but I will not be crawling anywhere. I'm good with my life. Now, I'd appreciate it if you would get the hell out of my shop."

"Your shop for now...we'll see how long that lasts." And with that, he walked out the door and I stood there dumbfounded.

What the hell just happened? Did Michael really expect me to fall to my knees for him? Did he really think I would take him back after all that has happened between us? Had I really been so blind to who Michael really had been all these years? I'm so over this bullshit. I gathered up my paperwork, grabbed my bags, locked the front door and headed out back to where my car was. Just as I started to unlock the door, I noticed a piece paper shoved under one of the wiper blades. I thought it was just another one of the "Save Our Downtown" flyers that had been floating around recently. Pulling the paper out, I quickly realized it wasn't the flyer. The note simply read: **YOU WON'T WIN.** What the hell did that mean and who left this? Win what? I shoved the note in my bag and got in my car. This had been a long day and all I wanted now was to get home, run a hot bath and settle down with my new romance book for the night. I just wanted to wash away this day and start fresh tomorrow.

*****

Piper: *Drinks?*

Me: *It's been a day girl!!! I think I just want to soak in my giant tub and read a romance.*

Piper: *Everything ok?*

Me: *No but I don't really want to get into it tonight. Lunch tomorrow?*

Piper: *You know it. Deli? I'm craving a turkey club.*

Me: *Oooh, that sounds perf.*

Piper: *Ok girlie. You sure you don't want me to come over tonight. We could have an old-fashioned* *slumber party **smiley face emoji***

Me: *I'm sure Pipes. I'm actually looking forward to some quiet time. I promise I'll tell you everything tomorrow at lunch.*

Piper: *Ok, love you bunches Gracie*

Me: *Love you back Pipes.*

Yesterday was rough and totally wiped me out. I had woken up this morning feeling like I'd been hit by a truck. Even though I'd come home and completely unplugged from the world, I still had an ominous feeling when I woke up this morning. Between Michael's unexpected visit and then the note left on my car, I spent my evening feeling totally unsettled. I was glad I was meeting Piper for lunch. I really needed some time with my BFF and filling her in on everything that went down yesterday. I hadn't even clued Nathan in on my day yet. He had already had plans to hang out with his crew to celebrate finally finishing their latest job and I really didn't want to burden him with everything that happened yesterday. I certainly wasn't looking forward to when I finally told him about my Michael conversation. That was not going to be fun.

Sitting in the deli, perusing my menu, I felt a tingling at the back of my neck. As if someone was watching me. I knew that was ridiculous but after that note yesterday, I was a little on edge. So much so that when Piper tapped my shoulder, I almost jumped straight out of my seat.

"Whoa girl, what's got you so jumpy." Piper sat across the table from me, a look of concern lacing her face.

"Sorry Pipes. Yesterday was just a crazy day and before you got here, I felt like someone was watching me. I know that sounds crazy but I just had this creepy feeling on the back of my neck. I'm sure I'm just being paranoid." I fiddled with the menu trying to calm my nerves.

"Damn girl, what the hell happened yesterday?"

Piper and I ordered our lunch and then I went into the whole story of how Michael popped by the bakery after work with his bullshit about missing me and making a mistake and then how after I kicked him out, I found the "You won't win" note on my car. By the time I finished telling her everything, Piper looked like she wanted to kill someone.

"What in the actual ass? I need a drink after that story. Too bad this is our lunch break. Who do you think left that note on your car?"

"I have no clue. I don't even know what it means. *You won't win.* Win what? Maybe someone left it on the wrong car and the note wasn't even meant for me." Piper shot me her best don't so stupid look. "I know, I know. Just wishful thinking. I just don't like the feeling that someone is out to get me. What could I have possible done?"

"Have you told Nathan what's going on?" Piper asked as the server brought our food over. I stayed quiet while my plate was placed in front of me and smiled at the waitress.

"I haven't had a chance to yet. He was hanging out with his crew last night and it didn't feel like I should text him the details of everything that happened yesterday. That felt like more of an in-person conversation if you know what I mean."

"He's going to be so pissed when he hears what Michael is trying to pull now. What is with that dickwad? He's never happy with what he has. Maybe he's tired of sleeping with a vampire every night." She took a giant bite of her sandwich and shrugged her shoulders.

I laughed and pushed my salad around my plate. "I don't know what I'm doing anymore Piper. I'm just so tired of everything Michael and Madison have been doing. I feel like I'm on the world's worst merry-go-round and I just want to be let off. I don't understand why they can't just move on with their lives."

Piper reached across the table and

squeezed my hand just as my phone vibrated with a new text message. I looked down and saw the message from Louisa and immediately opened it. Lousia never texted unless it was an emergency.

Louisa: *I hate to interrupt your lunch Gracie, but you need to get back to the bakery pronto. The health inspector just showed up with some bs about an anonymous tip and now we're having a surprise inspection.*

I couldn't believe what I was reading. Anonymous tip. Surprise inspection from the health department. What the hell was going on. I furiously started texting back and could feel Piper's concerned look.

Me: *Just great. Just what need. Anonymous tip. You and I both know that bakery is spotless. Let me just close out my bill here and I'll be right there.*

Louisa: *You got it boss. And I know this is bullshit. We've never had a complaint in all my years here. Someone is messing with you Gracie and if I find out who it is.....*

Me: *Thanks Louisa. I'll be there as fast as I can.*

I slammed my phone on the table and searched the deli for our server. This was the last thing I needed today. Seriously, how much more could a girl take.

"Gracie, you're scaring me. What's going

on?" Piper's voice cracked a bit as she switched seats so she was sitting right beside me.

"Louisa just texted that the health department got some kind of anonymous tip and now the bakery is under a surprise inspection. I need to get my bill so I can get over there ASAP."

Piper grabbed my phone and my bag and shoved them at me. "I've got the bill Gracie. You go handle your business. I'll head over to the bakery after I pay." She grabbed me and pulled me into a hug before shoving me towards the door.

"Love you mean it Gracie."

I could barely control the angry tears I could feel forming as I choked out, "Love you more Pipes" before I walked out the door and raced towards my bakery. Someone was fucking me and I was going to get to bottom of this mess if it's the last thing I did.

Chapter 19

Nathan

Piper: *You need to get to the bakery ASAP. Some bullshit is going down and Gracie needs you.*

Me: *What the hell is going on Piper. Is Gracie ok?*

Piper: *She's ok, just pissed. Some bullshit about an anonymous complaint to the health department and a surprise inspection. She's freaking out Nathan. I've never seen her like this before.*

Me: *Grabbing my keys now Piper. Thanks for the heads up.*

Piper: *Go help our girl Nathan. I'll meet you there. She needs all the support she can get!!!!*

Who the hell would've lodged a complaint against the bakery? Why was someone messing with Gracie's livelihood. I ran my fingers through my hair as I jumped in my truck. This was probably all Michael's doing. He couldn't mess with me anymore and he was moving on to Gracie. He was such a petty little boy. He couldn't stand to see that Gracie was happy with someone else even if he didn't want to be with her anymore. I wanted to find that asshole and punch him in his pretty boy face.

I raced down Main Street and pulled up in front of the bakery. Yanking the doors open, I raced in and grabbed Gracie around the waist. I just need to have her in my arms. Have her scent wrap around me and let her know that I would always be here for her.

Gracie pulled back to look up at me. "Whoa, that was quite an entrance. What are you doing here Nathan?" Damn this girl and those big whiskey brown eyes. My heart cracked that she always thought she had to go it alone. That she couldn't lean on me for help or support. That she would even question why I was here.

"What am I doing here? Gracie, Piper texted me and told me to get my ass down here. Why didn't you tell me what was happening? I know a thing or two about how these stupid inspector's work."

"Oh Nathan, everything happened so fast. I was at lunch with Piper and Louisa texted me that we had a surprise health inspection because of some stupid complaint. I literally had been here five minutes before you came racing through the doors. Damn sexy by the way." She waggled her eyebrows but I could tell she was trying to hide her worry with humor. Gracie was nervous this inspection wouldn't go her way.

"This complaint is utter bullshit Gracie and everybody who's anybody knows that. You know this town will have your back."

She placed her hand in mine and squeezed, "Thanks for that Nathan. I really needed to hear it. In my head I know there's no way this complaint is justified but the fact that someone still reported the bakery to health department...I just don't know what to think about that."

She blew out a deep breath just as the inspector headed towards the two of us.

"Ms. Henderson, I've finished my inspection and you'll receive a copy via e-mail in the next couple of days but I see no reason for concern. Whoever called in this complaint must of have been an unhappy customer. I can tell you; I wish I knew who it was so I could give them a piece of my mind. Total waste of my day and of county resources."

Gracie looked like she wanted to reach and hug the poor guy. She grabbed both of his hands and gave them a vigorous shaking. I could tell he was uncomfortable with her display of emotions because he pulled his hands back and began pushing his glasses up on his nose.

"Thank you, thank you so much for everything. You just don't know what a relief this is. I mean, I know that my bakery is up to code but just the fact that someone took it upon themselves to complain...I main, phew, that was stressful." She blew out another deep breath along with a chuckle.

I stepped behind Gracie and threw my arms around her chest. She reached up and wrapped her hands around my forearms. Damn, I loved this girl. She was my girl and my heart ached that someone had tried to hurt her.

The inspector began grabbing his things and made towards the door to leave. "I totally understand how stressful these inspections can be even when you know you're doing everything right. Don't worry, you're running a top-notch business here Ms. Henderson." With that, he nodded to both Gracie and me and walked out the doors just as Piper was walking in.

"Well...what the hell did I just miss?" Piper asked as she threw her hands up in the air. Gracie just shook her head and laughed, then she grabbed Piper for a giant hug.

"Crisis averted Pipes. The bakery passed with flying colors. That complaint was utter bullshit."

"Well of course it was bullshit. I was more worried that whoever complained had pulled some sneaky shit and messed with your kitchen so you wouldn't pass inspection. Especially after that note on your car yesterday."

My head shot to Gracie's face as soon as I heard those words. Note on her car. What the hell was Piper talking about and why the hell hadn't I heard anything about it? Gracie was biting her bottom lip, a sure sign that she was nervous.

I tried my best to keep my voice even and to keep my anger and fear hidden.

"What note is Piper talking about Gracie?"

"Umm...well...I had a note under my wipers yesterday after I closed up the bakery. I honestly didn't really think that much about it you know. I thought it was put on my car by mistake____"

"What did the note say Gracie?" I asked, anger lacing my voice.

Gracie chewed on her lower lip and whispered, "You won't win."

I clenched and unclenched my fists at my side. Who the fuck was messing with my girl. If this was that dipshit, Michael, I was going to kick is ass. I honestly hoped it was Michael. At least he was the enemy we knew. If this was some rando, that terrified me.

I grabbed Gracie and pulled her into my arms. "I'm packing some stuff and staying with you for a while Gracie. No arguments. I don't want you alone." I put my hand up and held her face in mine, "You're mine Gracie and I protect what's mine." I leaned down and placed a kiss on her sweet lips.

"Eww, get a room you too. This is too much for me." Piper groaned and threw herself into one of the chairs.

Both Gracie and I laughed before I said "Get used to it Pipes. I'm not going anywhere."

*****

A week went by and the drama seemed to settle down. No more anonymous complaints or notes left for Gracie. Life had been busy for the both of us. My crew was hired to do a remodel on a waterfront home and Gracie was swamped with holiday orders. With Thanksgiving just around the corner, Moonrise Bay had really come to life. Every storefront in downtown was decorated with fall leaves, hay bales and everything you think Thanksgiving should be. The final fall holiday before Christmas, which is a big event here in Moonrise Bay. Between holiday parades and holiday bazaars, the town of Moonrise Bay loves their holidays.

Gracie and I were still spending most of our nights together and I wasn't complaining. If you had asked me a few months ago if I thought this was where my life would be, I would have laughed at you. Practically living with Gracie. Sure I still went back and forth to my place to pick up clothes and check my mail but I was definitely spending more time at Gracie's house. My parents and sister had decided to spend the holiday in Moonrise Bay for the first time in years. I have a feeling my relationship with Gracie had something to do with it. Gracie and I were hosting at my house instead of hers because honestly I have more room but the sleeping situation was going to be interesting. Yes, I'm a grown man and don't have to answer to my parents anymore but it was certainly going to be awkward when they wake up in my house and I'm nowhere to be found. I guess that's a bridge we'll have to cross when we get to it.

I was excited for my family to meet Gracie. I just knew they were going to love her as much as I do. Honestly, I can't remember the last time I'd introduced my family to the woman I was dating. I guess no one had quite measured up or the relationships just weren't serious enough to bring home. For a long time, I was just going through the motions of life. No real serious relationships, mainly focused on work. Since Gracie has come along, I've realized what I was missing all those years. Someone to share a life with. Someone to come home to at the end of a long day. Even if Grace and I had only been together for a couple of months, we've settled into a nice routine together. I really could see myself spending the rest of my life with this woman. Babies with whiskey brown eyes and dark blond hair. Nothing would make me happier.

Gracie had been working hard all week and I wanted to do something special for her. Heading home, I stopped by the market to grab a few things for dinner so I could surprise Gracie. Wandering the aisles, trying to figure out what I was going to make, I was stopped in my tracks by the sounds of shouting. The small-town market wasn't usually the place where people got into disagreements. I turned my cart down the next aisle and run smack into the source of the yelling.... Michael and Madison in the midst of a very heated argument.

"What the fuck Michael. Why did Lila tell me she saw you skulking around Beach Buns a couple of weeks ago? Why are you still even talking to Gracie?"

What the actual fuck? Has Michael been hanging around the bakery? Why the hell didn't Gracie mentioned that to me? I know she's been busy but we've spending every night together and it's never come up once. What could that asshole possibly want from her?

"Baby, it was nothing. I was just there to discuss business. You know I don't want anybody but you."

I just rolled my eyes at this guy's bullshit. Any business he needed to conduct with Gracie could be done over the phone or through e-mail. He had no reason to hang around the bakery and I could see Madison wasn't buying it. Ole Mikey better watch out. Everybody knows that Madison Burke has a fiery temper and a violent streak.

Madison moved in close to Michael's face and poked her finger in his chest in jerky movements.

"You better not be lying to me Michael. If I find out you are, I'll have that precious dick of yours in a vise so fast, you won't know what hit you." Michael grabbed her finger with one hand and pulled Madison's ponytail with the other before crushing his lips to hers. It was gross to watch the two of them making out in the grocery aisle, so I just backed out and continued on with my shopping, hoping not to run into them again.

After getting everything I needed to make dinner, I got into my truck and headed towards Gracie's house. I needed to find out why she was hiding things from me and why the hell Michael had been hanging around the bakery. I had a feeling I wasn't going to like the answer to either of those questions.

Chapter 20

Gracie

Pulling up to my townhouse, I realized how utterly exhausted I was. It had been a crazy week at work. I was trying to get as many items assembled for the upcoming holiday rush as I could. I don't like to bake in advance and freeze that many baked items, but I could mix cookie dough, make pastry and pie shells and get those frozen. That always helped with the rush that descended upon the bakery between Thanksgiving and Christmas. Cakes of course, I always made to order. Sure cake layers could freeze well, but I preferred to make them the day before so I could get a good crumb layer of frosting before finishing the final product. I usually brought Piper in to help with any cake decorating. Between her, Lousia and Miquel, we could bust out the custom orders and keep up with the usual bakery traffic. Thank goodness for the off season. With fewer tourists coming in, we had time to catch our breath between orders.

Of course, that would all change the week of the big holiday bazaar. Each year it seemed to get bigger and bigger. I had a feeling that this year's bazaar would be the biggest one yet. Since news of the impending sale of the downtown buildings, the town of Moonrise Bay had really come out to show their support for these businesses. I guarantee that the town will be decked out in over-the-top decorations and that the townspeople will stop at nothing to make sure this is the biggest holiday bazaar Moonrise Bay has ever seen. They'll make Garrett Realty regret ever wanting to sell off their downtown holdings.

As I pulled up to my townhome, I couldn't stop the smile forming as I glanced Nathan's truck parked in the driveway. We had practically been living together these past couple of weeks without actually making anything official. This relationship with Nathan Sundry had truly come out of nowhere. Definitely not something I had ever expected. For the first time in my life, I felt true happiness. Nathan showed up for me in ways that no one ever has. Of course, I've always had Piper by my side but that was different. She and I have always been best friends and sure we've been partners in crime, but that isn't the same as having a partner to share your life with. Over the time I've been with Nathan, I've realized what it's like to have a real partner. Someone to come home to, someone who listens about your day or just someone to sit in a comfortable silence with.

When Michael had come to the bakery last week, it had really thrown me for a loop. Who the hell did he think he was? He cheated on me off and on for ten years and just now realized how much he needed me. WTF??? I know the game he's playing. He sees that I'm happy after all the bullshit he and Madison have put me through and he wants what he can't have. I hope he got my message loud and clear. I want no part of anything to do with him. He's burned this bridge and there is absolutely no repairing it.

I hadn't told Nathan about the visit from Michael. I hadn't been keeping it from him on purpose really. Things had just gotten crazy after it happened. Between the health inspector, to the note found on my car, Michael's visit really had just slipped my mind. It had been just a blip compared to everything else that had happened recently. I know I need to tell him. I just need to find the perfect time to slip that into a conversation. I know he's going to be pissed when he finds out and I guess I'm just trying to put that fight off for as long as possible.

Grabbing my bags and stepping through the front door, I'm surrounded by the most glorious smells making their way down the hallway from the kitchen. Mmm, Nathan must be making something delicious for dinner. I couldn't be more spoiled. I walk in the kitchen, putting my bags on the island and immediately wrap my arms around Nathan's waste.

"Hey babe, how was your day?" I feel him tense slightly before he turns in my arms and places a sweet kiss to the side of my mouth.

"Hey Gracie girl. My day was ok. I heard something interesting at the market today." His smile didn't quite reach his eyes and I could tell something was off with him.

"Oh yeah, what was that?"

"Well I happened to be turning down one of the aisles and I heard Michael and Madison arguing about something. She seemed to be pretty pissed that Michael's been hanging around the bakery lately. I've gotta say Gracie, that took me a little by surprise. It got me wondering why you haven't mentioned that Michael has been coming by."

Oh crap. He was pissed and honestly I couldn't blame him. He must think that I've been keeping this a secret from him which couldn't be further from the truth.

"Oh Nathan, I'm so sorry I didn't tell you. I promise you I wasn't keeping things from you. He came in the night that you were out with the guys and I didn't want to tell you about it in a text. Then everything happened with the health inspector and work has just been so busy, Michael's visit really just became a blip."

"I get we've both been busy lately but it's been a couple of weeks since that crap at the bakery and you've never said anything about Michael pestering you. I'm having a hard time believing that it's really slipped your mind."

He just stood there, in my kitchen, with his arms crossed over his chest. I could feel his anger. But I was getting angry now too. Did he really not believe me? What have I ever done to make Nathan think I wouldn't tell him the truth.

"Are you serious right now Nathan? I'm not a liar. I didn't tell you about Michael because he's so insignificant to me, I didn't put much stock into the visit. The fact that you don't trust me pisses me right the hell off more than anything. Honestly, if you can't believe me, then maybe you shouldn't even be here right now."

Nathan blew out a deep breath and pushed his hands through his hair pulling on the ends and taking a few steps towards me.

"Gracie, I do trust you but I'm not going to lie and say it didn't hurt to hear about Michael bothering you from someone else. I'm sorry for jumping to conclusions. You're right, you've never done anything to prove I can't trust you. That guy just grates on my nerves and I don't like the idea of him hanging around the bakery. Especially after that note you found on your car."

I reached out and grabbed Nathan's hand, twining my fingers with his.

"I know it hurts to find out information secondhand and for that I am truly sorry. Michael is nothing more than a spoiled child in a grown man's body and that's why it slipped my mind after all the other craziness. I really don't think he has it in him to leave a nasty note. He claims he misses me but let's get real. He only thinks he misses me and wants me back because he knows I've moved on to something better and he hates being told he can't have something."

I squeeze Nathan's hand with mine before saying, "I'm not interested in anything Michael has to say and I'm not worried about him hanging around the bakery. I promise Nathan, Louisa will come for him if he becomes a nuisance." We both laugh at the image of Louisa coming full stop for Michael. He's always been terrified of her and all it would take would be one look and Michael would run like the scared little boy that he is.

Nathan tugs me towards him with our hands still clasped and cradles my cheek with his other hand. Blowing out a deep breath, he leans his forehead onto mine and we just stay there like that for what feels like an eternity.

Nathan slowly pulls away from my forehead before placing his lips on mine. What begins as a sweet kiss quickly heats up as Nathan pours all of his emotions into this kiss. We're a tangle of lips and tongues. Sucking, nibbling, biting. He grabs me underneath my bottom and my legs automatically wrap around him. I'm placed on the island as we continue our breathless assaults on each other's mouths.

Panting, I break away and ask, "Nathan, what about dinner?"

I can feel his smile against the corner of my mouth as he says "I guess it's a dessert first kind of night. Don't worry Gracie girl, dinner will still be there once I've finished devouring you."

Nathan steps back and pulls my shirt over my head. Kissing his way down my neck, he licks my nipple through the lace of my bra before pulling the straps down my shoulder. He pulls one nipple into his mouth while working the other with his hands. Tugging and pinching. I toss my head back, hissing out a curse at the delicious pain being inflicted on my breasts. I can feel the wetness pooling between my legs as I begin to spread them wide apart, making room for Nathan to stand between them.

"Mmm, is someone feeling impatient? I'm taking my time tonight Gracie." Nathan tosses my bra to the floor and works his way down my stomach, licking and kissing as he goes.

Slowly, he pulls my leggings down, stopping only to pull off my sneakers before taking the pants off. Gliding his hands up my thighs, Nathan trails his fingers along the trim of my black lace panties. I begin panting and thrusting myself against his hand. Needing to feel him against that bundle of nerves between my legs. Nathan continues his torturous teasing, touching everywhere but where I need him to touch me.

Taking me right to the edge.

"God damn it Gracie, you're pussy is so fucking beautiful."

I can feel myself getting wetter at his teasing and exclamation and am all but dying here on this island, when he finally drags his tongue through my folds. I practically jump off the counter but Nathan grabs me by the ass firmly holding me in place. His licking and sucking intensifies as he drives two fingers inside me. Curling them in just the right motion.

I'm going crazy from all the sensations, feeling like a firework getting ready to explode. Nathan pulls me harder against his face, fucking me with his tongue and his fingers.

I grab him by the hair as I scream "Fuck Nathan, I'm going to come so fucking hard..."

Then it happens. Pure ecstasy as I almost detonate right off my beautiful quartz countertop. My whole body quivers and shakes and I swear I lose my vision for a hot second. This man never fails to deliver on the orgasms.

My eyes pop open at the sound of Nathan's shoes hitting the floor. I reach for the hem of his shirt but he just pushes my hands away. Reaching behind him, he pulls the shirt over his head and tosses it to the floor and his jeans quickly follow.

I don't think I'll ever get tired of seeing Nathan in all his naked glory. His body is a perfect specimen of muscle and beauty. I lick my lips at the site of his hard cock, wet from the precum escaping from his slit. I reach for it, wanting it in my mouth but again, Nathan pushes me away.

"I've got to be inside that pussy now Gracie." And he thrusts himself inside me, filling me completely to my core. He drives in and out, slowly at first but increases his intensity as my orgasm begins to build again. Nathan reaches between us and rubs his thumb against my clit and I start seeing stars.

Nathan pumping into me as he rubs my clit harder now.

My legs are quivering and I feel my inner walls begin to clamp down on Nathan's dick.

"That's it baby, come for me Gracie." I come with a scream like I've never come before, imbedding my nails into Nathan's back. He rides out my orgasm before filling me completely with an orgasm of his own. An orgasm so intense, I think we both blackout for a few seconds.

We stay there, connected, his come dripping down my leg. Neither of us willing to break apart.

Nathan finally pulls away and I immediately miss the fullness of him. He dashes to the bathroom just off the kitchen and returns with a warm hand towel. He places the towel between my legs and helps me clean myself. After cleaning himself, the two of get dressed and clean our mess in the kitchen and we get back to making dinner.

It hits me as we stand here doing such a mundane task as making dinner together that this is what a relationship is supposed to be. Yes, you fight and get angry with one another. That's the nature of being human but in the end, when two people love each other, the fights don't matter. It's the making up and forgiving each other that truly matters. I stood there in the kitchen, watching Nathan prepare the steaks for the grill, when it hit me. I don't want to wait anymore. I want to tell Nathan I love him.

I slowly turn to him and run my hand over

the scruff of his face. Nathan looks down and the look in his ocean grey eyes steals my breath away. I know he feels something deep for me. I feel it in the way he touches me, the way he moves inside me and the way he takes care of me. I'm not expecting him to say it back but it does take all my strength to work up the courage to say those three little words. The last man I said those words to almost ruined me and I don't know that I can pick up the pieces again if the same thing happens. What I do know is that I love Nathan Sundry and have probably been in love with him since that first night he slept on the couch with me. The night of the tropical storm party.

I take a deep breath and say the words that once they're out, there's no turning back.

"I love you Nathan."

Nathan blows out a deep breath and opens his mouth to speak but I put my hand up to stop him, "I'm not looking for you to say it back. I know it's a big step and we've only been seeing each other for a little over a month but I think I've loved you since that night of my little tropical storm party. That night that you let me fall asleep on your shoulder. Nathan, you've shown me what it feels like to really be cared for by someone and it's made me fall madly, deeply, head over heels in love with you."

Nathan takes my chin in his hands and tilts my face up to his. He takes a minute or two before he speaks but when he does he absolutely takes my breath away.

"Gracie Henderson, I've been in love with you since the moment you walked into our sophomore English class. You and Piper waltzed into class and the two of you were laughing at something. At the sound of your laugh, I looked up and saw the most beautiful girl I'd ever seen. I knew at that moment I was a goner for you. Your smile lit up the whole god damned room."

Nathan reached up and swiped away the tears that were forming at the corners of my eyes, "I love you so much it hurts sometimes Gracie. It hurt to watch you with that idiot Michael. It hurt knowing he wasn't good enough for you and killed me knowing that I played a part in him hurting you. I love you Gracie and I plan on loving you until my last breath."

I pop up on my tip toes and kiss Nathan gently whispering, "I love you Nathan Sundry... always."

Later that night as we lay on the deck under a blanket of stars, Nathan showed me how much he loved me. He worshipped every part of my body before pulling me to him and wrapping us in a blanket. We slept there under the stars that night knowing there was no going back. We loved each other truly and we were each other's happily ever after. It may have taken us years to get here but now that we finally had one another, this was going to be forever. He might not have proposed officially but he did say that he would love me until his last breath. So yeah, Nathan Sundry was my forever.

Chapter 21

Gracie

It was the morning of Thanksgiving and also the first night that Nathan and I had spent apart in weeks. I was swamped at the bakery last night finishing up last minute orders before the bakery took a weeklong break. Nathan had decided to spend the night with his family. His parents had driven down from Chapel Hill and his sister Landon had flown in from New York. Surprisingly she had flown in with Levi. I wonder how Piper is going to feel about seeing him again after their little fling. That will be interesting to watch for sure. Especially since Piper and her Gram will be joining us for the holiday too.

As long as I can remember, Piper and her grandmother, Gram, had spent every major holiday with my family. Honestly, Piper really is more of a sister than best friend. She grew up with shit parents but her Gram is a freaking national treasure. She stepped in when Piper's parents emotionally abandoned her. If not for

Gram, I don't know what would have happened to Piper. Piper came from money but not love. Her dad owns a tech company based in Raleigh but Piper and her mother lived in Moonrise Bay. Her mom had always been very distant. Caring more about appearances than spending time with her own daughter. Once her mother starting drinking, that was the beginning of the end for Piper. At that point, Gram stepped in and moved Piper in with her. I honestly don't know the last time Piper has spoken with either one of her parents even though they still live in their big house in the bougie part of Moonrise Bay. Interesting little side note, Piper's parents live next door to the Garretts. Gotta love small town living.

I'm not going to lie; this Thanksgiving has my nerves on high alert. Sure I've met Nathan's parents before but only in passing. Now I'm meeting them as his girlfriend. I hope I make a good first impression. I was hoping to be able to get to Nathan's after closing up the bakery, but it had been so late when Lousia and I finally finished everything, I was just too exhausted to do anything but go home and crash. Now, I'm standing in my closet, staring at every piece of clothing I own, trying to figure out what the best outfit is for a "meet the parent" scenario. After trying on about one hundred different outfit combinations, I settle on my dark wash skinny jeans, black cowl neck sweater and my camel-colored booties. With beach waves in my caramel brown locks, a swipe of light makeup and my favorite pink lip gloss, I'm ready to grab my various pies and get my mom before heading to Nathan's for Thanksgiving lunch.

As I step on the front porch, I run smack into a wall of man. Just not the man that I was anticipating seeing today. Standing at my door, arm raised ready to knock, is none other than Michael. I can't believe that today of all days, he's decided to show his face.

"What do you want now Michael? As you can see, I'm on my way out and my hands are full. I'm really not in the mood for a chat."

"Come on Gracie. Don't be like that. I just wanted to pop by and wish you and your mom Happy Thanksgiving. You know how much I love your mom. I miss her you know."

I stood there, mouth open, not believing what I was hearing. He honestly thinks he can just drop by, hoping to catch me and mom as if we would be happy to see him. He's the last person my mother has any interest in seeing. Or maybe she would. I know she's had a few choice words she's wanted to share with him since our breakup.

"You've got to be kidding me Michael. Do you honestly think my mother would welcome you with open arms? After everything you and Madison have been putting me through lately. After fucking my best friend and then trying to screw my business over. You are one delusional asshole." I laughed because it was all I could do. I really wanted to punch him in his smug face.

"Ok, ok" Michael throws his hands up in a display of surrender. "That's fair. Honestly, I just wanted to see your face Gracie. I told you before; I miss you. The holidays were always so much fun. Between you and your mom, Piper and Gram, it always showed me what I missed growing up in my family." On a deep sigh Michael continued, "I know I fucked up Gracie but I just want a chance to fix things. I just don't know how. I miss being a part of your family."

I stood there for a moment. Not knowing exactly what to say. I know Michael always felt a lot of pressure from his dad growing up. Maybe that's what made him such an insecure asshole. His family wasn't the most loving family either. Their house always felt cold and impersonal. Too clean almost. My house, on the other hand, was full of chaos. Mom usually had various papers and schoolwork scattered everywhere and dad's office was cluttered with books and papers for whatever he was researching for his next article. It may have been chaotic but it was a wonderful sort of chaos. I never wondered if I was good enough or loved. My parents showed me every day just how much they loved me. The way Michael's parents treated him created a monster. Constantly pitting him against his older brothers. Demanding that he play better football, make better grades. By the time Michael got to senior year, he had an ego the size of Texas. My teenage brain thought that was sexy. A teen boy with so much confidence. Looking back now, I really have no clue what I ever saw Michael.

"Go home Michael. There's nothing left for you here. You have Madison to spend your holidays with now."

Michael winced at the sound of Madison's name and just stood staring at me for a moment.

"Do you hate me Gracie? I don't think I could handle it if you hated me."

He looked like a little boy standing there with a slight pout on his face and I realized that I didn't hate him. I just felt indifferent towards him. Michael no longer had real estate anywhere in my life.

"I don't hate you Michael. I just don't care about you anymore." The look of relief quickly faded to disappointment. "Happy Thanksgiving Michael. I hope you have a nice holiday. I also hope this is the last time you decide to ambush me at home or at work. I don't wish you any ill will. If I see you out and about, I'll smile and say hello but I have no desire in having a friendship or rekindling any kind of relationship. Now if you'll just move out of my way, I'm already late picking up my mom."

Michael moved to the side, and I walked down the porch steps quickly, balancing everything in my hands. I never once looked back. Firmly putting Michael Garrett in my rearview mirror.

*****

To say I was nervous as mom and I approached Nathan's front door would be a giant understatement. I was absolutely terrified. I felt like an entire swarm of butterflies had taken up residence in my stomach. From behind me mom put her hand on my shoulder and gave me a reassuring squeeze.

"Nothing to be worried about sweet pea. His parents would be fools not to love you and I know his parents. They are not fools. Now open that door and let's go have a lovely Thanksgiving. I don't know about you, but I'm starving."

I looked back and she just winked at me. She was right. I could do this and I don't know why I'm so nervous. Deep breath, hand on the door and in we go. The moment we walk inside the immediate sounds of laughter fill our ears. I walk down the hallway to the back of Nathan's house that becomes a large open space encompassing the kitchen and family room area. Where my house is feminine with its white furniture, grey walls and pastel accent colors, Nathan's house is all masculine. From the dark wooden beams in the family room ceiling to the concrete countertops in his kitchen, his house screams man.

Piper and Gram are already here and Gram, it seems, is talking Levi's ear off. Piper on the other hand looks none too pleased that Levi is joining us for the holiday this year. I have to stifle the giggle that threatens to bubble out as Piper catches my eye. The look she sends my way tells me we'll be having words later. I just put a little smirk on my face and wave. Yup, she's going to kill me.

"Look Gram, Gracie and Alice are here. Excuse us Levi. I'm just going to head over and help Gracie. She looks like she has her hands full."

Levi's head turns in my direction, "Oh Gracie, it's so good to see again. This lovely young woman must be your sister." He says as he extends his hand towards my mother.

She laughs so hard I'm afraid she'll pull a muscle.

"So this must be the infamous Levi Anderson the town has been buzzing about. You are quite the charmer." She shakes his hand

and says, "Alice Henderson, Gracie's mom. It's a pleasure to meet you. My you are a handsome one and that's a firm grip you have there." She winks at Piper as she pulls her in for a hug. She whispers something only Piper can hear and then grabs the pies from my hands heading towards the kitchen.

I feel Nathan before I see him. He walks in the French doors that lead to his deck and his eyes immediately find me across the room. God, he takes my breath away every time I see him. Sometimes I think these feelings can't possibly be sustainable. There is no way I can feel this man to my very core every time we're in the same the room. I've never felt so much for one person in my life, not even Michael. Honestly, it terrifies me. I'm an utter goner for this man and I know I'll be irrevocably broken if things go south between us.

I shake away those thoughts and smile at Nathan as he makes his way towards where I'm standing with Gram, Piper and Levi. My mom is still in the kitchen. It appears that she's found Nathan's parents and they're standing around catching up on all the Moonrise Bay gossip.

Nathan reaches me and wraps his arm around my waist before dropping a sweet kiss to the top of my head.

"Hey babe. I've been waiting for you to

get here. Missed you last night." I blush as I feel everyone's eyes turn towards me.

"Missed you too. Sorry I wasn't able to come by after closing. The bakery was crazy busy and I was just so wiped by the time I finally left."

Nathan squeezes my hip and kisses me again.

"No worries Gracie. I took mom, dad and Landon out to dinner in Wilmington and then we came back here for an impromptu game night like old times. It was kind of nice to have us all under one roof. That hasn't happened since before Landon moved up to New York."

Nathan really did look happy. I know he's missed having his whole family close by. I don't know what I'd do without my mom just a few miles away. Since my dad died, she and I have leaned heavily on each other. She's more than a mom. Honestly, she's my other best friend. I'm glad Nathan has his whole family under one roof. Even if it's just for the holiday weekend.

While I remember Nathan's parents, his sister Landon is a bit of mystery. She was a freshman when we were seniors, so by the time I came home after college, she had already left for school up in New York. Nathan yells up the stairs for her to come down and meet everyone. I turn my head as I hear her walking down towards us and she could almost be Nathan's twin. Her sandy blonde hair full of waves. She has the same ocean grey eyes as Nathan and boy is she tall. Landon must be close to 5'9. I feel like a small child as she approaches me and brings me in for a hug.

"Gracie!!! It's so great to finally meet you. Nathan has been talking about you non-stop since we all got here. I feel like we're practically sisters now," she says with a light chuckle.

She's absolutely beautiful; looking like she just stepped off the runway in her pumpkin cowlneck sweater dress and mahogany brown knee-high boots.

I step back from the hug. "It's so nice to finally meet you too Landon. Nathan has been so excited to have all of us in one place for the holiday. I swear it's all he's talked about since Halloween."

"I gotta tell you Gracie, Thanksgiving is my favorite holiday. I mean Christmas is nice with all the decorations and gifts but Thanksgiving wins for the food alone. I cannot wait to try the delicious treats that Nathan has been promising you were bringing."

With a little laugh I say "Phew, not too much pressure then. I hope you like pie because I brought every pie we made for the holiday. We've got bourbon pecan, chocolate brownie, sweet potato, and of course the perennial favorite, pumpkin. I also brought a cookie plate and a few mini cupcakes. I may have gone a little overboard."

"Oh I think I'm going to like Nathan's girlfriend owning a bakery", Landon says as she swings her arm around my shoulder leading me into the kitchen. "Now let's go meet the parents and see when dinner will be ready."

Dinner goes off without a hitch. Nathan's mom made a turkey to rival my own mother's not to mention all the sides. Gram brought her signature baked macaroni and cheese which was delicious as usual. Piper brought a creamed spinach casserole that was to die for and of course we had mashed potatoes and sweet potato casserole. But for me, no Thanksgiving meal is complete without my mama's cornbread dressing. It has been and always will be my favorite part of the dinner.

Now we're all lounging around the family room letting our food digest and trying to fight off the desire for a turkey nap. Coffee and wine has been flowing and everything seems to good to be true.

"Gracie", Nathan's mom Linnie turns to me and says, "this bourbon pecan pie is absolutely sinful. Is there any way you're willing to part with the recipe?"

Right has a I begin to answer her, I'm stopped by a loud smashing sound outside along with sounds of tires peeling away quickly. Nathan and Levi both jump to their feet as Nathan says, "What the hell was that?" He and Levi both rush to the front door. The rest of us follow closely behind them. As soon as I reach the front porch, I can't believe what I'm seeing. The windshield on my Scout has been smashed out by what appears to be a brick with a note wrapped around it. Nathan grabs my arm to keep me from getting too close to the car.

"Gracie don't. Let's call the sheriff before we tamper with any of the evidence." He pulls me into his arms and I begin trembling as he holds me tightly against his chest, placing a sweet kiss to my forehead.

"I'm so sorry baby. I know how much your truck means to you."

He's right. Besides my bakery, that truck is my favorite thing in the world. It was my dad's and when he was getting close to the end, he made me promise to take good care of it. It's the place I feel my dad the most. It's why I love driving it so much. I can feel the tears welling in my eyes as Nathan rubs circles on my lower back. My mom steps in behind us and audibly gasps.

"Oh Gracie. Who would do such a horrible thing? Your daddy's truck." She begins rubbing my arms. "I'm so sorry sweet pea. If I find the jerk who did this, I'll run them over myself with this very truck."

I laugh through the tears because that's what my mom always does for me. She knows just what to say to make me feel better. I don't doubt for one minute that she would hunt down any person who she perceives to have wronged me. My parents weren't able to have more kids after me so my mom takes the protector role very seriously.

"Ok mom let's not do anything that would land you in the slammer. I'd hate for you to spend Thanksgiving weekend in jail. How would we go Christmas tree shopping?"

The rest of the group behinds us chuckles but there is still a bit of tension in the air. I can hear Piper on the phone with the sheriff's department explaining the situation and how we need a deputy out here as soon as possible. I'm in a state of utter disbelief. Why would someone do this to me? Was it Michael? I thought we were on okay terms when he left my house this afternoon. I know he's used to getting what he wants, but I can't imagine he would hurt me like this. He knows what this truck means to me. He knew my dad left it to me after he died.

"Okay, a deputy should be out soon to take a report. You okay Gracie?"

I turn to Piper and she looks like she straight up wants to kill somebody. I hope Levi's paying attention and can see it's never a good idea to get on her bad side.

"I'm okay Pipes. I just don't understand why this happened." She grabs my hands and squeezes.

"It's probably just stupid kids Gracie. We've had this group of punks terrorizing the library lately. It's gotten so bad; I've had a patrol car stationed out front to keep the stupid idiots from bothering my patrons."

"Jeez Louise. What's wrong with people these days?"

While we wait for the deputy to arrive, Nathan hustles his parents and Gram back into the house before coming outside to join me. From behind, he wraps his arms around my chest.

"We'll figure this out Gracie. I promise."

Just then the deputy arrives. He inspects the damage to my truck and bags the brick before coming over to take my statement.

The deputy is a guy we all went to school with and I'm immediately put at ease.

"Hey Gracie. Sorry about all this trouble. It doesn't look like this was a prank. It looks pretty personal to me. They wrapped a note around the brick before throwing it through the windshield."

"Hey Ryan. Thanks for coming so quickly. I wish we were seeing each other under better circumstances. Can I ask what the note said?"

Ryan grimaces for a second. Like he doesn't want to say what was in the note.

"Umm... it said WATCH YOUR BACK BITCH. I HAVE EYES EVERYWHERE."

From behind me I hear someone mutter "Fuck", realizing it must have been Nathan.

"Any idea who might have done this Gracie?"

Honestly I don't want to say it. My choices aren't that great. It's either my ex-fiance or my ex-best friend. I just don't want to think that either one of them dislikes me so much that they would do something like this. I cringe before answering Ryan because I know that Nathan isn't going to like what I'm getting ready to say. I wasn't going to mention anything about Michael's visit until after dinner. I didn't want any drama to ruin our first holiday together. I guess it's too late for that now.

"Well I did have a little run in with Michael before I came over here this afternoon. I thought I'd settled everything and he seemed okay after he left but maybe I was wrong."

I look at Nathan and can see his whole demeanor change. He's furious and I'm not sure if that anger is directed at just Michael, me or me and Michael.

"I promise Nathan, I was going to tell you tonight after we were finished with dinner and everything. I didn't want to ruin the holiday with Michael's bullshit."

"What. Did. He. Want. Gracie", Nathan asks through gritted teeth.

I pause for a second, feeling like everyone's eyes are me. I almost feel like I'm the one who's done something wrong. I take a deep breath and tell myself that the tension I'm feeling from everyone isn't because of me but for me. I know everyone here is just worried about what happened and in my mind I know no one blames me. It's just the anger radiating off of Nathan has my nerves on high alert.

"He said he was feeling nostalgic for past Thanksgiving's and he missed my family. I know he thinks that he wants back in my life but I promise you I told him there is no part of me that wants anything to do with him. I told him in no uncertain terms that while I may no longer hate him, I don't care about him at all. He may have looked dejected when I was leaving, but there was nothing in his body language to suggest he would throw a brick through my windshield."

Nathan just stands there for a minute, not saying anything, before turning and walking back inside the house. My heart breaks a little bit. I try to follow him but Ryan stops me with a few a more questions before I can.

"What about Madison? I think we all remember well what she was like in high school. Do you think she's behind this?"

"As much as I don't want it to be her, I wouldn't put anything past her. Madison has always felt like she was better than me. With Michael sniffing around, I'm sure she's not happy about that."

Ryan finishes up with his questions and reassures me that they'll question both Michael and Madison. He promises that he'll drive by my house and the bakery on his patrol to make sure that nothing weird is going on.

Standing outside Nathan's house, staring at the damage to my car, I've never felt more alone. I know my mom and Piper and Gram are here for me but watching Nathan walk away broke my heart a little. I know he's angry. Shit... I'm angry too. I didn't take him for the kind of guy that ran at the first sign of trouble.

Maybe I've rushed into this relationship with Nathan. Maybe I've gone into this with blinders on. Whatever the hell is going on, I won't be another man's doormat. I take a steadying breath and work up the courage to step back into Nathan's house.

The house goes silent the minute I walk through the door. Well, at least I don't have to wonder if everyone was in here talking about me. I bypass everyone mingling in the living room area and head straight for the kitchen. I gather up the various dishes that I brought with me and head towards Piper who is standing with Gram and my mom.

Addressing everyone in the room, I say "I'm so sorry for my drama spoiling what was a lovely holiday meal. I think I'm just going to head back to my house so I don't ruin the rest of the evening. Piper, do you think you could drop me and mom off seeing as I don't have a mode of transportation anymore?" I laugh uncomfortably as everyone else in the room just seems to stare at me.

Piper puts her arm around my shoulders and gives me a squeeze, "You got it girl. Anything for my boo. Just let me grab Gram's coat."

I make more apologies to Nathan's family and say my goodbyes. This whole time, Nathan hasn't said a word to me or even made eye contact with me. I guess that's how it's going to be now. I try to get out with my dignity intact and without crying. As I reach the door, I hear Nathan call my name. I stop momentarily and turn; a tear slowly escapes down my cheek.

When Nathan does nothing but stare at me, I know it's time to go. I turn away from him, closing the door behind me before turning to my mom and bursting into tears. This hurts one hundred times more than walking in on Michael and Madison.

Chapter 22

Nathan

Fuuuckkk. I didn't handle well and now Gracie just walked out the door with tears streaming down her face. After everything she's been through, and I act like a complete and total asshole. Fuck, what is wrong with me. The house had grown quiet with an awkward silence just before Landon walked up to me and slapped me across the back of the head.

"What the hell Nathan? How could you do that to Gracie and with everything that's happened to her lately. Are you a complete moron?"

I drag my fingers through my hair, pulling until the ends are sticking straight up in the air.

"I don't know what happened Landon. I heard Michael's name and all I could see was red. I love Gracie but..." I let out a huff that sounds more like a growl.

"If you truly love her Nathan, then there is no but. You're either all in or you aren't. I don't know Gracie that well, obviously, but I know she deserves more than some guy who's going to get pissed and run at the first sign of trouble. She already had that guy Nathan. Be better."

She pats me on the back, then heads upstairs. Both my parents follow shortly after, both expressing the same concerns.

I fix myself a tall glass of bourbon and head out to the back deck, not bothering with a jacket. I deserve to suffer out here in the freezing cold. I can't stop picturing the look on Gracie's face. Pure devastation is the only way to describe it and I did that that to her. She didn't even look that way when she saw the damage to her truck. No, I broke her heart, me and no one else.

I slam back the whiskey, needing to feel the burn as the amber liquid slides down my throat. I'm going to fix this, I tell myself. I have to fix this. I won't lose Gracie Henderson again. I've waited too long to make her mine and I'm not going to let this fuck up be what ends things between us. I know that a measly apology won't do. Nope. A grand gesture. That's what it's going to take to win my Gracie back.

******

I wake up the day after Thanksgiving and feel like I've been hit by a truck. Gracie hasn't answered any of my calls or responded to any of my text messages. I'm getting desperate at this point and decide it's time I call in the big guns. I finally have a moment to myself since mom and Landon are out shopping and dad is hanging with Uncle Jay. Today was supposed to be the day that Gracie and I picked out our Christmas tree but I totally ruined that with how I reacted to the Michael news yesterday. Shit, I still can't believe I let her leave without saying a fucking word to her. I let her think I was angry with her when it was really the situation Michael wouldn't stop putting her in that was actually pissing me off. I grab a bottle of water from the fridge and pull up Piper's contact on my phone. I just hope that she won't hang up on me or send my call straight to voicemail. I'm sure she's royally pissed at me too but I'm banking on our friendship and that she'll take pity on me.

"Well you royally fucked up my friend" is Piper's way of greeting me when she answers my call. "What the hell were thinking Nathan. I'm so pissed at you."

"I know, I know Piper. I really don't have a good explanation for what happened. I was so angry at Michael that night, I just couldn't get any words out. I just froze. I love Gracie so much but I feel like Michael is a constant thorn in our relationship."

"Well why the hell didn't you just say that to Gracie in the first place? She cried herself to sleep last night Nathan. I haven't seen her that upset since her dad died. Not even after she found Michael and Madison screwing in the kitchen. She really loves you, Nathan, and you broke her heart yesterday with that silent treatment bullshit you pulled."

"Fuuuckkk, Piper. How do I fix it? She won't even answer my calls or my texts. I really need to talk to her but I don't know if she even wants to hear me out."

Piper lets out a deep sigh before saying "I'm still at her house. I've finally convinced her to get out of bed and meet Miquel and Alan at the Moonrise for a little post-thanksgiving brunch. Maybe if we just happened to bump into you in a public place, she'll have no choice but to talk to you."

"I could kiss you right now Piper. I'll be there. I'm grabbing my keys now."

"Whoa, slow down there lover-boy Gracie hasn't even gotten out of the shower yet. Give us thirty minutes and then head on over to the diner. You're on your own from there pal."

Piper and I hung up and I paced my kitchen nervously. I really just hoped Gracie would give me a chance to explain why I reacted the way I did. I hope she can forgive me.

I park my truck about a block away from Moonrise Diner and head down main street working through what I want to say to Gracie in my head. There's a lot of activity in downtown Moonrise Bay this morning. Most of the store owners are gearing up and decorating for the Christmas bazaar that's starting in the next couple of weeks. The lamp poles are adorned with twinkle lights and garland. Storefronts have frosted windows giving the illusion of snow. Our little downtown has turned into a winter wonderland overnight.

My nerves are getting the better of me as I get closer to the diner. I know I've really screwed up where Gracie is concerned. I feel like I'm no better than Michael. How could I treat her the way I did yesterday with everything I know about how Michael treated Gracie? I'm such a dumbass. With shaky hands, I reach for the diner doors and walk inside, glancing around to find where Gracie is sitting. Miquel sees me first and just shakes his head at me as Gracie turns in her seat to see what he's looking at. Any hope I had of Gracie forgiving me are immediately dashed as I watch her face fall when she sees me. I'm heartbroken. I put that sadness on her face. I never wanted to be the person to do that to Gracie.

I begin to approach their table and Miquel stands putting his hand up towards me.

"Unh-uh man. You better keep on walking because no one at this table wants to hear anything you have to say."

I shake my head at him and turn to Gracie, "Please Gracie. I've been texting and calling all morning. I didn't sleep at all last night and I really just need to talk to you. Please just give me chance to explain and apologize."

Gracie can barely look me in eye before letting out a deep breath. Before she can say anything, Miquel is coming at me again.

"Oh poor Nathan. You hardly slept last night. How do you think Gracie's night went? You had your chance with her last night Nathan and you blew it my man. You're so lucky I wasn't there dude. Ooh I would have popped you right in the...."

Gracie puts her hand up to stop Miquel from continuing with his threat.

"It's okay Miquel," turning towards me, she says "I'll go outside and hear what you have to say Nathan. I'm not making any promises."

Once we get outside, Gracie just stands there with her arms crossed waiting for me to start. I don't really know what to do. I've never been in a situation like this before. I've honestly never felt what I feel for Gracie with any of the other women I've dated in the past. Now I'm standing here fighting for what I feel like is my life. I honestly can't imagine what a life looks like without Gracie. I reach my hands out to grab for hers but she pulls away. I put my hands in my pockets and begin explaining myself.

"God Gracie, I don't know where to begin. I really just want to say how sorry I am about last night. There is nothing I can say to you that will make what I did better. I'm just so sorry."

"What happened Nathan? I've never seen you act like that. I know I've kept it from you in the past when Michael was bothering me at the bakery but that's not what happened yesterday. I planned on telling you last night about Michael coming to my house but I wanted to wait until we were alone. I didn't want him spoiling our first Thanksgiving."

"No I guess I'm that one who did that didn't I? Shit, he just makes me so angry Gracie. I know in my head that he's not a threat but there's still that insecure part of me that thinks he's going to win. He always wins."

"But Nathan, I'm not a thing to be won. I'm a living, breathing person. There's no competition for my heart. This isn't the fricking bachelor for Christ's sake. This is real life and I'm tired of guarding my heart from being broken."

Fuck, things between Gracie and me were worse than I thought they were and my apology only seemed to be making things worse. I could feel myself losing her. I ran my fingers through my hair, pulling on the ends in an attempt not to reach out and pull Gracie into my arms.

"Gracie I know you're not an object to be won. I didn't mean it like that. Fuck, I'm not getting any of this right. I just really need you to know how sorry I am. I love you Gracie and I would never do anything to hurt you intentionally. Please believe me."

"I know that Nathan. I really do; but I need you to see where I'm coming from. I was barely out of a ten-year relationship before falling into another one with you. I was engaged for Christ's sake. I believe you love me. I love you too but...."

"No buts Gracie. We love each other and we can get passed this."

"I need some time Nathan. I, I think I need some time to focus on me. I'm sorry; I know that's not what you want to hear but that's what I need. I need a little breathing room to figure out where we go from here. Please just give me a little space."

I reached up to catch the tear that was falling down Gracie's cheek and this time she didn't pull away from my touch. She leaned her cheek into my palm and closed her eyes.

"I've waited for what feels like my whole life for you Gracie. I'd wait forever if I have to. Take the time you need to figure things out and I'll be here when you realize I'm what you want." I press a kiss to her lips and lean my forehead against hers.

"I love you Gracie girl."

I didn't give her a chance to say anything back. I couldn't. I just walked back to my truck, resisting the urge to punch my hand through the window. No I just got in my truck and drove back to my house, worried I'd screwed up my chance with Gracie for good.

Chapter 23

Gracie

I walked back into the diner and collapsed in my chair throwing my head on the table.

"Oh Boo, what happened?" Piper asked as she wrapped her arms around my shoulder. I took a long a breath, gaining the strength to explain what I had just done. Was it stupid? Did I just let something great walk away? I mean, I could understand where he was coming from. Michael, the ass that he is, was always going to be an obstacle for us, wasn't he? Was that something Nathan and I would never be able to move on from? Had I rushed this relationship with Nathan? Did I even know who I was if I didn't have someone in my life? I had never been on my own before so maybe I didn't even know myself.

I looked at the concerned faces at everyone at the table and I sucked my breath back in, steeling myself not to cry.

"I don't know what I'm doing anymore

Piper. Nathan said all the right words but none of what he said made me feel better and I don't really know why. What's wrong with me? Am I so broken that I'll never be able to be in a healthy relationship again? Do I even know what a healthy relationship looks like?"

"Babes, you're not broken but maybe you never really dealt with what Michael and Madison did to you. I know you think you're passed everything but maybe those hurts cut deeper than even you realized." Piper squeezed my shoulders as Miquel reached across the table and grabbed my hand"

"Listen Mama, you're one of the strongest people I know. I knew you in high school when you and that dirtbag started dating. I was here when your dad died and I was here when the shit hit the fan with asswhipe and hobag, so I know what I'm talking about. You're not broken and there is absolutely nothing wrong with you. Piper is right though. Maybe you just didn't take enough time to process everything that went down in the aftermath of the relationship ending."

"That's what I told Nathan you guys and the look on his face... I think I crushed him and I don't know what to do. I told him I need some space to breathe and figure things out."

"Ok and how did Nathan react to that?"

Piper asked quietly

Choking on the tears I'd been holding at bay, I said, "He told me he'd wait for me forever."

Everyone at the table gasped and both Miquel and Alan grasped their chests as if they were clutching pearls.

"Oooh girl, that Nathan Sundry is a romantic. He's what they call in the romance books a cinnamon roll boyfriend." Miquel said as he began to fan his face with a napkin.

Alan, chuckling at his boyfriend, added "I think what Miquel is trying to say is, Nathan might be a keeper my sweet one. He's respecting you enough to understand that you need some time to come to terms with everything that has happened to you in such a short time span. At the same time, he wants to reassure you that he's here, waiting in the wings for you when you're ready."

I knew that both Alan and Miquel were right but I was starting to question if I had made a stupid, impulsive decision. Had I let fear get the better of me?

Piper lifted her hand in the air, twirling her fingers in a circular motion.

"This calls for pitchers of mimosas. Waitress bring another round and make this one heavy on the prosecco. My girl needs to be tipsy when we walk out of here." The diner erupts in laughter and Rosie, our waitress, just shook her head at Piper.

"Piper Jackson, who are you calling waitress. I've known you since kindergarten. Cool your jets girl or you'll get no more mimosas and I'll make you pay for that muffin I know you stole when you walked in here."

Piper looked down at the table sheepishly "Sorry Rosie. You know I love you. If you look the other way on the muffin thing, I promise not to come after you for the shit ton of late fees you have on the "Fifty Shades of Grey" books."

Rosie's face turned red and you could almost see steam blowing out of her ears like a cartoon character when they're angry.

"Piper Jackson, I have no such thing. You know I don't read books like that." Rosie stalked off towards the back of the diner.

"Shit Piper, we'll be lucky if she doesn't spit in our pitcher of mimosas now. Girl you are nothing but trouble." Alan just shook his head and took another bite of his eggs benedict.

What would I do without these people sitting at this table with me. Piper always knows just how to pull me out of a funk. Between her snark and Miquel's sass, there was no shortage of laughter at this breakfast table. Living in a small town, it was hard knowing everyone in town was probably gossiping about every detail of your life. Lord knows, my life has given them plenty to gossip about these past couple of months. Everywhere I went in Moonrise Bay, I could always feel eyes on me; see people whispering when I walked by. Not these people at this table though. No these were the people who would sooner hurt someone than ever let anybody talk shit about me. Besides my mom, these friends are the reason I don't want to ever leave Moonrise Bay.

I reached for everyone's hands and pulled them towards the center of the table.

"I love you guys so much. Thank you so much for making me come here today and stop wallowing in my sad bed. I truly don't know what I would do without you guys."

"Well for one thing, you wouldn't look as fabulous as you do this morning. You'd probably be all snotty faced lying in a pile of tissues if hadn't been for me and Piper dragging you into the shower this morning." Miquel stuck out his tongue as I leaned across the table to smack him across the chest.

Rosie brought us the pitcher of mimosas Piper asked for giving her serious side eye as she passed by. Thankfully we determined Rosie hadn't spit in our drinks. The four of us continued laughing our way through brunch and

I left feeling a little lighter then when I'd left the house this morning. As we left the diner, I gave everyone a hug and thanks for helping me get out of my funk. I figured while I was close by, I would pop into the bakery to check in on things. We were closed for the next few days to give me and the staff a much-needed rest before the Christmas rush. Piper said she had some paperwork to catch up on at the library and would come back for me after she was finished since I had ridden with her to brunch this morning.

I walked through the bakery towards my office feeling a weird sensation crawling up my spine. Nothing seemed out of place but I just had a feeling someone had been in here. As I flicked on my office lights, I couldn't believe what I was seeing. Someone had completely tossed my office. Thankfully I had taken my laptop home but everything else in here was a disaster. Papers tossed everywhere; my desk had been toppled over and the pictures had been torn from the walls; glass from the frames shattered. What the hell was going on? First the note on my truck, then someone had broken all the windows out of the truck, and now someone had destroyed my office. I knew in my heart this was Madison's doing. I knew she was pissed that Michael was sniffing around me again. Of course I had no proof. I didn't have security cameras because I'd always believed the people of Moonrise Bay to be good people. I didn't think that now.

On instinct, I started to text Nathan but remembered I had asked for space. I couldn't lean on him now. I needed to figure this out on my own. I called the sheriff's office and then Piper. Might as well put on a pot of coffee with the sheriff's deputies on the way. Out of anger, I sent a fiery text to Michael. I was tired of this bullshit and he was the reason this was happening.

Me: *Get control of your girlfriend Michael. I'm tired of her fucking temper tantrums and ruining my shit.*

It took that coward a full ten minutes to respond.

Michael: *I don't know what you're talking about Gracie. Madison hasn't done anything to you.*

Me: **laughing emoji* Aside from the obvious you asshole, she left a threatening note on my truck, broke all the windows out of it and then tossed my office at the bakery. I know it's her. No one else would have any reason to be this angry with me.*

Michael: *Give me a break Gracie. I know Madison can be difficult but she's not vengeful. She has no reason to come after you. Besides, she was with me and my family all afternoon. Trust me when I say we were together all day and night.*

*Me: *barf emoji* She wasn't with you when you showed up on my doorstep yesterday morning now was she.*

I could almost feel guilt coming through the phone.

Michael: She doesn't know I was there, Gracie, and that was a mistake. It won't happen again.

Me: You're damn right it won't happen again Michael. I want this to be the last time we communicate with each other. Even for business purposes. Hear me when I say this Michael, I want you and Madison to stay away from me, my family, my home and my business. We are D.O.N.E. done.

I sent that last text and slammed my phone down on the counter. I didn't care what his response was. I was done being pushed around and done being the nice guy.

Ryan was again the deputy assigned to my office vandalism and after giving my statement and waiting for the scene to be processed, I was done for the day. Completely drained, I sent Piper a text letting her know what happened and that Ryan was driving me home. She promised to come by so I wouldn't have to be alone but that's exactly what I wanted to be. I just wanted to wallow in my misery with a bottle of wine, brownies and a bubble bath. Today was ending just how it had started. Complete and utter disaster.

Sitting in my tub in silence, I let the tears fall. I was so tired of crying but the tears felt never ending. How had I gotten myself here? Just a few months ago, I had been blissfully planning my wedding; unaware my fiancé and best friend were having an affair. Then I picked myself up and was on the road to happiness with Nathan just to have that fall apart too. Maybe I'm not meant for happiness. Maybe I'm not meant to fall in love and get a happily ever after. Maybe, just maybe, I'm supposed to be alone.

Chapter 24

Nathan

I was miserable and I was making everyone around me miserable. I refused to leave my house the rest of the Thanksgiving weekend. I didn't want to be around people. I didn't deserve to be around anyone. I'd hurt Gracie and that was killing me. She asked for some space and that scared the shit out of me. My family had given me a wide berth for the whole weekend. My parents spent most of their time with my aunt and uncle. Landon on the other hand spent her days working and giving me dirty looks. She was definitely team Gracie and honestly I didn't blame her. I knew I'd royally fucked up but I was going to do everything in my power to fix things.

I was trying to enjoy a quiet moment on the back deck with my coffee, thinking of how I was going to work things out with Gracie, when Landon came storming out on the porch.

"What the hell Nathan? How are you so calm this morning?"

Dumbfounded, I just stared at her. Landon was known in our family for her dramatics but I wasn't in the mood for it today.

"I'm not in the mood today Landon. So whatever it is, just leave me out if."

Landon huffed out a breath and threw her hands in the air, "Well if you don't care that someone vandalized Gracie's office at the bakery, then maybe there is no hope for you guys."

I gripped my coffee cup so hard I'm surprised the damn thing didn't shatter in my hands. I started running for the door on instinct. I had to get to Gracie. Fuckkkk, I'd screwed up so badly, she hadn't even wanted to tell me what happened? Would she ever trust me again? When she asked me for space it gutted me. Now that space had kept her from coming to me when I should be the one helping her with this bullshit. Whatever game Michael is playing with her; I should be there with her.

"Whoa, whoa, whoa, slow down buddy. You don't need to go off all half-cocked and show up raging at Gracie. You need to calm down first."

I took a deep breath and slowly blew it out. I know deep down that Landon was right. My running to Gracie's house all half-cocked won't solve anything. She would have called if she wanted me there. At least she would have texted.

Space. She'd asked me for space and I need to respect that. If want to earn back her trust, I know I need to respect what she asked for. Even if it's killing me.

"How did you find out Landon?"

"I was grabbing breakfast at the Moonrise this morning and I heard several people talking about what happened. Then I texted Piper to see how Gracie was handling things. I didn't want them to think we were a family of assholes", she said with a smirk.

I stopped before reaching the door and slumped down in one of the deck chairs. I felt utterly defeated. Gracie hadn't wanted my help. That was the plain and simple of things and it sucked. Landon sat down next to me and grabbed my hand.

"Nathan, you screwed up but you're not a bad guy. I know that Gracie asked for space but sometimes we don't really know what we need until it's gone. Right now, she's hurting and you walked away from her instead of fighting for her. She didn't tell you because she may have felt like you aren't in this with her 100%. You need to show her Nathan that you're all in. Michael and Madison be damned. Drop your insecurities and fight for Gracie. You love her Nathan. We all see it but you're scared to let her all the way in for some reason. You have to trust her feelings for her."

I knew Landon was right. This was all because I was afraid that I couldn't give Gracie the kind of life Michael could. I knew deep down that she had no interest in getting back together with Michael. I just needed to figure out a way to show Gracie that I was all in.

"When did you get so wise baby sister?"

"I've always been smarter than you big bro. You're just too stupid to see it." She swatted the back of my head as she headed back into the house. Before opening the door, she turned and said "Don't give up on her Nathan. You two love each other and love like the two of you have is worth fighting for." I couldn't help but see the sadness etched on Landon's face. Before I could ask her if everything was okay, she turned and went back into the house. I knew Landon was right, and I knew I was going to fight for Gracie.

****

Me: I know you wanted some space Gracie, but I just wanted to see how you're doing. I heard about your office being trashed.

I waited to see those three dots appear. I never wanted for something so much in my life. I knew that if those little dots showed up on my screen, there would be hope for Gracie and me. Minutes passed by but I swear it felt like hours, but those dots finally popped up. I'm not ashamed that I threw my hand up and may have fist pumped the air. I hadn't completely lost her after all.

Gracie: Thanks for checking Nathan. It was a mess but it's cleaned up. Called the sheriff and they sent Ryan out to deal with things. He helped me get everything cleaned up.

I couldn't help the low growl that escaped my throat. I was angry. Not that Ryan was there with Gracie. I know she's not interested in him and I know he was just doing his job as a deputy. I was angry that it wasn't me who was there for her. Knowing that I was the one to let her down...

Me: Can I see you Gracie? I promise I won't stay. I just need to lay eyes on you. I just need to know you're ok.

Gracie: I don't know Nathan. I'm not so sure that's a good idea. I promise I'm ok and I'm not alone. Piper is staying with me for a few days just to be safe. Thanks for checking on me.

I blew out a deep a breath. Not the response I was hoping for but at least I knew she was okay and not alone. I just wish I was the one who was with her. I missed the warmth of her body resting against mine. The last few days had been the worst night's sleep of my life. I just wanted her in my arms where I knew she belonged.

Me: *I miss you Gracie girl. I'm not pushing but I need you to know, I love you. I'm not giving up on us. I'll give you the space you asked for but I'm not giving up without fight. I waited too long for you to just give up and let you go. I wish I was saying this all to your face instead of in a stupid text message. I'm here Gracie. When you're ready, I'll be right here.*

I didn't expect a response back. I just needed Gracie to see the words. I just needed her to know that I was all in and would still be here when she was ready. I blew my chance with her in high school because I waited too long to tell her how I felt. I wouldn't make that mistake a second time around. I loved this girl with every fiber of my being. Being without her the past few days had made me realize just how truly lucky I was to have her in my life. This was a once in lifetime love. I knew that deep down in my soul. My chest tightened as those three dots appeared on my screen again.

Gracie: *Goodnight Nathan. Thank you again for checking on me. It means a lot to know you're there.*

Enough. I realized that would have to be enough for me for now.

Chapter 25

Gracie

I threw my phone down on the sofa beside me and placed both hands on my face. I felt the tears beginning to fall before my whole body was wracked with sobs. Gut wrenching sobs that I could no longer control. Tears for Nathan. Tears for me. Tears for this shitty situation I was currently living in. I felt strong arms wrap around my shoulders pulling me down onto their lap and I knew Piper was beside me.

"Oh babes, let it out. You've been put through the ringer these past few weeks. If anyone is entitled to a breakdown, it's you for sure."

I lifted myself off Piper's lap and pushed the hair back from my face. God, I was a total and utter mess.

"What am I doing Piper? Why am I pushing Nathan away? I know he screwed up the whole Thanksgiving debacle but I really have forgiven him for that. Why can't I let him back in? What's wrong with me?"

"Sshh Gracie boo. There's nothing wrong with you. It's not totally surprising that you're having trouble trusting Nathan. Michael put you through so much, not to mention with someone you thought was your friend. You're bound to have trust issues. What you need to do now is figure out if Nathan is worth putting your heart on the line again. I, for one, think he is but I can't make that choice for you."

I knew she was right. I was projecting all my fears from the past onto Nathan. He's not Michael. Nathan had done nothing to break my trust. It was actually the opposite. He had shown me time and time again that he was here for me. Whenever I needed him, he was there. Yet, the one time he showed the tiniest crack in his armor, I'd pushed him away. I'm a complete idiot.

"Ugh, Pipes you're right. I do have trust issues and that's not fair to put all my bullshit onto Nathan. He hasn't done anything to make me not be able to trust him. All he's ever done is show me over and over how much he loves me. But what do I do? I run at the first disagreement, I run away like a coward."

"Then you need to fix it Gracie. If Nathan is worth fighting for, then get in there and fight. Michael has already tried to take so much from you, don't let him ruin this for you too. Nathan loves you. He's not going anywhere until you tell him to. So what are you going to do about it?"

I knew Piper was right. Nathan said he was fighting for us so why wasn't I? I know that Nathan is everything I want and I'm letting Michael and Madison ruin that for me. I'm ruining it with all my stupid insecurities. No I'm not going to let that happen. I'm going to Nathan's and I'm going to take back what's mine.

I leapt up from the sofa and peaked at myself in the mirror. Ugh, I looked like a total nightmare.

"I'm going over there Pipes but first I need to fix what's happening here" I say as I circle my face with the palm of my hand. "Can you drive me? I just need to ten minutes to freshen up."

Piper threw her hand up for a high five. "Hell yeah girl. Throw on your sexiest outfit and let's go get your man."

I ran upstairs and tried to run a brush through my mess of hair. I gave up, putting my hair up in a sexy top knot instead. After some mouthwash, a quick swipe of makeup and an outfit change, Piper and I were out the door and in her Jeep heading towards Nathan's house. I was fucking nervous. Not quite sure why. Nathan told me in that last text he wasn't giving up on us but I still felt nerves in the pit of my stomach. I just need to see him, touch him and I know everything will be okay. I need to tell him I'm sorry for being so stupid. I know we'll fix this but I just need to put my eyes on Nathan's face.

Piper pulls in front of Nathan's house and puts the Jeep in park. She turns her body towards me.

"Okay babe, you got this. Go knock on that man's door and attack his face like your life depends on it."

Laughing I say, "Jesus Pipes, you certainly know how to paint a picture."

"Well girl, I guess you could just use your words but you know I really do believe actions definitely speak louder." She smirks and grabs my hand, squeezing gently. "You've got this Gracie. You know he loves you. You know he's not going to send you away. Now get out the car and go get your man. Love you boo."

"Love you more Pipes."

I jump out of the Jeep and head up the driveway. The house is dark except for the porch lights. I instantly start to regret this decision. Especially as I see Piper's headlights driving away in the distance. I guess she's confident I won't need a ride home. I'm definitely rethinking my spontaneity. I have no plan and don't have a clue what I'm going to say when Nathan answers the door. My feet are moving faster than my brain but there's no turning back now. It's a long walk back to my townhouse.

Standing at the front door, I inhale deeply working up the courage to ring the doorbell. "Here goes nothing" I whisper as I push the bell. It feels like an eternity before Nathan answers the door. The moment I see his face; I feel the air rush out of my lungs.

"Hey Nathan" I say drawing up all the courage I can muster.

Nathan smiles faintly as he shoves his hands in the pockets of his sweatpants, shoulder leaning against the doorjamb. "Hey Gracie, want to come inside?"

I nod and Nathan steps to the side as I slip past him and into the entryway of his house. My arm lightly brushes against his and that same zap of electricity is there. I know in my heart that this is where I've always belonged. This is where I'm supposed to be. Nathan leads me down the hallway into his kitchen. God does he look good with his low-slung sweatpants resting just on his hips. What I wouldn't give to just rip those pants right off him.

I pull out one his barstools and take a seat at the island.

"Can I get you anything to drink, Gracie?" Nathan asks as he reaches for his beer resting on the counter.

"Umm, sparking water if you have it" I say as I sit nervously twisting my fingers. Nathan hands me a Perrier and leans against the counter. He just watches me for a minute. Like he's trying to see directly into my mind. It's almost unnerving how he does that. I'm so god damned nervous. I just want to reach out and grab him by his shirt and fucking kiss him like there's no tomorrow.

"Not that I'm not happy to see you Gracie, but what are you doing here?" There's no anger in his voice, just curiosity. I can understand that. I am the one sending mixed signals. I'm the one that pushed him away and asked for space just a couple of days ago and now here I am sitting in his kitchen. I would be curious too if I was him.

"I don't know where to begin Nathan. I guess maybe with an apology." Nathan quirks his eyebrow and takes a long sip of his beer. I watch; entranced by the working of his Adam's apple as he swallows. Memories of me licking a trail from his throat down his chest flickers through my mind and I squeeze my thighs together, squirming on the barstool.

"I'm so sorry for my reaction at the diner the other day. I was hurt by how you acted on Thanksgiving but that wasn't an unforgivable offense. I just... I don't know, I think I lost sight of who you are and put all my insecurities from Michael unto you. That wasn't fair of me,

Nathan, and I'm really sorry. I don't know why I said I needed space. I got scared I guess. This____ what's happening between the two of us scares the shit out of me. I've never had such intense feelings for someone so fast before Nathan. Not even Michael. What I feel for you, it's like I can't breathe without you. I didn't know what to do with those feelings and instead of embracing them, I pushed you away. I'm an idiot Nathan. Can you forgive me? I don't want space; I just want you."

Nathan is quiet for minute before setting his beer down. He stalks to my side of the island like a predator, turning my seat so I'm facing him. He slides between my legs, placing his thumb under my chin as he lifts my face so our eyes meet.

"What took you so long Gracie girl?" His lips crash against mine and I'm lost in the beauty of his kiss. I open for him as Nathan's tongue slips inside swirling with mine. Groaning against his mouth, I feel Nathan harden against my thigh. God, I've missed this man's kiss. His touch. The way he lights me on fire with just one touch. With just a look. He places one hand on the nape of my neck as the other rests against my check. His thumb gently rubbing my jawline. We break apart and Nathan rests his forehead against mine. His breath hot on my skin causing goosebumps to pop up across my body.

"Fuck Gracie. I thought I'd lost you. The way you ended our last text conversation; I thought this was over. I'm so fucking happy you showed up on my porch tonight."

I grab his hand and brush a soft kiss against his knuckles.

"Nathan, I can't apologize enough for making you feel that way. Even though I was in a relationship with someone for ten years, it still feels like I'm new to this."

Nathan exhales a deep breath as he kisses the top of my head. "Gracie, we're going to screw up sometimes. I know that I will. What's important is that we're honest with each other and we don't run away when times get hard. I'm kind of new to this whole relationship business too but I meant what I said Gracie. I'm all in. I'm so fucking in love you that I can't imagine a world where you aren't mine. You own a piece of my heart Gracie girl and I don't want it back."

I can feel the beginning of tears burning in the corner of my eyes. "I love you too Nathan. So fucking much it scares the shit out me. I'm all in too. I want your face to be the first thing I see in the morning and I want it to be the last thing I see before closing my eyes at night. You've become my best friend Nathan and my world would be empty without you in it."

Nathan grabs me by the waist and lifts

me from the barstool. My legs instantly wrap themselves around his body.

"I'm so happy you rang that doorbell tonight." He squeezes my hips and slides his hands down, grabbing my ass.

I lift my eyebrows and say "Oh yeah Nathan? You gonna show me how happy you are or you just going to stand there?"

With my challenge thrown down, Nathan pulls my wrapped legs from his waist and throws me over his shoulder fireman style, slapping my ass as I squeal with delight.

"Careful what you wish for Gracie girl" and he takes the stairs two at a time only stopping in the doorway of his bedroom to slide me down his shoulders and fling me on the bed. I sit up on my elbows and watch as Nathan stalks towards. He stands there for a moment just staring at me. His piercing blue-grey eyes dance in the glow of the moonlight.

He reaches behind his head and pulls his shirt off one handed. I'll never get tired of that move. So fucking hot.

"I'm taking my time with you tonight Gracie. Hope you weren't planning on getting a lot of sleep. Now that I have you here, back in my bed, I'm never letting you go."

My tongue darts out and I slowly lick my

lips. God, the way this man makes my body sing with just his words.

I reach my hand to the waist of his sweatpants but Nathan puts his hand out, shakes his head and stops me.

"Patience Gracie" he says as he pulls the top knot out of my hairs and lets my caramel locks fall around my shoulders. "I'm going to undress you piece by piece until you're almost coming just from me taking your clothes off."

My eyes roll back in my head and I moan with anticipation. The things this man's words do to me. I love his dirty fucking mouth. My shirt is pulled over my head and I'm so fucking happy I wore my good bra today.

"God, but you're beautiful Gracie." Nathan's hands make their way slowly down my body. One hand holding me gently by the throat as the other pulls my bra down; stroking my nipples.

I hiss as Nathan pinches and tugs. "Fuck Nathan, you're going to make me come just from doing that."

He laughs softly, "that's ok Gracie girl. We've got all night and I promise that won't be the only time you come tonight." His mouth crashes with mine and we're a tangle of tongues. Nathan unclasps my bra and it falls to the floor. Our mouths never leaving each other. While one hand is working my nipples, his other hand makes its way down my body and slips under the waistband of my yoga pants. Fingers slipping inside my lace panties.

"Jesus Gracie, you're so wet for me already."

"Always Nathan" I reply panting because I can't seem to catch my breath. Nathan has my body under his complete control. I'm ravenous for him.

"Please Nathan" I beg.

"What baby? Tell me what you need."

"I need you Nathan. I only need you." And just like that, my pants and underwear hit the floor as I scoot further up on the bed. Nathan's sweatpants and boxer briefs quickly join my pile of clothes, his dick springing free as he dips a finger inside my wet folds.

"Oh my god Nathan, yes" I scream unable to hold it in any longer. The way his fingers fill me so completely. He dips another finger into my pussy and my back arches off the bed. It's all I can do to keep myself from coming undone. His fingers dipping in and out of my wet cunt. I'm spiraling out of control. My sensitive clit barely able to handle the touch of his thumb.

"That's it baby. God, I can feel how swollen your clit is. You like that don't you baby."

Nathan's stroking inside my pussy intensifies as his thumb begins to rub circles on my clit. I feel completely out of control. It's utterly euphoric. It's like nothing I've ever experienced in my life. How this man can make me come in mere minutes is beyond my comprehension.

My legs begin to tremble as I feel myself tumbling towards the bliss of my orgasm.

"That's it Gracie, come on my hand" and I shatter on those words. Blinding white lights hitting in the back of my eyes. Nathan puts his fingers in his mouth, sucking the taste of my arousal from them. "Fuck baby, you taste so good. I crave your pussy morning, noon and night. You're my favorite meal." Nathan winks and strokes up and down the length of my thigh.

The world almost silent except for the sounds of our mixed heavy breathing. I want it to always be like this. Just like this moment for the rest of my life.

Chapter 26

Nathan

I stare at the glow on Gracie's face, tracing a line up and down her jawline. "Fuck you're beautiful when you come Gracie. I'll never get enough of that look, the glow in your eyes." Looking down into her whiskey brown eyes, I'm stunned that she's mine. I take a moment just to breathe her in. That signature scent of cinnamon and vanilla. Always so sweet. The taste of her is fucking craveable.

"This is how I want it to always be between us Gracie. Just like this moment. I swear to God, there's no better feeling than lying naked with you. No better feeling than your skin against mine."

"I promise Nathan, it will always be like this with us" Gracie smiles as her hand reaches down between our bodies and grabs my cock. With the tip of her thumb, she rubs the precum that has seeped out over the head of my dick.

"Fuck" I hiss and that seemed to make

Gracie rub harder. She stroked the length of me, working me up and down, I didn't think I could feel any better than her warm hand, wet from my leaking tip, rubbing my smooth tip, and tugging my shaft. Nothing could feel better until Gracie switched positions and licked me from tip to balls. Her pussy staring me in the face. God, I needed to get my mouth on that delicious pussy again. Gripping her ass cheeks in palms, I brought her glistening lips to mouth and sucked her clit, nibbling her pretty pussy.

"Fuck.... Nathan" Gracie groaned with my cock between her lips. Those lips pulling my shaft in and out; her tongue licking the length of my cock. She sucked harder and faster as I teased her clit with my tongue. I pushed my fingers in her hot sex and she hissed, sucking even harder making me thrust until my length hit the back of throat.

"Oh fuck Grace, feels so good baby." I moaned around her clit making her moan even louder.

"Baby, I don't want to come in your mouth. I want to come in your beautiful pussy." I grab her, flipping her over so I'm staring down in her beautiful, glowing face and line the tip of my cock up with her entrance. I watch her as I push myself inside, her eyes rolling back.

"Yes Nathan. I need you, all you." Her

nails claw at my shoulders and down the length of my back as I rock my hips into her.

"This is where I belong Gracie. Your pussy was made just for me. You're mine."

"Always Nathan. I'm yours."

I slow my pace for moment. Staring down at the beautiful woman who had chosen me. I was in awe of her beauty. I can see it. Feel it. All the years of wanting this woman.

Gracie wrapped her legs around my waist and pulled me into her. "Move Nathan. I need to feel you." I begin pumping in and out of her sweet, wet pussy. Watching as we join together. The sight of my cock sliding between her dripping wet folds. God, I could come just watching that.

"Fuck Gracie, we look so fucking good together. I love watching my dick pump in and out of that pretty pink pussy. Your lips are so wet and swollen baby."

Gracie moans my name and I begin to thrust faster. Fucking her with abandon. I can feel sweat beading at my temples. Our slick bodies colliding as one. I don't want tonight to end. I just want to stay here, bodies connected, our souls becoming one.

I feel Gracie clamping my cock between her pussy lips and know she's ready to burst.

"Come with me Nathan. I need to feel you."

With Gracie's pleading, my eyes roll back in my head. My back muscles clinch in anticipation. I can feel the tightness in my balls right before I explode. Unleashing every drop of my desire for Gracie. White dots light up my brain and I swear to God, it's as if I enter another universe. It's an orgasm like nothing I've ever experienced before. I roll so that Gracie is on top of me. Our slick bodies still joined. I can't bring myself to pull out of her. Not yet. I need to be connected just a few moments longer.

"God if makeup sex is always like that, then maybe we should fight more often" Gracie chuckles as she draws a star pattern on my sweaty chest.

"Maybe we can just pretend to fight. I don't want to go through another week like that again Gracie. I was fucking miserable." She draws closer to my side and nuzzles my neck. Her breath warm and sweet. I hadn't slept in days without her in my bed. With her tucked tight against my body, I could feel my eyes growing heavy. This was perfection. Gracie in my bed. This was how it was supposed to always be.

Gracie's hand slowly makes it way to the scruff on my jaw, rubbing small circles with her fingers.

"Nathan, I love you so much. You are what

I've been wanting my whole life but didn't think I deserved to have. I just... I don't know if I can say it enough. Before you, I thought Michael was all I was good enough for. But over the past two months, you've let me see myself in your eyes. You've shown me what it's really like to be loved by someone. You've become the first person I want to see in the morning and the last one I want to see before I close my eyes at night. I just want you to know that I'll choose you over and over again. In this life and the next. I love you." I single tear slides down her face and I reach to brush it away with the tip of my thumb.

I feel like she's just knocked the breath from my lungs. Never in a million years did I ever expect to hear those words from Gracie Henderson's mouth. I reach for her hand, kissing her palm before placing her right above my heart.

"Do you feel that Gracie? That beating in my chest? My heart beats for you... only you Gracie. You won my heart all those years ago. Just from the sound of you laughing. Just from the smile on your beautiful face. I've loved you for as long as I can remember but never did I imagine you would ever feel the same way about me. It's a god damned gift that I will treasure for a lifetime. These are sweet beginnings Gracie Girl." We lay there, facing each other, her head nuzzled just underneath my chin. The only sound in the room is our steadying breaths. I pull Gracie closer, clutching her to my chest. No more words need to be said. Just this moment. This feeling of her in my arms. That's all I need. Just this. Just us.

*****

I wake up, Gracie in my arms, thanking God last night wasn't just a dream. It's real and she's still here sleeping peacefully next to me. I don't know what I did in my life to deserve this much happiness but I'm sure as shit not going to tempt fate by continuing to question it. I slowly and begrudgingly pull myself from Gracie's arms and throw on my sweatpants from the night before. I quietly creep out of the bedroom so I don't wake Gracie up. From the dark circles she had under her eyes, I could tell she had been sleeping just about as shitty as I had the past few nights. I knew she needed to get a good night's sleep. I turned to take one little glance at her naked body strewn across my bed. That beautiful caramel brown hair spread across the pillow. Her sleeping face so peaceful.

I made my way down to the kitchen and got a pot of coffee brewing. Gazing out the back window, the morning felt calm and serene. The fog was rising over the water and there was a slight frost on the rails of the deck. It was a beautiful late fall morning and I was so grateful to be able to spend it with Gracie. Hopefully in bed for most of the day. I was so lost in the thought; I didn't even hear Gracie make her way down to the kitchen. I jolted as her hands wrapped around my waist, her lips pressing a kiss against my bare back. I tokk her arms that are wrapped around my chest and rubbed up the length of her arms.

"Morning Gracie girl. Sleep well?"

"Mmm, perfectly" she hummed against my skin, setting the nerves in my spine on fire.

Turning around, trapping her in my arms, I placed a kiss to the top of her forehead. "Got plans today? I know the bakery is closed for the week, so I was hoping I could convince you to spend the day here with me. In bed maybe?" I wiggle my eyebrows and smile "we have a lot of making up to do after all."

Gracie chuckles as she massages up my spine, "I think I could be convinced to spend the day here in bed with you. On one condition though."

"Anything you want you Gracie girl. Just name it."

"Feed me first Nathan. We worked up quite an appetite last night. I need food and a cup of that delicious smelling coffee."

I kiss her again and smack her ass. She

feigns a surprise look before tossing her head back and laughing.

"One cup of hot coffee and a breakfast to feed an army coming right up." The two of us work together in the kitchen gathering all the ingredients for a lumberjack special. Eggs, bacon, pancakes, hashbrowns. You name it, we made it.

We spend the morning, laughing through breakfast, making love through the morning hours stopping only for small naps and showers that turn into more sex. By the time night is falling, we're exhausted, sore and possibly dehydrated. We lay together in the mess of our bed under the glow of the moonlight just beyond the bedroom window.

"Thank you for today Nathan. Thank you for forgiving me for being a complete idiot."

I smooth the sweaty hair that is sticking to her forehead away from her face, "there was nothing to forgive Gracie. We're going to fuck up from time to time. I'm not perfect, you're not perfect but that doesn't mean we don't love each other. Perfection in a relationship is an illusion. This____ right here, between you and me. This is all that matters. Communication, calling each other on our bullshit, forgiving when something needs to be forgiven. That's what makes a strong relationship. We'll stumble along the way, but we'll always be here to catch each other before we fall."

"I love you Nathan, always."

"I love you too Gracie, forever."

Chapter 27

Gracie

Nothing felt more right than waking in Nathan's arm, his bed, his house. Since the night of our epic makeup, I have spent every night in Nathan's bed. Ever so slowly, more and more of my things were making their way over to Nathan's house. I was beginning to feel at home here. Like this was the place we could build our lives together. I'm not going to lie___ that thought scared the shit of me. Was I rushing this? Was it too soon to even be thinking about something like living together?

From the beginning, this thing between me and Nathan moved at lightspeed. Shouldn't that worry me? Most people would say this relationship was just a rebound but I knew that wasn't true. There was something deep in my bones that told me Nathan was it. The real deal. Endgame. Even when I said yes to marrying Michael, it didn't feel like this. Sure, there was excitement but if I really thought about it, wouldn't we have moved further along in our wedding plans? We were supposed to be getting married in February and we hadn't even booked a venue. We hadn't even talked about what we wanted our wedding to look like. Never made a single plan beyond setting a date. We just settled back into our day-to-day existence. I spent most of my time at the bakery and he was always working too. I really didn't have time to notice that Michael and I had stopped being a couple. Sure we had sex from time to time. We had the odd date night here or there but for the most part, the two of just existed in the same space. This feeling in my heart, I've never felt for anyone before. Not even Michael. Michael was puppy love. Just love that a naïve eighteen-year-old girl felt for a cocky eighteen-year- old boy. This___ this love I feel for Nathan is an all-consuming kind of love. The kind that eats you up. Toe curling, smiling for no reason kind of love. The kind of love people wait a lifetime for. So why was I still scared? It's not Nathan's feelings for me. I feel that love down deep in my soul. Is it me I'm questioning? Do I not feel like I'm worthy of love like that?

Reaching for my phone, I shoot off a message to Piper. She's always been my best sounding board.

Me: *Piper, s.o.s. I'm spiraling again and I need you to talk me off the ledge.*

It takes a few minutes but the tension in my body eases as I see those three dots appear on the screen

Piper: *Aww babes, meet me at The Cozy Café. I think you and I both could use a little afternoon caffeine pick me up. I can be there in ten.*

Me: *Thanks Pipes. Grabbing my keys now. Love you *kissy face emoji**

Piper: *Anytime Boo. Love you, mean it *heart eyes emoji**

Ten minutes, I'm just pulling in a parking spot not far from The Cozy Café, when I feel eyes on me. I know it's probably just my imagination but with everything that's happened lately, I can't help but take a moment to look around to see where this feeling is coming from. I don't see anything that would give me pause so I turn back and head inside the coffee shop. Piper already has two pumpkin spice cold brew's and what looks like gingersnap muffins waiting for me. This little café has stepped up their pastry game over the last couple of months. I may have to talk to Sally, the owner, about a recipe swap. That gingersnap muffin is absolutely to die for.

"Hey boo. I got you your favorites" Piper grabs me and pulls me in for a big hug. We both sit down before I start in on my downward spiral.

"Thanks Pipes" I breath in the sweet smells of pumpkin spice and freshly brewed coffee, my nerves instantly calmed by their comforting scents. "I really needed this."

"What's up babes? Why the spiraling? I thought things were going great with you and Nathan this week?"

Letting out a heavy exhale, I start telling Piper what's churning in my brain. "I don't know what's going on with me Pipes. Don't get me wrong, everything with Nathan is wonderful and I do mean *everything*. Sometimes I just get all in my head and think all of this is too good to be true. What's so special about me?" I throw my head down and the table and Piper runs her hand through my ponytail.

"Gracie Henderson, WTF!!! What's so special about you? What's so special about you? EVERYTHING. EVERY. FUCKING. THING. Do you hear me Gracie. Stop talking badly about my ride or die."

"I think everyone in the café heard you Piper." I say grimacing while glancing around the café to see if indeed everyone is looking at our table.

"Good. The only person I care about hearing me though is you Gracie. You've always done this. You doubt you're worthy of anything good and I don't know why. You have such a kind heart Gracie. Remember when I was little and my dad was away on business, mom was drunk and I had no one to take care of me? I was too afraid to tell Gram but you always knew and would make sure I came home for dinner at your house or you'd share you lunch with me. You deserve good things Gracie because you're a good person. You're the best person. Don't let what the douche canoe and slutbag did make you think any less of yourself."

I laugh, grabbing Piper's hand and squeezing it. I truly love Piper with all my heart. She's the sister I never had growing up but she's my sister just the same. Piper didn't have an easy life. At least not until she finally got the courage to tell Gram about her home life. Gram immediately moved Piper into her house and the rest is history.

"I hear you Piper, I really do but there is still a part of me that, with the whirlwind this relationship has been, is just waiting for the other shoe to drop."

"Babe, I think the other shoe did drop. Don't forget the Thanksgiving debacle, but you guys worked through that and came out the other side a stronger couple."

"Yeah, I know you're right. I'm just being stupid. I just feel off you know. When I got out my car, I could swear I felt someone watching me. It just feels like something is coming but I just don't know what it is."

Piper gives me a thoughtful look, considering everything I've just told her. "That's totally understandable with everything that's happened recently. It's probably just nerves that's got you spooked babe."

"Yeah, you're probably right. I'll feel so much better once we catch whoever has been messing with me in the act."

"We both know who it is. It's that bitch Madison. Just let me catch her in the act..." We both laugh so hard I almost pee my pants. The whole café is looking at us now because we are straight up cackling and snorting. This isn't pretty laughing but it feels so good. Completely distracts me from all my anxious thoughts.

******

Moonrise Bay was in full Christmas mode all across the town. Now that Thanksgiving had passed, Christmas Tree lots had popped up everywhere, streets are lined with holiday decorations, storefronts are full of lights and garland. It truly makes the town look magical. The months of September through December are my absolute favorites. Of course, I always wish we could get a white Christmas here in Moonrise but that rarely happens on the North Carolina coast. A girl can have her dreams though.

I love this time of year because of all the creations that I get to fill the bakery case with.

The smells of cinnamon rolls and gingerbread baking. Sugar cookies in every holiday shape you can imagine. Not to mention the specialty cakes we have. Eggnog, Peppermint Mocha, Cranberry Orange, you name it we make it. I love having the little kids come in and decorate gingerbread houses that they can take home to proudly display. I know it's hokey, but it really is the most wonderful time of the year.

This year feels different. There's the obvious worry of what the fate of downtown will be. We've all been served with notices that the Garrett Realty holdings have sold. Now we're all waiting on bated breath to find out what will become of our businesses. I know that's why the town is stopping at nothing to show the new owners how quaint our little downtown area is. The town council has been hard at work trying to make this holiday bazaar the best it's ever been. We're even starting it earlier. I've been hard at work baking up a storm in preparation for tonight's annual tree lighting ceremony. It's what kicks off the whole bazaar. Next up we'll have the holiday parade, which is always a hoot. The mayor and his wife dress as Santa and Mrs. Claus and throw candy to the kids lining the parade route. I really love this little town. Yes, everybody whose anybody is in your business, but when push comes to shove, this town is here for its citizens.

I'm terrified of what's going to happen if the new building owner decides to raise rent on my business. Sure I do a good amount of business during the summer months to hold me over through the off season but I don't know if that will be the same if my rent goes up. I survive in the off season on holiday orders but after December, business slows down dramatically until spring. Valentine's Day does a decent job but business is really just locals coming for the odd treat from January until Easter hits. If rent gets increased, I'll probably have to find some kind of job I could do from home to help supplement things until the busy season kicks in. The thought of that worries me. I'm a girl who majored in art and makes her living baking cakes and pastries. Sure I run my own business but I'm not really sure what kind of job that would qualify me for. I'm honestly hoping for a Christmas miracle.

Nathan walks through the door looking like a dream just as I'm closing up the shop to meet him at the tree lighting.

Dark wash jeans, topped with a heather grey cable knit sweater. Just the right amount of scruff lining his jaw. God damn is this man gorgeous and he's all mine.

He saunters towards me, grabs me by the waist and places a not so chaste kiss to my lips.

"Hey baby. How's my girl doing?"

It's all I can do to keep my legs from buckling. Will I ever not have this reaction when Nathan touches me? God I hope not.

"This is a nice surprise Nathan. I was just getting ready to close up shop so I could head out and meet you at the tree lighting." Nathan grins as I continue, "If you don't mind, I thought after the lighting we could head back here and get together some treats and hot cocoa for the crowd when its over."

Smiling, Nathan looks down at me, nothing but love radiating from his gaze. "Put me to work Gracie Girl. The quicker we can get everything finished up here, the quicker I can get home and have my treat."

I swear to God, I almost faint right then and there. The look this man is giving me, tells me there won't be a lick of sleeping happening tonight. I don't mind it one bit. Not. One. Bit.

Twining Nathan's hand with mine, I flip off the lights and lock the bakery door. "Come on Nathan, let's go see this tree lighting." Walking hand and hand, we stroll down the block towards the growing crowd and I've truly never been happier in my life.

Chapter 28

Nathan

Strolling through our little town, you could feel a buzzing energy with every person we passed. Moonrise Bay folks really do love their holiday celebrations. Every shop and street corner was decorated. No space had been left untouched. It was as if a Christmas town had exploded here overnight but I loved it. I loved this the small town and I loved the woman walking with me, hand tucked into mine.

Looking at Gracie, I was so grateful that she had been able to forgive me and that we were working our way out from under the Michael and Madison situation. Honestly, Gracie really did have bigger things to worry about. I know when she received the notice of her building being sold, her anxiety level peaked to an all-time high. I wish I could make things better for her. I truly wished I had been able to come up with a solution for her. None of us were able to find out anything about who the new owners were. The town council was keeping everything very hush

hush. That was definitely out of the norm for the people of Moonrise Bay. I even tried getting Levi involved again but was told by his assistant that he was out of the office and had asked not to be disturbed. I hoped everything was ok with him. I'd tried sending him several texts but they all went unanswered. It was all really strange and not typical Levi behavior.

As Gracie and I made our way down Main Street, we were stopped by just about every person we passed. Everyone was curious about what was going to happen to the downtown businesses. Poor Gracie. I could see the stress tugging away at her the more people asked. She really had no more information than the rest of the town. All she had received was an email notice from Garret Realty letting her know they had closed a deal with an out-of-town developer and more information would be made public soon. No other communication had been shared and it was frustrating for Gracie to say the least.

Making sure to keep Gracie's hand firmly twined with mine, I navigated her away from the crowd as we made our way to where the tree lighting was being held.

"Hey Nathan, Gracie. Over here." I turned to where I heard my name called and looked over to see Piper, Gram and Gracie's mom Alice standing down on the boardwalk bundled up and waiting for the ceremony to start. The three of them were excitedly waving us over. With her hand in mine, Gracie pulled me over to where everyone was waiting.

"Hey y'all. You guys managed to grab a great spot. One of you must have been waiting here for hours." Gracie laughed as she gave everyone a hug.

"Well my brilliant granddaughter skipped out of work early and held down the spot. Your mom and I were more than happy to supply the warm drinks and snacks. Speaking of... I've got hot apple cider if anyone's interested. I added a little something extra to keep us warm." Gram said with a wink. I knew what that something extra was. Gram was known for her "special cider" recipe. The secret ingredient being whiskey. We used to sneak it for beach bonfires when we were in high school.

"Gram, you know no one can resist your cider" I replied with a chuckle.

Gram reached up and squeezed my cheeks like I was a toddler. "You sure are a charmer Nathan Sundry. Watch out Gracie, I just might have to steal this cute fella from you." I could feel my cheeks heating with embarrassment as I poured everyone a cup of cider.

"If I only I knew you were interested Gram, I may have asked you out instead of Gracie." I turned and winked at Gracie as she bent over laughing.

"Nathan you flirt.   You'll make an old woman blush."   The five of us stood around laughing and sharing stories of tree lightings in the past. All of us wondering what things would look like this time next year.   No one knowing if the town of Moonrise Bay would ever look the same.

A hush came over the growing crowd as the mayor and a few members of the town council made their way to the front of the town's decorated tree.

"Welcome   everyone   to   the   annual Moonrise Bay Christmas Tree lighting.   It's pleasure to see so many of our citizens in attendance tonight for the first night of our annual holiday bazaar.   What makes this night even more special is the guest we have flipping the switch for us tonight.   Without further ado, let me introduce everyone to Levi Anderson of LJA Global Associates.   The new investor of our beautiful downtown Moonrise Bay."

It was if you could hear a pin drop amongst our group.   Was this why Levi hadn't returned any of my calls and texts?   That sneaky bastard.   This was the best news that could have come out of this whole debacle.   I knew Levi would leave everything as it was for the business owners and he was truly just investing in the town itself.

"Did you know about this Nathan?" Gracie asked, eyes wide and a tentative smile on her face.

"I had no clue. I've been trying to reach him for days but he wasn't returning my messages. He really kept this one under wraps." I could feel Piper stewing behind me and knew she wasn't thrilled Levi was back in Moonrise Bay. I, on the other hand, couldn't have been happier. I knew Levi would do right by Gracie and the other business owners. "I can tell you this much though, I know this is a good thing. Levi is a shrewd businessman and he wouldn't have bought those building just to kick the businesses out. He bought them because he knows they'll make money for him."

I could see the relief wash over Gracie and her mom's faces. I knew this was a huge burden taken off her shoulders.

"Thank God" Gracie responded as she blew out a deep breath. "Finally something going my way after all the bullshit I've been through the last few weeks."

"It's about damn time. The only thing that would make this moment sweeter would be to see the look on Michael and Madison's faces. I'd love to watch that smug smile fall right off that bitch's face." Piper laughed manically.

"Damn Piper, remind to stay on your good side." I huffed out, pulling Gracie to my chest and wrapping her into a hug.

"Is it really over Nathan. Is my business really safe." Gracie looked up; her eyes so full of hope. I placed a kiss on her forehead and one of the tip of nose before lightly brushing my lips against hers.

"I think so Gracie girl. I think everything is going to be ok now." We all stood there, almost stupefied as Levi flipped the switch to light the town tree. The crowd cheered and our group cheered along with them. This really was turning into a great night. I could only see good things ahead for Gracie and me.

With the switch flipped, the town tree bursts to life in an array of colors and the whole town cheered. Not just for the lighting of the tree but because our downtown was safe and our little bay town wouldn't change. We would still be full of the small-town charm that drew more and more tourists here every year. You could almost feel the collective sigh that had descended upon the crowd tonight.

Our little group, huddled close together singing along to Christmas carols and drinking cider, was too preoccupied to hear Levi approach.

"I hope everyone was pleasantly surprised by the town announcement." Levi said as he smirked Piper's way.

"Jeez Levi, if you wanted another date all you had to do was ask. You didn't have to buy a whole town to see me again." Piper responded as she brought her cider to her lips, smirking right back at Levi.   There was something between these two that neither one wanted to admit. Part of me wondered if Piper wasn't one of the reasons Levi had made his investment in Moonrise Bay.

I turned to Levi with my hand ready to shake his "Hey man. That was some surprise. I guess that's why you've been ditching my calls and texts."

Taking my hand with a sheepish grin "Yeah, sorry about that Nate. I just didn't want to give away the surprise. No hard feelings?"

"Nah man, this was a great surprise. I know it's a big relief, right Gracie?" I turned to Gracie and she was still wiping away tears. I wrapped my arm around her waist and drew her in close to my side.

"Oh my gosh Levi, you have no idea. I was so worried that whoever was coming to buy up the downtown buildings would come in and kick all the businesses out and maybe bulldoze our beautiful downtown. I'm so happy that someone like you is my new landlord."

"Well Gracie, I wanted to talk to you about

that. I'm not going to be your landlord... I'm" but before he could finish Piper was jumping in Levi's face, spitting mad and screaming at the top of her lungs.

"What the hell do you mean you're not going to be her landlord. You double crossing asshole. You're kicking Gracie out? Of course you are. You come in here with all your money and take what doesn't belong to you. You can go all the way to hell Levi Anderson. Do. Not. Pass. Go."

Levi just laughed. Straight up, doubling over laughter. "Are you finished Piper, or do you think you can let me finish what I was saying to Gracie before you oh so fabulously interrupted me? As I was saying, Gracie, I'm not keeping your building. Yours is the only one that I've put in someone else's name and that someone is you Gracie. You now own that building fair and square."

Levi took some papers that he had been holding behind his back and handed them to Gracie. Her hands shook as she took the paperwork from Levi and more tears began to fall down her cheeks.

"Levi, oh my God. Is this real? Are you serious? I'm not going to lie. I'm totally freaking out here" Gracie pulled Levi in for a shaky hug. I looked around and everyone but Piper had tears in their eyes. She looked rightfully ashamed that she had jumped to conclusions about Levi's motives. Me... I was stunned silent. I knew Levi was a good guy and a smart businessman but I never thought he would be so generous as to sign over Gracie's building to her.

"I'm dead serious Gracie. It was a dick move for Michael to try and sell that building without offering it to you at a fair market value. It felt dirty and the fact that he threw the other buildings in too, that dude's a complete asshole. Just so you know, yours was the only building he tried to sell above market value. He was really trying to stick it to you Gracie. That's why I bought that building in your name."

Fucking Michael. If he can't get his way, he'll make everyone miserable until he does. I really wish I could take those papers from Gracie and shove them straight down his throat. I could tell from the look on Piper's face that she was feeling the same way.

As if she could sense the same thing, Gram turned to her granddaughter "Don't even think about it Piper. I can see the violence in your eyes and I don't have the money to bail you out tonight."

Throwing an arm around Gram's shoulders and smiling right at Piper, Levi drawls "Oh don't worry Gram, I've got Piper covered if she decides to play dirty."

"Woowee, did someone turn up the temperature out here. I'm sweating more than a whore in church watching you two look at each other. Come on Alice, let's go wander around the bazaar and leave these young people to have a fun time."

Gram grabbed Alice by the arm and started dragging her into the crowd towards the craft booths as Alice waved to all of us. "By kids, have fun but not too much fun. If you do, promise to name it after me." She laughed as she let Gram pull her away.

"Ugh mom, love you." Gracie shook her head and laughed as her mom disappeared into the crowd. "Hey guys, why don't we go to my new building and celebrate. Hot cocoa and Christmas treats are on the house."

The four of us made our way to the bakery, laughing all the way. Tonight was not what Gracie and I had been expecting but it was a great way to end the evening. The town felt magical; like Gracie and I had overcome all the obstacles that had been standing in the way and nothing could harm us now. We only had the future to look forward to you and I knew, looking at Gracie, that she was all I wanted in my future. Gracie Henderson was my endgame. She was my everything.

Chapter 29

Gracie

It was a few days after the tree lighting, and I still couldn't believe this building was mine free and clear. It still felt like a dream. I kept thinking back on everything that had happened to me over the past few months; Michael cheating and getting engaged to Madison, the threat of losing my business, the damage to my car and bakery but best of all, falling completely, utterly, madly, head of heels in love with Nathan Sundry. Logically, I know our relationship shouldn't have happened as quickly as it did. I'm sure most people looking in from the outside think he's just my rebound but I know better than that. None of that matters to me. Nathan Sundry has been the best god damned surprise of my life and I will be forever grateful for him. Without Nathan I would never have met Levi Anderson and without Levi Anderson, I wouldn't be standing here not only a business owner but I own this whole damned building. No more rent, no mortgage, it is mine free and clear.

It was nearing closing time and I was wrestling with how much work I wanted to leave until the morning when I heard Miquel calling from the back room.

"Hey Mama, Louisa, Alan and I are all heading out to walk around the bazaar tonight. I think there are a few new pop-up restaurants to check out. All the kitchen prep is finished up and you know you can't look at another invoice or your eyes are gonna start bleeding. Come on, girl. Come out with us. I'll hit up Piper too. You know Miss Thang needs a night out now that sexy suit left town."

Glancing down at the stack of paperwork, I knew Miquel was right. I really didn't want to look at another invoice or stack of orders that need to be completed.

"You're right, let me pack up this stuff to take home with me later and you text Pipes to see what she's up to. You guys go ahead and head out and I'll meet y'all down there."

Miquel grabbed his bags and headed for the front door where Alan was waiting for him. "Ok girlie, shoot us a text when you're on the way and we'll tell you where to meet. But drinks on are you tonight baby girl." He laughed and pushed through the door grabbing Alan by the arm and dragging him down the street.

I pack up all the paperwork and start

digging through my bag for my phone when I hear the chime of the front door opening. Thinking it's probably Miquel coming back for something, I don't even look up as I say, "Did you forget something" and I chuckle until hear the voice that answers back. My hand stills in my bag as I slowly glance up towards the door.

"You've never learned to take a hint have you Gracie?" Fucking Madison, standing there in her Alexander McQueen suit and Louboutin heels. Strawberry blonde hair perfectly swept back in a chignon, eyes seething with anger.

Slowly pulling my hand from my bag, I walk towards Madison. Rage coursing through every inch of my body.

"What the hell are you doing here Madison? The deal is done. Levi Anderson bought up the downtown properties. Whatever little scheme you and Michael cooked up to hurt me, failed. We don't have to be a part of each other lives anymore. Get the hell out of my bakery."

The look in Madison's eyes is pure fury. While the rest of her body conveys composure, her eyes scream hatred. I cannot fathom what happened in our friendship over the years that has brought us to this moment. Women who were good friends at one time, torn apart because of a stupid man.

"You think you've won Gracie" she sneered, lip curling into a snarl, "you've won nothing."

"What are you talking about Madison. I never said I won; I said this was over. I said you and Michael failed in ripping my business away from me but I never said I won. This wasn't my doing. You and Michael turned this into some kind of vendetta against me for God knows why. You two were the ones screwing behind my back and lying to my face. I'm the injured party here Madison, not you."

I could feel my face turning red and hands shaking with rage. I've had enough with this bitch and it was ending here, tonight.

"I know it was you, Madison, who trashed my truck and my office. I know you called in the phony the complaint to the health inspector. I know you're the one who left a threatening note on my car."

"Yeah, you can't do anything without proof bitch."

"What did I ever do to you Madison? I was your friend. Even when you and Piper weren't getting along, I didn't take sides. Why would you do this to me? Is it jealousy? I had something you wanted and you just couldn't stand it. For fuck's sake Madison, you were the fucking head cheerleader in high school. You had every guy you ever wanted."

"Every guy but one Gracie and you made sure of that didn't you?"

I stood there staring at her incredulously. Was she serious right now? Had she harbored these feelings since high school?

"You know what your problem is Madison. You peaked in high school. While the rest of us were figuring out how to make it through and find our paths, you reached all you were ever going to be in high school. You've absolutely had no growth since you were eighteen years old and that's sad."

"Shut the fuck up Gracie. You know nothing about me. You don't know…"

"I know everything about you Madison because you're not that deep. Poor Madison didn't get to date the high school quarterback. Boo fucking hoo. That was ten years ago. Time to move on."

"I've got him now though don't I." She sneered again, as if she had won some great prize. Michael Garrett was no prize.

I began a slow clap as I approached where Madison was standing.

"Yup, you got me on that one Madison. You win the prize. You get the washed-up high school quarterback turned mediocre real estate mogul" throwing the back of my hand up against my forehead feigning distress, "Whatever will I do without having to fake my orgasms. Trust and believe Madison, I don't want Michael back. He's all yours."

It happened before I had a chance to register what was going on. Madison pulled a gun from her bag and aimed it straight at my face. I stood there stunned...completely unable to move. I didn't recognize this woman standing in front of me. This wasn't the Madison that I had been friends with. The look in her eyes was terrifying. All I could see was rage. Seething rage.

"Say that again Gracie" Madison spit the words at me as she laughed manically. "Tell me again how you're so much better than me. Not better than me now are you bitch?" She screamed as she waved the gun in my face.

I threw my hands up defensively. "Madison, what the hell? What are we doing? Are you really going to shoot me over a guy? Over Michael fucking Garrett?"

"Don't you fucking dare talk about him like that. Like you don't want him back. Like you're not just slumming it with Nathan to make Michael jealous."

She shoved the gun further in my face

pushing me further into the bakery. I could see there was no trace of the Madison I knew left in her eyes. Something had snapped in her. I knew I needed to rethink my tactic where Madison was concerned. I needed to try and reassure her that I wanted nothing to do with Michael without insulting him. I needed to turn things around to make me look like the loser she so obviously needed me to be.

So obviously thought I was.

Keeping my hands up almost like I was surrendering, I began to try and talk Madison down from her breakdown.

"You're right Madison, you're right. Part of me probably always knew he didn't belong with me; that I wasn't good enough for him. But he's yours now Madison. You won. He'll never want me. I'm not good enough for him and he knows that now. Why do you think he's with you? He chose you not me. He didn't even fight for us. He let me go. Don't you see that?"

"NO, NO, NO. You've been teasing him by waltzing around town flaunting your relationship with Nathan and you know it. You thought if you slept with his friend the way he did with yours that he'd come running back. I know he's been hanging around the bakery. I know he showed up on your doorstep on Thanksgiving. And you're just loving it...not giving a shit about who you hurt in the process."

I knew I had to choose my next words carefully. Madison was growing more unhinged by the minute.

"He doesn't care about me and Nathan, Madison. You've got it wrong. He only comes here to rub it my face about how happy he is with you. He tells me how miserable I made him and that Nathan and I deserve each other because...

"Stop lying bitch! I know he tried to sabotage Nathan's business when the two of you started fucking."

I blanched at her harsh words; making what Nathan and I had seem dirty. I was done trying to talk Madison down. Down dealing with her bullshit. One way or another, this confrontation was over. I just hoped I didn't wind up shot or worse dead when all was said and done.

Chapter 30

Nathan

Piper: *Have you heard from Gracie? She was supposed to meet me, Miquel and Alan at the bazaar for some shopping and treats but she's not answering her phone and she hasn't responded to any of our texts.*

Nathan: *I haven't spoken to her since this morning. Has anyone checked the bakery? I'm just down the block at the hardware store. I'm heading that way now*

Piper: *We'll meet you there. I've got a bad feeling Nathan*

The pit in my stomach grew with every step I took. Gracie just had to be ok. We had finally gotten our lives settled. Her business was safe, our relationship was better than ever and the threats against her had stopped. They had stopped hadn't they? Gracie hadn't mentioned anything to me lately. There was no way she would keep something like that from me again. Especially after the fight we'd had the last time she kept information to herself. I was gripped with fear at the thought that Gracie might be hurt and alone at the bakery. I completely ignored the looks from everyone I passed on the street; my only concern was reaching Gracie in time.

I could see the bakery was mostly dark as I approached the front window but what I saw at the door made my heart plummet. Madison frantically waving a gun in Gracie's face.

Gracie looked terrified. I felt frozen; not knowing what to do. I knew if I went rushing through the front door, that damn bell would chime as soon as I opened it. I could see that Gracie was trying to keep Madison distracted, attempting to talk her down.

I grabbed my phone, firing off a quick text to Piper

Me: *No time to explain. Call the Sheriff and tell them to get someone down to the bakery ASAP. Madison is holding Gracie at gunpoint.*

I shoved my phone back in my pocket; ignoring the incoming text that I knew was from Piper. I didn't have time to respond. I needed to figure out how I was going to help Gracie.

Time stood still for a moment as I watched Gracie launch herself at Madison. It was now or never. Hopefully me bursting through the door would give Gracie the distraction she needed to get the gun away from Madison.

With the sound of sirens in the distance, I burst through the bakery door. As soon as the bell chimed, Madison turned her fury on me just as Gracie flung her body into Madison.

It happened to fast; I didn't have time to register the pain.

The bang of a gunshot, both Gracie and Madison screaming; the shouts and yells from Sheriff deputies and Piper in the mix. I barely felt it as the bullet passed through my shoulder knocking me to the floor.

Ryan, the sheriff's deputy we all knew from high school, had Madison pinned to the ground, slapping handcuffs on her wrists. Gracie flew to my side, tears streaming down her cheeks.

"Nathan, oh my God! She shot you, oh my God, she fucking shot you!"

I took her trembling hands in mine, trying to reassure her I was okay. Even with the adrenaline coursing through my body, the gunshot hurt like a sonofabitch but I didn't want Gracie to know how much pain I was in. I could hear someone calling for the medic as I reached out to stroke Gracie's face.

"Baby, baby. I'm okay. I think the bullet when straight through." I winced as one of the paramedics moved my shirt to assess the damage.

"It seems to be a clean shot but we need to get you to the hospital to make sure there's been no arterial damage." The paramedic said as she wrapped a bandage around my wound.

"Can I ride in the ambulance with him?" Gracie asked on a shaky breath. Her tear-stained face had grown pale as she watched the paramedic attend to my injury.

"I'm sorry miss, you can't ride with us but you can follow behind us. We need to get him in the ambulance now. He may need surgery when we get there." She helped me onto the stretcher and rolled me to the waiting ambulance. Gracie still clutching my hand, never leaving my side. The scene inside the bakery was complete chaos but I only had eyes for Gracie.

"I love you Nathan. I love you so much. I'll be right behind you. I promise." She lifted my hand to her lips and pressed a gentle kiss to my knuckles. I brushed her face with my hand, tucking a strand of hair behind her ear.

"I love you too Gracie girl. Always." With that, Gracie dropped my hand and stepped back from the ambulance as the doors slammed closed. I was alone with nothing but my thoughts and the paramedic to keep me company.

My shoulder fucking hurt with every jostle of the ambulance, but all I could focus on was how grateful I was that Gracie wasn't the one lying in this ambulance.

Chapter 31

Gracie

I felt like I was moving in slow motion. Nathan being lifted into the ambulance.

Piper rushing to me.

Someone helping me move towards a car.

All the while, I felt paralyzed by terror.

I kept replaying the scene over and over again. Launching myself at Madison just as Nathan pushed his way through the door. Madison turning and shooting him. It all happened so fast; I felt like time was standing still. I know Nathan said he was going to be ok. I know it was a good a sign he was talking and moving on his own. I know the paramedics said it looked like a through and through gunshot wound but there had been so much blood. I don't even remember getting in the car, or the drive to the hospital. I don't remember walking into the waiting area or sitting in this damned chair. All I could see was Nathan's blood, stained on my hands, caked under my nails.

"Babe, you're going to rub you skin off if keep rubbing at the blood like that. Let me see if I can find a bathroom for you to get cleaned up." Piper gently placed my hands in my lap and made her way to the nurses station.

I hated this place. The sounds of the machines, the smell of disinfectant. I didn't want to be here. I didn't want Nathan to be here. I was so fucking angry; I just wanted to scream. Strong arms wrapped themselves around my shoulders before I could register Gram sitting next me, taking the seat that Piper had just vacated.

"It's okay to let the tears fall Gracie. You're not meant to carry the world on your shoulders. It's okay to lean on your people in times like this."

"It's my fault Gram. This is all my fault. All these years, Madison has hated me and I never saw it. She was just biding her time until I got what she thought I deserved. If Nathan and I hadn't started dating, he wouldn't be here. It would be me. It should be me." I threw my hands up to cover the tears that had begun to fall. My shoulders shaking with the sobs.

Gram's strong hands reached up, taking my hands from my face and placing them in hers

"That's bullshit Gracie Henderson and you know it my sweet girl. The only person to blame for this situation is Madison Burke. She's obviously been off her rocker for a while and nothing you could have done would have stopped her. She was intent on taking from you. Maybe it wasn't part of the plan to hurt Nathan but she sure as shit was hoping to take your life. How do you think Nathan would feel if he were sitting in these chairs, worrying about you? Would you want him to blame himself... no you wouldn't."

"But Gram...."

"But nothing Gracie. Love isn't just the easy times. Loving someone comes with everything___ the good stuff, the bad stuff. Without pain, there can't really be love. I loved Piper's grandad with all that I had. I still love that man and I'll love him still when we meet again. If I had known he was going to die on me so early, do you think I would change a thing? That man gave me all the good things I have in the world, so I would gladly suffer that pain all over again. I know that Nathan feels the same way about you. He knew what he was doing when he came rushing into that building. He knew the likelihood was he would be hurt but he did it anyway. He'd do it again and again Gracie. That's love my darlin."

I knew what Gram was saying was right. I knew you couldn't have love without pain but I was struggling with the part that I had caused the pain. If Madison didn't hate me so much, none of this would've happened and Nathan wouldn't have a fucking hole in his shoulder.

"It just hurts so much Gram. It hurts so fucking much."

"Let me tell you something my girl; this pain you feel, it's proof that your heart is alive. That you're brave enough to care. And that's no small thing. Love doesn't just heal; it grows stronger in the cracks. The hurt doesn't mean it's broken; it means it's real. Hold on to that love, nurture it, and let it teach you. Time and tenderness work wonders, my darlin. And you'll see—the heart has a way of mending itself stronger than before."

Gram wrapped her arms around me and I let the fear and anger wash away in the warmth of her arms.

"Babes, I found a small bathroom where you can clean up. I checked on Nathan while I was at the nurse's desk. He's still in surgery for some minor arterial repairs. It's going to be awhile before a doctor comes out to update us. Let's get you cleaned up, maybe some food."

I let Piper lead me towards the bathroom, still in somewhat of a daze. "Thanks Piper. Thank you so much for being here. For calling Gram and my mom. Calling Nathan's parents. I don't know what I would've done if you hadn't been there when everything happened."

"Gracie boo, where else would I have

been. I've got you; no matter what. I just wish I would've been able to beat the shit out of Madison but I guess knowing she's going to spend a lot of years dressed in prison orange will have to be all the revenge I get."

We both laugh and that keeps me from bursting into tears.

"God I love you Piper."

"Love you, mean it Gracie boo. Now go. Get cleaned up. I'll be waiting right outside for you."

I got my hands as clean as they were going to be and stepped out of the bathroom. Just as I was walking towards our group I heard someone say, "Is anyone here for Nathan Sundry?"

I turned to see the doctor who must be treating Nathan standing nearby.

"Me, I'm here for Nathan, doctor."

"We've got him in recovery now and he's doing nicely. There was no real artery damage, and we've got him on an IV to administer antibiotics and fluids. We'll keep him here for a couple of days to make sure no infections set in but I expect a full recovery."

The waiting room filled with a collective sigh, as everyone let out a deep breath.

"Can I see him now?"

"Sure, I'll take you there myself. Don't be alarmed when you see him. He's lost a lot of blood and been through quite a trauma but I promise, he's going to be just fine."

****

I sat by Nathan's bed, gripping his hand in mine. He was so pale but looked so peaceful at the same time. I traced a star on the back of his hand over and over again- hoping and praying he would just open his eyes for me.

"Gracie" Nathan's voice was nothing more than a whisper.

"Shh Nathan, don't try to speak. Let me get you some ice chips." I grabbed the cup from the side table and rubbed the ice on Nathan's cracked lips and spooned a few chips in his mouth.

"What... what happened? Was I shot?"

"Yeah baby you were. I'm so, so sorry. It should be me lying in that bed, not you."

Nathan squeezed the hand I was holding and gently reached for my face with his other hand..

"Stop Gracie girl. This wasn't your fault. Madison is the only one to blame."

"I love you Nathan. When I saw her shoot you and thought for a moment that I might lose you..."

"I'm right here baby and I'm not going anywhere. I love you Gracie girl; you're stuck with me."

I looked into Nathan's eyes and knew what he saying, what he was promising with those words. This, us was endgame. I knew it deep in my soul that this was the man I was meant to spend the rest of my life with.

"No one I'd rather be stuck with." We sat there for a moment in silence, me tracing a star on the back of his hand over and over again before Nathan spoke.

"Why do you do that?"

I stilled, not understanding the question. "Do what?"

"Sometimes, when we're quiet, you'll hold my hand and trace a star on the back of it, why?"

"Unh, I guess it's something I do without even thinking about it." I sat there for a minute pondering what Nathan was asking. It came to me in a flash and I knew what it meant.

"It's something my dad did when I was little. I remember him tracing a star on the back of my hand as he read bedtime stories to me. He started it up again when he was sick and we would lie in his and mom's bed. I asked him about it once... he pointed to his heart and said, 'because you're my north star Gracie and I know that you and your mom will always lead me home'. That was the last thing he said to me right before he died."

I hadn't even realized I was crying until Nathan wiped the tears that had begun to fall down my face.

"You're my north star Nathan. You're my home and I know wherever you are is where I'm meant to be."

Nathan gently leaned forward and pressed his forehead to mine.

"Forever Gracie."

"Forever Nathan."

****

Epilogue

Nathan

Two Months Later

It had been two months since the shooting and life was finally getting back to normal. Madison had been arrested that night and later charged with attempted murder along with various charges stemming from the vandalism to Gracie's truck and bakery. Hopefully she will spend many years in jail. Thankfully Michael's dad had been so embarrassed that one of his employees, not to mention his son's girlfriend, had committed such a heinous crime, he transferred Michael to their Charleston, South Carolina office. Michael tucked his tail and left town without even attempting any contact with Gracie.

As for me and Gracie, we were better than ever. After my release from the hospital, Gracie had moved in with me and we were in the process of leasing out her townhouse. She had considered selling it but we both decided it would be a great rental property. For now Levi was staying in the townhouse until he found something or some land to build on.

After investing in the downtown area of Moonrise Bay, he decided he wanted to split his time between here and Manhattan. Let's just say, a certain librarian wasn't too happy with the situation. Knowing Levi, he'll be able to wear he down before too long.

These past two months haven't been the easiest. Even though my shoulder wound wasn't life threatening, I did have a lot of physical therapy and recuperation I had to deal with. Gracie and I had also hadn't been able to have sex these past months and that was going to end tonight. Gracie had been busy at the bakery the last couple of days. It was Valentine's Week and business had picked up with everyone wanting a special treat for their special someone. Not to mention, Gracie had a huge wedding order she was working on for the weekend.

I, on the other hand, had yet to return to full working hours. I've only been putting in half days for the past couple of months, with Pete picking up the slack for me. I really am lucky to have such a great crew pitching in to keep things afloat while I'm recovering.

I spent the morning cleaning house and running to the market to get everything to make

Gracie's favorite dinner. My girl loved ribeye's on the grill, creamed spinach and au gratin potatoes and that's what was on the menu tonight. That, paired with her favorite pinot noir and whatever treat she brought home from the bakery and tonight was going to be the perfect night. I had a little something up my sleeve that Gracie was not going to see coming.

The front door clicked shut and I smiled as heard humming her favorite Lainey Wilson song.

"Hey babe, it smells great in here. It's been a day and I'm so ready for comfy clothes that aren't covered in flour and a huge glass of wine." Gracie wrapped her arms around my waist and burrowed her face into the crook of my neck.

"Glass of wine is poured baby. Why don't you grab it and go make yourself comfortable. Dinner is almost ready." She reached up and placed what was supposed to be a simple kiss on lips but the minute I tasted her; I knew I needed more. I slid my tongue along the seam of her mouth and she opened for me with a moan. Before I knew it, the kiss had gotten away from us and I was moments away from saying screw dinner, hauling Gracie upstairs and ripping all her clothes off. But there was time for that later and tonight was not a night for rushing.

Tonight was about savoring.

I begrudgingly pulled away from her, placing my hands on her shoulders. "Baby," I rasped "we have time to do all the dirty things I want to do to you but first I want to have this delicious dinner with you to celebrate finally getting our lives back to normal."

I turned her away from me and gently pushed her towards the staircase.

"Go baby, before I change my mind and tear off your clothes right here in the kitchen."

"Mmm, Nathan you know I do have a thing for you and kitchens." She glanced over her shoulder, a sly smile playing on her face.

"Don't you dare Gracie girl. I have plans for you later and you're ruining them you temptress."

Throwing up her hands in surrender, Gracie ran upstairs and turned on the shower. It took all my control to not run right up the stairs after her but I really didn't want anything to derail the evening I'd planned.

I plated our food and placed everything on the table including my special Valentine's Day surprise and boy was Gracie going to be surprised.

"Ok Nathan I'm comfy, starving and ready for this dinner that you say is better than letting me jump your bones in the kitchen." Gracie shouted from her perch on the stairs.

I poured her another glass wine and ushered her to the table placing my gift bag in front of her.

"Nathan, what's this?　I thought we weren't doing gifts?" Gracie grabbed for the bag on the table.

"I know Gracie girl, but I just couldn't help myself. After the past few months that we had, I just had to celebrate us."

Gracie pulled at the tissue paper in the bag and pulled out a black velvet jewelers box, big enough to hold a ring. She popped open the box and sucked in a breath.

"Nathan, oh my god, what did you do?" When she looked up from the ring, silver lined the rims of eyes, I had moved in front of her and gotten down on one knee. I took her hand in mine.

"Gracie, I know we haven't been a couple for long but these past few months with you have been the best of my life even with the challenges we've faced. You've been my calm in the chaos, my light in the dark. You're the reason I wake up excited to see what's ahead. I know people will say this is fast but it's not Gracie; it's always been you. Gracie, we've known each other most of our lives and even when we were "just friends" I knew you were the girl for me. I can't imagine my life without you and I don't want to. You are my home, my safe place, my forever... what I'm asking Gracie is will you marry me?"

She jumped from her chair and got down on her knees in front of me, throwing her arms around my neck.

"Yes Nathan, yes. A thousand times yes."

Her lips were on mine and this time as the kiss intensified, I did not to stop it. Later that night, we would have our Valentine's dinner but for now, in this moment I was going to savor the woman I love and relish the moment she promised to spend forever with me.

Playlist

Want to hear the music that inspired Sweet Beginnings... Here's a list of the songs that inspired Gracie and Nathan's story.

... How Did It End?... Taylor Swift

my tears ricochet... Taylor Swift

tolerate it... Taylor Swift

I Did Something Bad... Taylor Swift

...Ready For It?... Taylor Swift

Interlude (full length) Kelsea Ballerini

I Bet You Think About Me (featuring Christ Stapleton) ... Taylor Swift

Mountain With A View... Kelsea Ballerini

Weak-End... Lainey Wilson

How Do I Do This... Kelsea Ballerini

The Good I'll Do... Zach Bryan

I Swear (To God) ... Tyler Childers

Feathered Indians... Tyler Childers

IF YOU GO DOWN (I'M GOIN' DOWN TOO) ... Kelsea Ballerini

This Love (Taylor's Version) ... Taylor Swift

Butterflies... Kacey Musgraves

Mine Again... Zach Bryan

Deeper Well... Kacey Musgraves

Sun to Me... Zach Bryan

Paper Rings... Taylor Swift

Ride... Carey Brothers

Run... Matt Nathanson, Sugarland

Stubborn Love... The Lumineers

Time after Time... Lennon Stella

Dirty Looks... Lainey Wilson

Acknowledgements

I don't even know where to begin. This book has truly been a labor of love. I've been writing since I was a little girl but it took me until my oldest kid's senior year of high school for me to buckle down and really focus on writing. Funny thing is romance novels aren't even my first love. When the Covid-19 pandemic hit the world felt so dark and heavy. I turned to the romance genre to get me through those dark days. I fell in love with romance books through the works of Robyn Carr, Lucy Score, Tricia O'Malley, Claire Kingsley, Meghan Quinn, and Catherine Cowles. Honestly the list could go on forever. I would like to thank those authors as well as all romance authors across the genre for sharing their worlds with me. I have truly enjoyed the ride.

I want to thank my loving, kind, funny, honest and patient husband, Kevin. Without you babe, this book wouldn't be possible. While Nathan isn't exactly you, you are and will always be my forever book boyfriend. They broke the mold when you were made and honestly no one will ever measure up to the man you are. I love you always and forever and you are my north star.

Thanks to my daughter, Makena, who is the one I turn to when I need a laugh, fashion advice, make-up advice or any advice in general. Without you kid, some of the dialogue in this book wouldn't have been possible. You helped me give Miquel a voice. I love you to the moon and back kiddo and miss you everyday you're away at school.

Thanks to my son, Matthew who is always in my corner and always reminding me to dream big. I love you kid and wouldn't be able to be this brave without your encouragement.

Thank you to Kaliyah Davis, my forever book bestie. I love our book chats and sharing a love of reading with you. You have been one of my biggest cheerleaders and I don't know if I would have made it as far as I have without you encouraging me. I'm so lucky that you are part of our family and I love you dearly.

To my beta readers, Page and Evie. Two of the most honest people I know and the people whose opinions I trust the most. Thank you for taking the time to read this labor of love and give your honest feedback to make this book a better story.

To Kelsey, my ride or die and bestie for life. Without you in my life there would be no Gracie and Piper. Our friendship has been inspirational and I love you boo boo. Love you mean it girl.

Lastly, thank you to the readers who took a chance on my book. I hope you fell in love with the town of Moonrise Bay as much as I did. It has been a pleasure to share this story with you.

Want More
Moonrise Bay

Coming Soon: Champagne Problems

Want to find out what happens when a certain billionaire needs the help of one small town Moonrise Bay librarian? Stay tuned for Piper and Levi's fake fiancé story coming to you soon.

About the Author

Beth Curley is a wife, mom of two kids and two dogs. When she's not facetiming with her college aged daughter, watching her teenage son play high school football, she enjoys reading spicey romance novels, watching Food Network and HGTV and hanging on her back porch with her husband. She lives somewhere in North Carolina and dreams of one day having her own little cottage on the water near coastal NC.

Made in United States
Troutdale, OR
04/13/2025